A STORM RISES

BLOODLINES LEGACY
BOOK ONE

USA TODAY BESTELLING AUTHOR
ROSE GARCIA

DEDICATION

For My Jake!
Thank you so much for waiting for this book.
I hope you love it!

THE FAE REALM OF
FAEVENLY

TORCH
LAKE

STRONG
HAVEN RUINS

SUMMIT
RANGE

GREEN
FALLS

THE MORNING SEA

Author's Note

A Storm Rises is set in the beautiful yet dangerous fae realm of Faevenly and features palace politics, warring families, and a deadly royal hunt. As a result, the book contains the following which may be sensitive to some readers: death, near-death, assault, death of wild animals.

In addition, the prologue includes a scene with birthing complications, death of a mother, and near-death of an infant. This scene is revisited in minor flashbacks in chapters 11 and 25.

PROLOGUE

Princess Gabriela Avila Strong exhaled with a groan and turned to her side. "The pain." The last remaining heir of House Strong of Strong Haven pressed into her midsection with both hands. "It returns." She clenched her teeth and squeezed the sheets. "Worse this time."

"My dear lady. Hang in there," Maid Gidna said soothingly as she wiped Gabriela's wet forehead with a soft cotton cloth. "Help is on the way. It should arrive any moment."

Gabriela panted in bursts. Her breathing grew shallow. "It's all wrong." She looked to Maid Gidna for help. "Please... My baby is not due to arrive for another month." Tears streamed down her face as she shook her head from side to side. "It is too soon."

The stocky and faithful dwarf had served the Strong family, and then Gabriela and Lord Leaf, for almost one hundred years. Her lady had never endured such pain. It was all too much. "All will be well. I am sure Lady Sonia is on her way. She will fix you right up."

Maid Gidna prayed to the Stars Lady Sonia would arrive soon. But who knew when the hard-to-locate witch-healer would show.

"And Leaf?" A hard swallow and then Gabriela asked again. "What of Leaf?"

Gidna glanced at a maidservant huddling in the shadows of the bedchamber's corner. The young and tiny maiden clutched her fitted white dress skirt in her small hands. The flowers that usually adorned her short-clipped brown hair had fallen away. With wide eyes, she moved her head from side to side.

Hiding a gulp, Gidna reported the progress to the princess. "Surely, our raven has reached him and he races home now. I have no doubt."

Gabriela dug her nails into the feather mattress. With jaws clenched, her face contorted. When the wave passed, she gasped for more air, and her head fell back against the pillow. "I am breaking in half. I need help."

She wiped Gabriela's chin with the square of cotton and pulled the long white-streaked brown hair away from her lady's face. She stroked Gabriela's moist and cool cheek. "You are not breaking, my princess."

Seventy years ago, Gidna had stepped in and filled the void after Gabriela's mother, Princess Celyse, went to the Passing Place. Five years later, Gidna assisted with the paternal role when Gabriela's father, Lord Julio, died in a car crash. He paid the ultimate price while visiting the human realm. She and others suspected responsibility lay with House Kane or those aligned with them. Yet, there had been no way to prove it, of course.

"I love you, Gidna." Gabriela locked eyes with her servant and best friend, then squeezed her hand. "You are my family."

The dwarf blinked and then harrumphed. Her lady

mustn't start with that talk. "You will be fine, my lady. I know it. I can feel it with every sense inside me."

Ignoring Gidna, Gabriela went on. "Do you remember when we first met?"

"Sun, Moon, and Stars, my lady. Of course, I do."

The princess smiled, and her eyes took on a faraway look. "I was seventeen when I came here from the human realm. I hardly knew anything about Faevenly. But you..." Gabriela swallowed and winced as if the pain had jabbed her again. "You helped me. Because of you, I learned the balance between the human and fae realm." She threw her head back and unleashed a throaty wail that echoed throughout the small room.

This time, Gidna could not stop herself. Tears fell from her eyes. They trailed down her cheeks like a mighty river carving through the rocky mountain range. If Lady Sonia didn't appear soon all would be lost. The princess could not take much more of this agony. Neither could the baby. Disaster loomed, and Gidna was determined to stop it.

She hollered over her shoulder. "Send more guards! Find Lady Sonia at once!" She turned to the shy maidservant in the corner. "And where is Manny!?" Gidna did not know how to help the princess. She could not save the baby from coming early, and she was woefully unprepared.

The maidservant scurried away and left Princess Gabriela to her ragged and shallow breathing. "My Uncle Manny...is probably...fishing somewhere. He's surely lost in a daydream."

"It would not surprise me in the least." Gidna flashed

her a half-hearted smile. Manny spent countless hours fishing and wasting time. "Daydreamer, that one. But full of nothing but love for you."

"I know." Gabriela struggled to prop herself on her forearms. "You must promise me something."

"My lady, please, none of that talk. Lady Sonia will be—"

"Please, Gidna!"

Gidna's mouth dropped open. Her next words hung in her clogged throat. Giving in to Gabriela's plea, she exhaled and pursed her lips. "Anything, my lady."

"If I do not make it, you must know that Leaf will perish too."

"Your soul is linked to Leaf's. I have not forgotten what that evil witch Draven did to you both."

Gabriela clutched the platinum cross hanging from her neck. She stroked the smooth edges of the precious heirloom. Her father passed it on to her when she was a child. It was all that remained of him—a powerful symbol of his human faith and a reminder of the powers held within her human bloodline. "If my baby survives, this must be passed on. This represents great power. The child will need it throughout life and beyond."

Gabriela's mother had foretold in a dream that her child—the Only One—would restore peace throughout Faevenly. Gidna knew and trusted that prophecy. She had seen the power within Gabriela. Her father, Lord Julio, possessed it too. "Your word is my command, my lady."

With a deep, guttural grunt, Gabriela struggled to remove the chain from around her neck. She placed it on

Gidna's warm, thick palm and then closed Gidna's trembling fingers around the cross. "Faith is a warrior."

She nodded. "It is."

The princess's head fell back. "When you have no other choice, you must share my letter with the child. You know where it is, right?" Gabriela motioned toward a glass of water on the bedside table.

"I do, my lady." Gidna held the glass to her lips. "I know the spot."

The princess took several small sips and then waved the glass away. "Do not use the Strong or Avila name for my child. Tell Manny he must keep the child and raise my baby using only his name—Vela."

"Yes, my princess. Of course, I will do as you command until my heart's last beat."

"If the Kanes or their allies learn that Leaf and I conceived a child..." She groaned, and her voice lowered. "Assuming our baby lives, they will stop at nothing to kill it. Their hatred for me and my family runs deep. They do not want the prophecy realized."

Fifteen years ago, Gidna was present when Gabriela and Leaf abandoned Strong Haven and moved to the Sublands. Her heart hurt at the memory of that awful day. Though over time they had all grown to love the red and rocky province. "I will protect and defend your child with my life. Manny will, too. We all will."

Gabriela moaned and shifted to her other side, her purple nightgown wet and clinging to her tanned skin. "Trust only in Manny and Lady Sonia. No one else."

"No one else," Gidna repeated the command.

Outside, the day was closing, the sun's golden hues

giving way to the dusky colors of twilight. Shadows stretched across the dull and dirty stone floor as finality settled in Gabriela and Leaf's simple bedchamber. With each passing minute, Gidna's hope for Lady Sonia's timely arrival and her lady's salvation waned.

Like the setting sun, Gabriela would soon face her final moments. Gidna could see it in the princess's paling skin and hear it in her failing breaths.

But for the baby...there was still hope. Gidna rubbed the cross and prayed for a miracle. "For peace in Faevenly, let this child survive."

Over the distant hills and drifting through High Meadow, the raven's message arrived on a chilly gust of wind. *Hurry home.* A flush of heat and Leaf's stomach roiled. He yanked the reins. "Silverhoof, home!"

Silverhoof's muscles tensed. She clamped the bit, steam bursting from her flaring nostrils as she jetted forward.

Leaf crouched low and leaned forward as the muscles of the powerful steed bounced beneath him. The rushing wind forced his eyes into a squint while the landscape of High Meadow zoomed past. With each strike of Silverhoof's hooves, he drew closer to the rocky Sublands.

Hurry home.

Gabriela and their unborn child were in trouble. He knew it. His heart quivered. His chest knotted like a ball of breeding snakes. He should have never left. If something happened to them, he would never forgive himself. He prayed to the Sun, Moon, and Stars that he would make it home in time.

But the worst scenarios always seemed to find them.

"Hold on, my love." Tears slipped from the corners of his eyes. "Please, hold on."

Silverhoof weaved her way around tall trees and thick underbrush. She leaped over jagged boulders and skimmed across glistening streams. Any faster and Silverhoof would have taken flight. She loved Gabriela too and must have sensed the danger.

The greenery and colorful wildflowers of High Meadow thinned. The red and orange desert landscape of the Sublands took over. A sliver of hope entered Leaf's heavy heart. "Almost there!"

But something else entered and resided within him— a long ago binding from the wicked Draven Midlothian.

The fae witch had almost conquered Faevenly when Gabriela and her human witch abilities and blue energy power ended Draven. But that victory came at great cost. Many died during that uncertain and tumultuous time. Leaf almost met his end too, but Gabriela saved him. That selfless act linked their souls forever.

A tickle of cold gathered at the top of Leaf's head. Like an icy tendril, the sensation trailed through his body and down to his feet, sapping his energy. Listless, he slumped over, gasping and clutching his chest. He knew what was happening.

Gabriela was dying...and so was he, and there wasn't anything he could do to change that.

He threaded his fingers through Silverhoof's long

mane. Although Leaf lacked the power to tug the thick, coarse hair, the trusty steed knew what he needed. Silverhoof slowed to a standstill. Her head hung low, and her ears drooped. She stomped her hooves and neighed.

Leaf slipped his boots from the stirrups. He slid from his mount, his face smacking against the cold, rocky ground with a thud. This was it. He would never rise and retake that saddle.

Silverhoof whinnied and lowered herself one leg at a time. She inched closer and nudged her soft, warm muzzle against Leaf's fast-freezing cheek. Silverhoof gave him a gentle, loving nudge.

"I cannot." Leaf stared into the steed's violet eyes. "I am sorry, my friend."

Silverhoof's head swayed and then snuggled against Leaf.

"We shall meet again in the Passing Place. But not yet. You must find Gabriela. She and our baby need you. You must go to them. You must protect them." Leaf tried to prod Silverhoof but could not lift his hand. "Go home, my friend. Help our princess. Be quick."

Silverhoof stayed close for several long seconds before she nudged Leaf goodbye. She scooted back and raised herself upright. She stomped her hooves and circled Leaf.

"Go!" Leaf pleaded in a weak voice. "Do not disobey —not now."

His horse huffed and whinnied before slowly trotting away.

"I will miss you too, my beloved friend."

Leaf lay firmly planted on the ground. His black

trousers, long-sleeved green tunic, and black cape provided no protection from the cold rushing within his body. He could not even feel his feet inside his boots anymore. Death had come for him.

The retreating sun rays stained the sky in a collage of red and orange. A trail of puffy white clouds floated by. He watched the tufts pull apart as his heart slowed and his breathing grew shallow.

He closed his eyes and pictured Gabriela's soft tan skin and her big brown eyes. He hated that he was not there for her during her time of need. As her one true love, that was his duty. He hoped she would not suffer at her end. He prayed their child was not meeting their end, too. He would find out soon enough in the Passing Place.

"I am coming, my love." His vision tunneled, and a soft light led the way. "I...am..."

CHAPTER ONE

When you read this, know that your father and I love you more than life itself. I pray you accept this with peace and understanding in your heart.

Mateo Vela perched atop Spirit Butte. He sat at the edge of the wide plateau and watched as the setting sun cast a sea of red, pink, and orange across the horizon. The colorful glow resembled flames—the kind that soothed, not burned, and made the cold desert nights more comfortable.

"Everything is on fire." He scooped up a handful of pebbly red dirt and tossed it into the gentle breeze. "And so am I."

He visited this spot almost every evening to escape the bustle and noise of Sandhaven Village. On Spirit Butte, he wasn't a lowborn part fae, part human. Here, his bloodline didn't matter. He could be whoever he wanted.

Sometimes he imagined himself coming from a royal family with the power to make Faevenly a better place. Uniting the bloodlines would be his first order of business. He would elevate the Sublands to a place worthy of respect and position, and everyone would know his name. Other times, his restlessness and anger left him wanting to be a villain. He would own the heads of every member of ruling House Stromm—shove them on spikes so everyone would see.

Faevenly would be a better place without them.

A rustle sounded from behind, and he turned to find his best friends, Lirien and Gareth, approaching. Like him, they wore their usual black pants and long-sleeved green tunics with tall brown boots. Lirien's silver hair draped down his back while Gareth's red hair was tied back in a thick, long braid. They were like his brothers, and lowborn too.

"Sandhaven is busy today." Lirien adjusted the dagger at his waist and sat next to Mateo on a sheared-off but unyielding rock. Daggers were Lirien's favorite. When traveling, he kept several sheathed at his waist, one in each boot, and a few tucked in his tunic. But at home in the Sublands he carried little, if any.

"Too busy," Mateo grumbled.

Gareth did not sit. Like a sentry, he stayed upright and crossed his thick arms.

Lirien scooped up a rock and tossed it in Mateo's direction. "You nervous about the hunt?"

Mateo kept his gaze on the horizon. *The Summit Range Hunt.* High King Sylrik Stromm had established the hunt years ago after eliminating every member of House Strong. It was his way of celebrating his new rule —a demonstration of ultimate control. Since the hunt's inception, the Sublands had been denied participation because of their close ties with the Strongs and their sympathetic views toward lowborns and human blooded. So, to be included this time around was huge. Mateo outsmarted and outlasted the other Sublanders and earned the coveted spot.

He blew out a labored breath. If he finished first, he would receive favor and the coveted rewards. The losing competitors would receive nothing. They would be waiting five years for another hunt.

The internal pressure to perform mounted in Mateo. Anger followed. He would show the treacherous Stromms and everyone else what he and the Sublands were made of. He would come home with the rewards. Gold. Precious stones. Rich fabrics. Healing seeds for his father and little sister, Floriana. The Sublands might even regain a seat on the Faevenly Council when Mateo won the hunt.

The Summit Range Hunt meant...everything.

Frenetic nerves fluttered in his stomach like a swarm of lightning bugs. He scooped up a small pebble and rubbed it between his thumb and forefinger. "Nervous?" He chuckled. "What a joke. I'm not nervous. I'm *ready*."

He had been preparing for the hunt his entire life, somehow knowing it would happen one day. Day and night, he had sprinted the vast canyons and dry riverbeds of the Sublands and neighboring provinces. He built his stamina and planned his hydration and nutrition. Under the velvety night sky and the light of the glowing moon, he tracked, hunted, and killed elk and boar. Now, at nineteen, his desire to compete in the hunt had come true. But could he win against highborns? That would be tougher than it sounded.

"You will show them all." Lirien patted Mateo on the back. "They have no clue about your speed."

Gareth grunted. Born mute, he communicated with the occasional guttural sound, but mostly with his hands. He pointed both index fingers at Mateo, letting Mateo know he agreed with Lirien.

Lirien took out his dagger and poked the dirt. He flashed Mateo a teasing grin. "Think you'll see the ice princess?" All of Faevenly knew that name.

Mateo drew in his chin and balked. "Avalynn Stromm?" The ice princess with a heart so cold she couldn't even bother to look lowborns in the eye. "I certainly hope not."

"Yeah, she'll probably be in a high tower somewhere ordering people around." Lirien laughed. "Counting her piles of silver and gold coins."

Gareth poked Mateo's back, then held out his fingers near his face, touched his thumb to his chin, and swiped his fingers across his face until his hand closed.

"Pfft, pretty?" Mateo threw a pebble at Gareth. "Who cares? She is a Stromm."

Lirien's attention stayed glued on the small hole he was digging. "I bet she looks like a harpy, but everyone has to say she's pretty or they'll be hanged."

Laughter burst out of them. The kind that eased doubts and worries. Mateo's heart warmed, and his nerves cooled. He nodded at his friends, then tossed the rock he'd been holding. "Ugly or not, I will show her and all the Stromms soon enough what we Sublanders are made of."

Mateo, Lirien, and Gareth made their way down the craggy path. They maneuvered the familiar trail with ease, their sharp eyes tweaking and adapting to the darkening sky. Though lowborn, their fae side dominated the three best friends. They were tall and lean with keen senses, athletic prowess, and graceful dexterity.

A large black wolf with a white streak down her back leaped from a prickly brush patch and took her usual place at Mateo's side. The thin, long tail of a field rat hung from her sharp teeth. Stormshroud bucked her head and toyed with her snack. With one swallow, she gulped it down. Even rats were scarce in the Sublands.

The trio entered Mateo's modest home. Usually, it bustled with activity, but tonight Mateo found his home empty. Mateo's father, Manny, wasn't cooking. His older sister, Camilla, wasn't reading to his sickly little sister, Floriana. Gareth's sisters weren't visiting.

"Where is everyone?" Lirien asked.

Mateo glanced around. "Maybe at the market for more seeds. Floriana's cough has been getting worse by the day."

Lirien turned away. His voice trailed off. "We are low too."

Gareth grunted with a nod. They were low on seeds as well. But nobody's bowl was lower than Mateo's and his family's. Their dismal supply of healing seeds dwindled faster than anyone else's.

Dim light from the sun's last remnants filtered

through a row of tiny windows set deep within the thick beige stone walls. Blue and purple woven rugs covered the rocky floors. They provided warmth on cool nights and soft padding for bare feet.

With nightfall a blink away, Mateo made his way to the fireplace. He struck a long match from the wooden mantle and used the flickering flame to start a fire. Then, he lit the oil lamps hanging from the walls.

When Mateo finished the last lamp, the back door opened and then closed. Camilla rushed in with little Floriana at her heels. Their small-framed father, Manny, followed. Puffy eyes. Red noses. They had been crying.

Mateo's gut clenched. "What is it?" His heart pounded like a blind man's cane. "What happened?"

Little Floriana ran for Mateo and clutched his leg. Tears burst from Camilla's soft brown eyes. "Oh, Mateo." She held out a crumpled parchment paper. "It's awful." Her hands shook as he snatched the note.

He cleared his throat and read it to himself. The words chilled him to the bone. "No, no, no—this cannot be."

"What does it say?" Lirien moved closer. With his hand on Mateo's shoulder, he inspected the note.

Body trembling, Mateo swallowed a huge gulp of stale air and read aloud. "The High King of Faevenly does hereby proclaim by royal decree that the last place finisher in the Summit Range Hunt will earn the penalty of death. There will be no exceptions or excuses. Let it be known far and wide throughout the realm. Signed, High King Sylrik Stromm."

Silence fell on the room as if everyone had been

instantly suffocated. For years, the Sublands' elders had petitioned for a spot on the hunt. Not only so they could be seen, but in hopes of winning the much-needed rewards as well. Now that the Sublands had joined the hunt, of course the Stromms imposed a death penalty decree. Honor, fairness, and dignity knew no home with the Stromm family.

Camilla gripped Mateo's arm. "You are not hunting."

"You are not doing it," little Floriana cried.

"I agree, *Mijo*," his father added and grasped his shoulder. "It is way too dangerous."

Lirien and Gareth nodded while Stormshroud whimpered at Mateo's heels.

Mateo stepped away, searching for the right words. He would never back down to highborns or a Stromm. Not now. Not after such an unfair edict from the High King. He turned to face them. "We need those rewards. All of us. So, I am in. No matter what."

His older sister's eyes widened. A rigid furrow formed on her smooth forehead. "No!"

"Yes, Camilla. I am competing. I can win. I know it." He shook the note in front of her. "They will not get the satisfaction of taking me out of the hunt. I am sick of being controlled!" He crumpled the parchment and tossed it into the flickering flames of the fireplace. "Aren't you?"

His father shuffled closer. "Of course, she is. We all are. But *Mijo*, this is different." His shoulders slumped as his voice lowered to a whisper. "This is your *life*."

"Life?" He almost laughed. "It is always about life here in the Sublands. You know that. Mother's life and

—" Floriana grasped his leg harder, and he held his tongue. He didn't want her to know how desperately he worried about her health.

His father waved him off. "Enough, enough."

A full-blooded human, Mateo's father came to Faevenly during the Strong era after he and his best friend Julio found a portal. He liked the realm so much he decided to stay. Without the potion he sipped daily from the mysterious healer Lady Sonia, Manny would've departed this life for the Passing Place decades ago.

Still, the potion did not have the same effect as before. Like the healing seeds, it was running low and almost empty.

Deep lines etched his father's dark tan face. His almost fully gray hair hung past his shoulders. He often complained about back pain. But most concerning was his developing cough. It sounded like the beginnings of the dreaded Dragon's Bellow—the same as Floriana's cough. The disease had claimed Faeryn, Mateo's fae mother, ten years earlier. Mateo wasn't about to lose Manny or Floriana. Not after what happened to his mother.

"Father, please." He needed and wanted his father's support but was ready to go forward without it. "Winning would do so much for us and the people of the Sublands."

His father sighed. "The Stromms only know hate." He held his back and eased into his favorite plush chair. "Hate for humans." He rubbed his stubbled face. "Hate for the Strongs who sought refuge here so many years ago." He gripped the chair and gritted his teeth. "Hate for everyone in the Sublands. We are the lowest of the low to them." His hacking cough returned with a vengeance. Camilla rushed to his side, but he shooed her away. With a swallow, he managed a few final words. "Who we are will never change."

Mateo kissed the top of Floriana's head. He pulled her away from his leg but kept her close as he bent a knee and took his father's hand. "Yes, Father. But we must try. Doing nothing is not an option."

"You will risk death for the chance to compete?" His father's sad eyes pleaded for a different response. "Is that what you're saying, *Mijo*?"

"Yes, Father. That's what I am saying."

"My boy." Tears slid from Manny's eyes. He wiped them with dark, weathered hands. "Then I will stand by you no matter what."

Camilla put her hand on Mateo's shoulder. "Me too."

"If that is what you want," Floriana whispered, wrapping her small arms around Mateo's neck.

His friends joined in. "Count us in," Lirien said.

Together they had weathered more storms than Spirit Butte. With their support, a surge of hope sprouted inside Mateo. A tidal wave of expectation and desire that nothing could stop him. He prayed to the Sun, Moon, and Stars that he was right.

CHAPTER TWO

To appreciate your birthright, it's important to start at the beginning. Before you were conceived.

Mateo could not remember sleeping. His head throbbed as if he were an oak tree claimed by a relentless woodpecker. His sore eyes stung. His achy legs twitched. He fluffed his feather pillow and turned from side to side. He had been ecstatic about the hunt. Couldn't wait to be in those mountains putting all the other hunters to shame. But the night and the darkness brought with them thoughts of the last place death penalty. His empty gut twisted tighter. All excitement had evaporated, replaced by the weight of winning and the fear of losing.

He didn't want to let his family down or go to the Passing Place.

Early morning stillness filled his bedchamber. The hush of nightfall clung to the stone and sun-dried mud bricks of Mateo's home. His gaze roamed the pressing darkness, landing where Stormshroud lay curled in a ball. He didn't have to see her to know she breathed slowly, her paws twitching while she dreamed. Those things were a given. Maybe she chased a mouse or a rabbit. Maybe she fled the Passing Place.

A hazy and soft light began seeping into the room from his narrow window. Inch by inch it brought Stormshroud into full view. A ball of strong, sleek muscles with a fluffy black coat with that streak of white. She weighed over one hundred pounds and stood nearly seven feet tall on her hind legs—Mateo's height. But when he and his father had found her, she barely fit his hand.

They were hunting deep in the Sublands, far from the village. While they were sleeping in a cave, a raging storm rolled in. Through the deluge and over the thunderclaps, they heard whimpering from within their rocky shelter.

Deep in the cave, they found a decimated litter of wolf pups. All had perished, except for one. No larger than a fist, the pup could not have been more than a few days old. Eyes closed, she was helpless and barely had any fur. Mateo and his father brought her home, and she's faithfully served them since—the best wolfhound in the Sublands.

With the morning light growing brighter, Stormshroud recognized the new day. She lifted her head and yawned. Mateo yawned too and then flung off his thin cotton cover and rose from his narrow bed. The steward of the Sublands, Lady Verona, would be picking him up and escorting him to the Stromm Palace, where the Summit Range Hunt would begin.

Time was running out. He might as well get ready.

After a stop at the washroom, he put on his best travel clothes—dark pants, a long-sleeved silver shirt, and his newly polished black boots. He had already packed his weapons and clothing the night before. Yet, he added two more things from his bedside table—the black scarf his mother made for him when he was little and a wood carving of a cross his father had whittled one winter during a human time known as Christmas. These two items would either carry him to victory or join in death's defeat. Wherever he went, they went as well.

Head tilted, Stormshroud cast a stare at Mateo. His loyal wolf knew he would soon be leaving. "It will be okay, Stormy." He stroked her behind the prickly ears. "I will be back in no time."

He would've taken her if he could, but the hunt allowed for hunters and their weapons only. Stormy would've been the best weapon he could have taken from the Sublands. That, and the best companion.

The carriage ride from the Sublands to Summit Range Palace would take three days. Once there, he would endure the arrival festivities. The day after that, he'd attend the Gala of the Hunter's Moon. The next morning, the hunt would commence.

His mind zipped to the possibility of coming in last. How would the last place finisher be executed? His hand paused in the middle of stroking Stormshroud's back. Forget about that. It wouldn't be him anyway. That honor would surely go to highborn scum. Mateo would see to it.

He whistled and jerked his chin. "Come on, Stormy girl." Leaving his bedchamber, he headed for the cook-room. "We have lots to do."

With a yelp, Stormshroud dashed ahead of Mateo and disappeared around the corridor's corner. In the wolf's wake came Camilla. She held a mug of tea in her hand. A trail of steam floated from the top like a white lace ribbon. She favored their father with her small frame, big brown eyes, and long wavy hair. But she'd also inherited much from their fae mother. Pointed ears. Sharpened fae senses. Innate abilities with herbs and alchemy. She made the best herbal drinks.

She eyed Mateo while handing over the tea. "Sun, Moon, and Stars. Did you get any sleep last night?"

"Some." He brought the mug closer. The smell of mint and sage swirled around his nose. He took a slight sip. The flavors provided a pleasing warmth, and he perked up instantly but not completely. Camilla's flavored tea in the morning would've put him two steps in front of Stormshroud on most days. But today was far from typical.

"You can sleep in the carriage on the ride." She glanced over her shoulder at the cookroom. She moved closer to Mateo. "Please be gentle with Father and Floriana this morning." She raised her pleading eyebrows. "They are worried about the last place penalty."

Mateo lowered his mug and nodded. "Of course. How are their coughs?" They needed those healing seeds. He had no choice but to risk it all to get them.

Camilla's eyes watered. "The same. I have even gotten word from Gareth's mother that little Poppy is coughing."

His gut sank. "Now you see why I have to go?" His point had been proven. No further talk was necessary.

She wiped away a tear that had slid onto her face. "I do. But I still do not like it."

He wrapped his arm around her. "I know." He knew and accepted that his family would worry themselves, but Mateo could handle it. He would save his family and the Sublands. Or face his end trying.

After a quiet breakfast, Mateo's family gathered together around the crackling fireplace in the sitting room. His travel bags rested by the door while Stormshroud sulked in the corner. They stared at the flames and avoided talking about the hunt while waiting for Lady Verona. The tension was concrete and solid. Like a fortress.

His father broke the deafening silence. "We will throw the biggest party when you get back, *Mijo*." He smiled wide. "Everyone will be invited." He scooted to the edge of his seat. "We'll have food and drink and games!" Manny was more than a good father. He was a good man.

Taking his lead, Camilla piped in. "I will make those powdery cookies." She put her hand on her father's shoulder. "Those little ones you love from the human realm."

Father smiled back. "Camilla's delicious *pan de polvo*. It's been a while."

"I will color flowers for decorations and hang them on

the walls." Floriana covered her mouth while she coughed but kept a sparkle in her brown eyes. "I can also make a *piñata* from the human realm, like Father showed us." His little sister was the reason he could never say he wouldn't participate in the hunt. As long as she was in need, he could not and would not rest.

Talk of coming home to a celebration filled Mateo with hope. Knowing he had the full support of the ones he loved meant even more. "A party sounds great. And the cookies—"

Stormshroud leaped to her feet, ears on alert. She howled at the door.

His father's smile dropped as reality intruded. He glanced at Mateo before he closed his eyes and swallowed. "They are here."

They rose, and his father started rattling off reminders. Mateo knew the exact words before they landed in his ears. "Stay true to who you are, *Mijo*." Manny folded his hands under his chin, as if praying with each word. "Be as pleasant as possible to everyone you meet, but do not trust anybody."

Mateo nodded. "I know, Father." Manny always issued the same reminders in uncertain times. And there was no time more uncertain than this.

He interrupted Mateo and pursed his lips. "Fae are cunning, manipulative, and devious. They cannot lie, but they do not have to. ¿*Entiendes*?"

"*Entiendo*," Mateo answered back in his father's native language, one Mateo had come to love, honor, and respect.

He pulled Mateo closer. "There is great strength

inside of you." He moved his hand from Mateo's forehead, down to his chest, and then across from shoulder to shoulder. The sign of the cross—a symbol of his human beliefs. "Have faith in our Heavenly Father above. All will be as He wills it. Remember that. And always, always remember who you are."

Usually, Mateo scoffed at his father's human views on faith and religion. Not today. He welcomed all assistance, from any deity, from any realm. He wrapped his arms around his father's small and fragile frame. "I will remember who I am—the son of Manny Vela of the Sublands."

He brought his sisters in to join them. Soft whimpering came from Camilla while louder cries came from little Floriana. "Shhh. It will be alright. I will be back so fast it will seem like I have only been camping in Spirit Butte."

Mateo knelt in front of his faithful shadow, Stormshroud. "You be good, Stormy. Take care of Father and the girls. Don't let me down."

She nudged him with her snout and then licked Mateo from chin to forehead. He begged off with a smile. "Okay, okay. That's enough."

Ka-dunk! Ka-dunk! A hard knock banged at the deadwood door. Father wiped his glistening eyes. He nodded to his children, then opened it. Two guards clad in all black stepped inside and took positions beside the entry. His time at home had ended. He would face whatever lay beyond that door with the grace and strength he'd been taught inside this home.

Lady Verona walked in. She tipped her head. "Manny."

"Lady Verona." His father returned the gesture.

Her copper-colored pants and long-sleeved shirt matched the rock and stone of the Sublands. Her long and dark, shiny hair was pulled up in the front. The thick remainder hung loose and reached the small of her back. Her piercing, sapphire blue eyes fixed on Mateo. "I am proud and most pleased to escort our first Summit Range Hunter, Mateo Vela, to the Stromm Palace."

Unsure how to respond, Mateo figured Lady Verona despised him. He, Lirien, and Gareth had appeared before her several times in their youth for pranks gone awry. Hardcore, she had never gone easy on them. "I am the one who is honored, Lady Verona. I am grateful for your escort."

"Indeed." Lady Verona spoke with her usual brusqueness. "Let us get on with it, then." She commanded her guards with a wave to take Mateo's things. "Daylight's wasting."

Stormshroud circled his legs, taking her place next to him. He patted her head. "Not this time, Stormy. I will see you again, but it will be in a few days, when I return to the Sublands."

Floriana and his father lowered themselves to the ground and wrapped their arms around the neck of the wolf. "Go on. We got her," his father said.

"I will take care of her for you," Floriana said in a tear-filled voice.

Mateo cast his eyes down at his boots. He did not want them to see the hint of sadness and twinge of heartache in his gaze. He also did not want to see the same emotions echoed in theirs. It would only make things worse. A clean break benefited everyone.

With a quick step, he followed Lady Verona out of the house and shut the door behind him. There was no going back now.

With the bags secured to the top of the carriage, Mateo climbed aboard first. He froze when he entered—not because of the simplicity of the wood interior, or the plain brown fabric on the flat benches that faced each other, or the rectangular wooden table in between those benches.

He froze when he saw the witch sitting inside.

Pale-faced, with red hair and white brows, she wore a lengthy brown dress with a short black cloak. She studied Mateo with sparkling black crystal eyes. He had heard of witches with crystal eyes, from his father mostly.

Manny often spoke of an evil soul-sucking witch named Draven who had tried to kill him and his friends when they arrived in Faevenly all those years ago. Did this witch belong to Draven's coven? Was she evil? And why was she with Lady Verona? All questions Mateo needed answered.

He clutched the cracked leather hand strap and cleared his throat, unsure of where to sit. "I uh..."

"Were you not expecting me?" the witch asked in a silky voice.

Mateo paused, then remembered his manners. "No,

my lady." He nodded and smiled. "Apologies for my rudeness."

"No apologies necessary. I would have reacted the same way."

He lowered himself onto the bench across from her. He kept his gaze down and his hands on his knees. Lady Verona boarded soon after and sat next to the witch.

A crack of a whip and the carriage lurched forward. After a few bumpy turns, they rolled down the main road of the village. Shouting and clapping filled the air. Mateo peered out the window, seeing rows of villagers throwing flowers and beaming with pride. These people added to the reasons why Mateo could not stay home for fear of last place. They knew him and knew he was not only capable but likely to win the hunt for the honor and glory of the Sublands. They believed in him.

"Son of the Sublands." Lady Verona nodded. "They honor you."

He swallowed. He was not worthy of praise, not at all. But seeing the hope in their faces lifted his spirits and his resolve. "I will do my best to earn their honor."

With the crowd thinning out, the last faces he saw were Lirien's and Gareth's and their families. Lirien cupped his hands around his mouth, hooting and hollering. Gareth held his youngest sister, Poppy, on his shoulders while she tossed an armful of wildflowers.

Mateo waved until he lost sight of them, his heart overflowing. He sat back. "My friends," he said with a smile. "They mean a lot to me."

Lady Verona nodded. "They are good people. The Sublands love and honor their hunter."

With the village behind them, the bouncy carriage settled into a steady pace. Lady Verona took off her short black gloves, one finger at a time, settling in for the long ride. "With the pomp and circumstance behind us, allow me to introduce my friend and adviser, Rhyka. She will accompany us to Summit Range." She placed her gloves on her lap. "She possesses wisdom and counsel regarding the hunt and will share it so you do not finish last."

Relieved, Mateo cleared his throat. "Thank you. I appreciate any assistance." He shifted in his seat. "I only learned of the execution penalty last night."

"That was by design," Lady Verona said.

He tilted his head. "What do you mean, by design?"

Lady Verona and Rhyka exchanged knowing glances. Lady Verona folded her hands in her lap and held her head higher than usual. "I knew of the penalty because I asked for it."

Mateo's stomach dropped as if he were in freefall. What did she say? He needed to hear it once more because he did not believe his ears.

"You did what?"

"The Sublands asked for the death penalty."

His nerves skyrocketed. Why would she do that? He drew in slow, steady breaths and held his tongue while his mind processed her words. As steward of the Sublands, Lady Verona controlled the province to the extent allowed by the Stromms. But more than that, she loved the land and its people. He had heard tales of how she'd stood by the Strongs and defended the Sublands from Draven the Witch. Risking the life of a Sublander ran contrary to what he knew of Lady Verona.

Mateo's voice remained steady. He wanted to make sure he understood what he had heard, but needed to mind his manners. He promised his father to be pleasant. "You asked for the one who finishes last to be executed?"

"I did." She studied Mateo with a keen focus. "It was the only way we were allowed a competitor in the hunt."

"So, you wanted to put me at risk?" Forget being pleasant. His voice rose as he leaned forward. "To possibly die?" That made no sense at all to Mateo.

"Not at all. We want you to win." Lady Verona leaned forward and pointed her finger at him. "And show everyone who you really are."

Mateo backed away from Lady Verona as much as he could. *Who he really is?* He narrowed his stare. "What do you mean?"

Lady Verona motioned to the witch, and Rhyka took over. She lowered her voice as if sharing an ancient secret. "I see many things, and I have seen that you are destined to rise as a savior of the Sublands. Like a powerful storm. Not only to save our people, but to restore peace in Faevenly."

A chill swooped through Mateo. It sent his spine tingling and his stomach tumbling. "A savior?"

The witch's voice grew even softer. "Yes, a savior. The hunt is only the first step."

He had no doubt in his abilities to win the hunt, but Rhyka was claiming something more. Something he did not exactly believe. "Why me? I am only a lowborn."

"Because"—she held out the word like a hissing insect —"Strong blood runs in your veins."

Strong as in Strong Haven? He gripped his knees.

His knuckles turned white. He made eye contact with Lady Verona and used a steady yet forceful tone. Fae could not lie, but somehow Rhyka's witchery was allowing her to spew untruths like a fountain. "Lies. I am not a Strong. That bloodline does not even exist today."

Rhyka sat back. She flashed Lady Verona a side glance. "He is not ready to hear the truth."

His pulse thrummed like the mighty blow of a blacksmith's hammer. He did not believe her deceiving tongue. Not for a minute. "There is only one truth here. I am Mateo Vela of the Sublands, son of human Manny Vela and fae Faeryn Vela. And I am going to win that hunt."

Finally, everything he wanted was coming true. The Sublands being included in the hunt. Him being selected. But now everything was spinning out of control. The death penalty for last place. Some so-called premonition about him being a Strong and some sort of savior. None of it made sense. Or maybe Lady Verona and the witch were manipulating him for their own gain somehow. His father did say to trust no one. Did that include Lady Verona? Everyone meant all people, including these two.

"We are on your side, Mateo," Lady Verona said. "I assure you."

His mind scrambled for a response. His ultimate plan was to take first, avoid last, get those seeds, and then go home. When he got back, he would tell Father and let him deal with Lady Verona and the witch.

His breathing steadied. He cleared his throat. "Lady Verona, I am grateful to have you as an escort, but I do not want to hear any more of this. All I want to do is win the hunt."

Rhyka sat back in the seat, angling away from Mateo. "You will come to me when you are ready." She fixed her gaze on the desolate terrain as they passed by towering spires of eroded red and orange rock formations.

No way. He would not be going to her for anything. He almost told her so but held his tongue lest he end up a toad...or worse.

Lady Verona huffed. "Your only worry should be Lord Engrendorn. He represents House Stromm and is highly skilled. We recommend you stay on his tail. You should strike hard and fast if you aim to beat him."

Now they were getting somewhere. Perhaps these ladies had more to offer than a ride filled with deception. "Good. And the other hunters?"

"No other hunter matters," Rhyka said, her eyes remaining on the desert scenery.

He cocked his head sideways. "What does that mean?"

Rhyka turned from the window and glared at Mateo. "I have foreseen that you and the hunter from House Stromm will be linked in the hunt." She threaded her fingers and folded them into a joined fist. "Two destinies tied, making one future."

The witch's premonition landed like a venomous kiss. His scalp prickled, followed by a slight shiver. Mateo's destiny tied to House Stromm? No way. His skin crawled like a thousand tiny spiders scurried beneath the surface. He'd rather be executed.

His logical brain screamed, but he bit his tongue.

Rhyka's premonition was yet another change in plans, another surprise for Mateo and the hunt, and clearly a deception because he would never associate himself with a Stromm for any reason. He tossed the witch's words aside and took away her power. No one decided his fate but himself—not a witch, and certainly not a Stromm.

"Let him rest," Lady Verona said at last, diffusing the uncomfortable tension in the carriage.

Relieved, he muttered a thanks and angled himself away from the ladies. He folded his arms across his chest and closed his eyes. Even though he tried to push away Rhyka's words, they were all he thought about as he struggled to find sleep.

Something else was at work here, something larger than himself, and he had no idea what.

CHAPTER THREE

At one time, there existed harmony between the fae realm and the human realm, with access to both realms made possible through shimmery portals.

Avalynn Stromm hiked up the skirt of her green nightgown. She jammed her boot through the vines that covered the lattice to her second-story bedchamber. Her sharp eyes peered up through the dark night as she considered the path to her open window. "I should have worn pants." She grabbed the lattice, and the spindly thorns scraped her skin. "And gloves."

Despite the barbed woodwork, she climbed swiftly and with purpose. She needed to reach her bedchamber before anyone discovered her missing and reported her absence to her father, the High King. His strict rules against roaming the palace grounds at night were legendary, and he made exceptions for no one. A year ago, her cousin from Sand Bluff left his room during the night to see the newly installed selkie fountain. He was never seen again.

Her excursion did not honor a fountain, though. She was not *that* foolish. She had snuck out to ride a magical creature. For months, beyond the landscaped gardens and expansive lawns of Stromm Palace, she had watched the white Enbarr horse. It appeared when the moon shone bright in the sky, and it pranced and played alone. She had never seen one up close, and it soon became her heart's desire, so much so that she felt a kindred spirit with the Enbarr.

And tonight was her chance. She would've never passed on the opportunity.

The graceful creature had meandered close to the Stromm property line, almost beckoning her to come out. So, she did. She snuck out through her window—which was way easier to climb down than up. She tiptoed her way through the garden's shadows until she was face-to-face with her new friend. Tall and lean, it carried a graceful neck and the longest eyelashes. Lowering on its front legs, it asked her to climb on. How could she say no?

They galloped all night from the Morning Sea to the Evening Sea, even throughout the Majestic Chasm. Glorious. Magical. Invigorating. Wind against her face, hair flowing in the breeze, exhilaration coursing through her veins. She had never felt so alive. She could not wait to do it again, but she needed to get back to her room before daybreak. Getting caught would've ended her magical, mysterious encounters with the creature and seen her endure some sort of awful punishment at her father's order.

With each grueling step up the lattice, she grew closer until she finally reached her window's ledge. She hoisted her legs over the windowsill, fell into her room, and sprawled on the marble floor, smiling. "Made it." It wasn't pretty, but she'd gotten the job done.

Or had she?

Cuts lined and blood streaked across her hands. Her sweat-stained nightgown had ripped on the lattice, and mud caked her boots. "Thunderation." She had marked herself as evidence of her forbidden jaunt with the magical Enbarr.

Scurrying to her washroom, she tore off her boots, nightgown, and underclothes. She shoved the wad to the bottom of her dirty clothes basket. Quickly, she washed her hands and face at the water basin. Slipping on a fresh nightgown, she exhaled. "Now I made it."

With a yawn and a scratch of her head, she returned to her open window. She wiped the ledge with a rag then perched herself on her ivy-strewn window bench. A new day was dawning at Stromm Palace.

The morning sun lit the indigo sky with a soft silvery glow. In the distance a chirp sounded, followed by another. Nestled within the maples and dogwoods, birds were announcing the day. The cool, crisp honeysuckle and rose-scented air meant Stromm Palace awakened. The silver in the horizon made way for pink tints and matte shades of orange and gold. Birds zigzagged through the lush garden, seeking food and drink. Along the gravel pathways, she spied gardeners dressed in their all-green attire along with maidservants in their customary white, all trooping along to attend to their duties.

She could no longer see her new friend—the Enbarr —out in the forest. Perhaps it rested under a large tree or dense shrubbery, settling in for some shuteye after their night of wild play, which was not a bad idea. Sleep, if only for a short while, sounded better than none at all. At least until her maidservant Nia arrived and prodded her awake for the day.

She headed to her plush and comfortable bed when the heavy wood-carved door flung open. *Whoosh!* The orbs floating along her gilded ceiling illuminated. Her father strode in without knocking, wearing silver pants with a pale blue tunic buttoned up to his chin. His long black hair hung down his back while his morning crown of thin silver and crystal circled his head. He rested his hand at his waist on the hilt of the black onyx dagger. His piercing green eyes narrowed on her.

"Father." Avalynn glanced behind him, waiting for her High Queen mother or Maid Nia. But he was alone, which signaled a bad omen for Avalynn. No telling what he might do if angered by something like her sneaking out and riding an Enbarr.

"We must talk." His deep baritone voice filled the bedchamber. He slammed the door behind him. "I need your full attention."

She stopped breathing. Her heart skipped a beat. She wrung her wrists. He must have found out about her frolic. Calm... Stay calm. Redirect his energy to something else. "Of course, Father."

With her head held high, she kicked back her shoulders. If he knew what she had done, would he be so cool and reserved? She smoothed her long, dark hair away from her face and snatched the robe draped on the bed's footboard. Was he toying with her? She pulled on the robe, cinched it at her waist, and stepped in front of his looming form, which nearly touched the wood archway separating her sleeping area from her sitting room. Imposing would've been an understatement for his demeanor.

She motioned toward the white plush chairs in front of the fireplace. "We can sit here if you would like."

With a wave of her hand, the logs flamed like they always did for her. Palace magic designed by the gnomes who secretly maintained the gardens and the lighting for the palace. She sat and rested her hands on her lap. Hiding her superficial skin cuts from the thorny vines, she angled her hands inward.

Her father remained standing and staring.

The fire crackled and popped but offered little warmth. Too much anxiety had built inside her, blocking the soothing heat of the flames. She waited for her father to speak.

"We must talk about the Summit Range Hunt."

She perked up, and her eyes widened. "Yes, Father?"

Avalynn had always wanted to compete in the prestigious hunt. She had been too young to enter the qualifiers, until this year. Preparing for the chance, she'd trained with fierce abandon. Running. Hunting. Archery. She was so skilled with her aim she earned the nickname Arrow Whisperer from her trainers. But it was Summit Range's fiercest warrior, Engrendorn, who beat her with his so-called speed. That, and her foolish glance at a fluttering butterfly, gave him the needed edge. She lost the hunt qualifier due to her own failures, not the excellence of another.

Father shook his head and sighed. "I have received word that Engrendorn is no more."

A quiet gasp escaped her lips. She blinked. "No more?" Their hunter was dead?

"Killed—while investigating the dragon sightings in the far north."

"Sun, Moon, and Stars," she whispered. Her mind picked apart the information, unsure of which thing to latch on to first—the sightings or the death. Both were alarming. But with Engrendorn out of the way, surely her father meant to include her in the hunt. Her time had come after all. She needed to be careful with her words. Her father hated it when she made assumptions. "I was unaware Engrendorn had gone to the north...or that dragons were back."

His nostrils flared, and he gripped the hilt of his dagger at his waist. "You would know of their return if you paid attention to the palace updates."

She bit the inside of her lip but remained sitting tall. She knew he was right, she often ignored the boring palace updates. Much to her father's displeasure, she could not help it. Her mind preferred more interesting things, such as the hunt, but her father needed placating. "You are right, Father. I do not pay well enough attention. I will do better."

He exhaled and grunted. "It would make your rule one day so much easier to know what is happening in Faevenly, my child." He removed his hand from his weapon and glanced at his perfectly groomed nails. "*If* you rule."

When the Strongs and Kanes battled for control of

Faevenly, her father rose as a lord under his father, Lord Thornwick Stromm. His father claimed that when the Strongs and Kanes were done with each other, the Stromms would rise above all others. And he was right.

After the Strongs were wiped out by the Kanes, her grandfather mysteriously disappeared. Her father stepped in to rule the house and sent the land's fiercest witch, Raelor, to kill the highest lords of House Kane. Her father made the remaining heirs and other houses bow to him and crowned himself High King. Now, House Stromm ruled all of Faevenly, and every province answered to them. She was next in line and then Lily, her younger sister. The line of succession was well known and set in stone.

"I pray I gain your favor, Father." Her stomach turned. She had to say that or face his wrath. She knew deep in her heart that she would never truly win him over. For some unknown reason, he seemed to hate his firstborn daughter.

His lip curled with satisfaction. He shifted his stance, blocking even more of the fire with his tall and sleek frame. "The Summit Range Hunt is in two days. The sudden loss of Engrendorn has me searching for a new hunter to replace him." He folded his arms. "Someone who is skilled, capable, and above all else, loyal." He moved closer and stared her down like his pet rabbit. "Someone who will do as I command without question."

Without question? She wasn't sure about that part, but she wanted to prove herself in the hunt. She had the best aim in Summit Range, probably all of Faevenly. Though she despised her father's tactics and manner, she remained a Stromm—loyal to her house and name. A win might make her father view her as an equal, someone worthy of inheriting the crown without groveling. With her position secured, she'd spare her little sister from her father's cruel eye. "I can do it. I can win."

He held up his hand and paused her words. "Before I select the hunter, there are matters that must be acknowledged and accepted."

"Yes?" Her body tensed as she prepared herself for whatever he had in mind.

"The Sublands have been invited to participate in this year's competition." He tightened the grip on his dagger's hilt. "They are sending a hunter to the palace as we speak."

She drew in her chin. "A lowborn?" Father always said they were not worthy of standing beside highborns. "Why? What changed?"

"A bargain has been struck." He paused as if waiting for her reaction. She had none, not yet. The revelation had taken her words. Bargains were dangerous work, especially with her father. "They have asked to be included in exchange for a new rule, the penalty of death for last place."

Avalynn squinted and shook her head. The Sublanders had made a silly wager. Lowborns had no chance against highborns. "Why would they do that?" It made no sense. Everyone knew their human blood made them weak. They were sure to come in last. "Why sacrifice one of their own?"

His grip tightened on his dagger's hilt. "We do not know the skill set of their hunter, though it appears they have great confidence in their chosen one." Tension strained his broad shoulders. "My advisers and I believe they are plotting something."

"But Father, if they—"

"Silence!" he interrupted with his neck veins bulging over his collar. "We will control this outcome, no one else!"

She wanted to yell right back, threaten him with her own dagger, but kept still. The last time she defied him, he confined her to the dungeon for a full moon cycle. She thought she would meet death there and wished for it at times. "Of course, we will. I did not mean to suggest otherwise."

He breathed heavily. "The Stromm hunter will not compete to win. He or she must ensure the Sublands lose. Engrendorn knew this. His replacement must follow his lead."

"Not win?" She wanted to win more than anything. Her skills far surpassed any hunter, and would especially surpass any Sublander. Now, she had to *not win* on purpose? "I do not understand, Father."

His brows furrowed into a formidable V-shape, casting deep shadows over his eyes. "You do not need to understand anything. Only obey." He leaned forward and control brimmed from his cruel eyes. Was he about to compel her? "The hunter's mission will be to sabotage the Sublander. Nothing more."

Nothing more? She did not think so. In the time he gave the directive, she'd already figured it out. She would make sure the Sublander came in last while still finding a way to win. It should not be that hard.

She would do it all—win and prove her worth to her father. "I can do that."

He stepped away from her and moved closer to the fire. "If you fail, you could be facing the death penalty for finishing last."

Fail? She had never failed at anything in her life. She would not start with the hunt. But since her father was including her, he had stamped her as expendable. That's what he was saying. She swallowed, a deep knot forming in her throat. "I will not be last."

He circled the room with slow and deliberate steps, like he was a hunter and she, his prey. She didn't appreciate being put in that position, especially by her own flesh and blood, her own father. Rising, she clasped her hands behind her back and waited for her father's next move.

"Silence is required. You may share that you will be replacing Engrendorn. But you will tell no one your true purpose, other than the Master of the Blade. You will not mention this to your mother or your sister. Or the maids who serve you. Or the other hunters." He tightened his circular path until he practically brushed against her with each step. "You will not even discuss it with me after I leave this room." He stopped in front of her. "Do you understand?"

His stance, the tidal wave of darkness behind his eyes, and the growing depth in his voice—he was one blink away from compelling her. Then, she would be forced to obey regardless of choice. She did not want that and avoided it at all costs.

She squared her shoulders and tamped down the rising fear inside her. "I will tell no one."

"Good. It is agreed. You are appointed the Summit Range Hunter for House Stromm." Before leaving her bedchamber, he looked back. "Do not fail me."

"I will not fail."

The door shut behind him, and a surge of radical emotions raced through her. Excitement at competing, anger at her father's willingness to put her at risk, fear that something would go wrong. But one emotion overrode all the others—determination. She would succeed at all costs.

That Sublander hunter was as good as dead.

CHAPTER FOUR

Over time, humans sought to conquer the fae,
which culminated in the Great Shimmer War.
But humans were no match for the fae.

Avalynn traced the thin cuts on her hands while her father's rich oak, moss, and clove scent lingered. The urgent pulse of her new reality overshadowed the joy of riding the Enbarr. Her mind fixed on her new mission. She needed to learn everything about her fellow competitors. Especially the Sublander. Her life and the honor of House Stromm depended on it.

Her door opened, and Maid Nia whisked in. A white dress hugged her slender and petite frame. A thin blue headband kept her long, silver hair out of her heart-shaped face. She approached, easily balancing the cup and saucer on the gold tray.

"Your father visited early." Nia set the tray on the marble table between the chairs. With lips pursed, her eyes scanned the area. "Is everything all right?"

Her maid knew and understood her father's viciousness for she too had been the victim of his wrath. It was long ago when Avalynn found Nia huddled in the corner, crying. Though too young to grasp the nuances of it all, Avalynn never forgotten the fear on Nia's face. Or the red mark across her cheek.

Avalynn wanted to tell everything but did not dare cross her father or put Nia at risk. Instead, she settled on sharing the bare minimum. "Engrendorn is dead. The role of hunter for House Stromm falls on me now." The less her trusted maid knew, the better.

Nia covered her small mouth with her blue-painted fingernails. "What happened?"

"Dragons." Avalynn raised the delicate glass cup. "In the North." The warm lemon tea touched her lips and kicked her thirst into high gear. She gulped the rest, then set the cup down with a clink. "My father, he—" She stopped and searched for the right hint.

"I can guess." Nia's eager eyes suggested the solution. "You will not have to say the actual words."

Avalynn shook her head. Even a guess might endanger her friend. "I am in the hunt. And that is all you need to know."

Nia pulled her shoulders back and nodded. "Yes, my princess." Her long lashes fluttered like butterfly wings. "How may I assist?"

Pushing aside her father's words, excitement budded inside of her. She was competing in the hunt at last. A grin spread across her face. "Notify the Master of the Blade. Have him meet me in the training circle in one hour."

"Yes, my princess." She smoothed out her skirt. "I will set out your clothing, then notify Master Kragar."

She pointed at Avalynn's hands. "I will bring a salve for those cuts and an energy potion since you lack sleep."

Was it the dark circles under her eyes? The bed she had not slept in? Avalynn rose to her feet and hugged Nia. "You always take such good care of me. I have no idea what I would do without you."

"I am honored and blessed to be with you, my princess." She clapped her hands together with a twinkle in her eye. "Now, let us get you ready."

After a quick wash, Avalynn returned to her bed and found her clothes laid out. Brown training pants, a matching brown tunic, and a thick black belt. Beside her outfit rested the salve and energy potion.

She dressed without delay, her fluid movements matching her rapid-beating heart. She threaded her leather belt through her pant loops. What did Kragar know about the penalty for last place? She sat on the white plush chair and slipped on her black boots. Did he know anything about the Sublander? She needed answers to her pressing questions.

She rubbed the salve on her hand and then gulped down the minty potion. A surge of vitality raced through her fae veins. She whiffed the crystal vial. Hints of the Green Falls water swirled in her nose mixed with herbs she could not quite identify. Whatever it was, it would help in the hunt. She would ask Nia to make more.

A soft rustle whisked through the silent room. Setting

the vial down, she turned and saw an envelope. It rested by her door on the marble floor. She hurried to the door and yanked it open. Nobody. She went back inside her room and examined the plain white envelope. She opened it and removed the note.

Trust your instincts, not your past.

She lowered the note. Who sent this? What did it mean? The hunt. It had to involve the hunt. But how? She put the note back into the envelope and shoved it under her mattress. She tucked it as far as she could reach. The note was her secret, and she'd ask Nia about it later. Now she had to focus on Kragar. Duty and destiny called her name. She would answer that call with a resounding victory.

Avalynn stepped from her bedchamber and marched down the sparkling white corridor. She passed rows of gardenia-filled vases. The blooms filled the air with that rich and velvety sweet aroma. She trotted down the winding staircase, crossed the foyer, and exited the glass doors. Her mind raced toward the training meadow at the edge of the palace grounds when a pair of slender arms slipped around her waist from behind and hugged her. She turned and saw her ten-year-old sister, Lily.

She smiled from ear to ear, as if she had found buried treasure. "I heard the news! You are a hunter!"

Lily had spent hours watching Avalynn train. When

she didn't win the qualifier, it broke her little sister's heart worse than her own. Inconsolable, Lily cried for days.

"Yes, my little princess. Always remember...hard work and honor pay off."

"I knew it would. I prayed to the Stars above."

"And it worked." She tucked Lily's long silver hair behind her sharply pointed ears and kissed the top of her head. "I am headed to meet Master Kragar. Want to come?" She would take her little sister with her anywhere.

"Sure. But will you look at my dress first?" Lily held out her lilac-colored dress skirt and spun. "Is it pretty?"

"It is! You are the prettiest princess in all of Faevenly."

The sisters clasped hands and continued along the crushed gravel path toward the training circle. "What kind of training are you doing?" Lily asked.

They passed a group of gardeners tending to a row of blooming azalea bushes. "I'm not sure. But I think today will be mostly strategy since the hunt is only a few days away," Avalynn replied.

Lily slowed her pace. "Strategy? No training? Sounds boring."

Avalynn stopped and pulled Lily closer. "It may sound boring, but it is the most important thing in hunting and even ruling a kingdom. Sound strategy makes for a successful hunt and, later, a successful queen." These were words of wisdom for her sister. She waited to see if she would listen.

Lily scrunched up her nose. "Um, I have something

else to do." She pulled her hand from Avalynn's grasp. "Have fun with your strategy."

As Avalynn suspected... She chuckled as Lily skipped away. "I will." Her little sister had plenty of time to become a warrior princess. Maybe another day.

The gravel path wound through a variety of towering oak trees. Their mossy, gnarled branches crisscrossed overhead. They cast patterns of shade and light with each of Avalynn's steps. Beneath the green canopy rested rows of towering rhododendrons with clusters of pink and lavender bell-shaped flowers. In the distance loomed the blue-hued mountain tops. The challenge lay before her eyes. Summit Range. Her destiny had been defined.

Avalynn's heart raced at the sight of the hunting ground. A triumphant purple glow gathered in her chest. She would be out there soon—winning.

Stepping along, a whistling whoosh buzzed past her ear. She ducked, and another arrow whizzed over her head. It thudded into a tree trunk. She darted for cover and crouched behind a concrete bench. Who in thunderation was shooting arrows at her? On palace ground no less? "I will have your head!"

"I will have yours first!"

She peeked over the back of the bench. She spotted a tuft of red ducking between the bushes. Kragar and another surprise training session. The Master of the Blade loved spontaneous encounters. "Stop, Master!" A third arrow sailed her way, brushing the hair on top of her head. "I am weaponless!"

"Enemies do not care if you are weaponless!"

She spotted a cluster of rocks. She lunged, rolled, and

snatched two fist-sized chunks. She righted herself with a hop. Her sharp eyes found the fourth arrow racing straight for her. The thin wood spun. The sun glinted against the silver arrowhead. She threw her makeshift weapon. Aim on point, her rock collided with the arrow's tip and knocked it to the ground. She held the other rock at the ready. She had bested the dwarf Master Kragar and was eager to do it again.

He popped out from behind a magnolia cluster. Half elf, half dwarf, and she also suspected part troll, Kragar stood almost five feet and a half and wore all green, like an overgrown, maniacal garden gnome.

She lowered her rock. "Have you lost your mind?" She could've killed him or vice versa.

He grabbed his sides and bellowed. "Of course, I have lost my mind!" He flicked his long red beard. It landed next to the clump of red hair atop his head. "You should lose yours sometime." He left the misplaced and wayward beard wisp. "It is way beyond liberating."

Avalynn shook her head with a chuckle. "Master Kragar, this is not the time for jesting." She joined him on the path. "Have you heard from my father?" Perhaps Kragar had further information her father wouldn't part with.

He fastened the bow to the sheath at his waist. "I have." He stashed his arrow in the quiver on his back. "You are going into the hunt, like you have always desired." Patting her back, he slung his axe onto his shoulder. "Your time has finally come."

A deep breath and her lungs expanded to their

fullest. Kragar believed in her and understood her desire to succeed. "I will show them all."

"I have no doubt. You are House Stromm's best chance." He clicked his tongue and winked. "Does not hurt that I have trained you."

She laughed. "No, it does not."

The green open space was not set up for target practice or agility training. Instead, a large crate rested in the middle of the field. Inside, a small beast circled. Master Kragar spread out his arms, as if presenting her with a special treat. "Feast your eyes."

She approached the crate. "Ooh! Is that what we are hunting?"

Kragar nodded. "It is." He made direct eye contact with Avalynn. "The hunters will see it as a group after arrival." His grin conveyed a secret advantage. "But you are a Stromm. You will see it now." He wiggled his eyebrows. "And you can ask all the questions you so desire." He leaned in. "Make them count."

She crept closer to the crate. Every hunt featured a different animal. Elk. Boar. Goblins. Harpies. What animal would be featured this year? Inside the crate, a beast the size of a small wolf circled. Its long bushy tail curled up to its back. Its dark fur shimmered with an iridescent, ethereal glow reminiscent of the midnight sky. She had never seen this creature.

Kragar tugged the back of her tunic. "Not too close."

"I will keep my distance." She bent down and looked inside the crate. The creature zipped from the back of the cage to the front. She stared into the beady and molten eyes that looked her over like doomed prey. "It is beautiful. And I sense it is smart. What is it called? And where is it from?"

"It is a Shadowblood Fox." His thick eyebrows rose and peaked on his rippled forehead. "They come from the far north. Cunning. Quick. Not to be fooled with...or trusted."

Her fingers twitched, wanting to pet it, but she knew better. The deadliest creatures roamed the far north. Like dragons. *Poor Engrendorn.* She moved closer. "The name 'shadow' must come from its dark color. But what does the 'blood' part mean?"

"Good question," he said with a smile.

The Shadowblood Fox hissed, and its fangs elongated. Its eyes flashed red. It jabbed a long paw through the bars and swiped, missing Avalynn's nose by a fingernail. "Whoa!" She tumbled onto her backside. That vicious creature almost took her snout right off her face.

Kragar slammed his fist on the top of the cage and growled. "You will be dead soon enough!"

The fox scampered to the far end of its crated prison.

Avalynn checked her face and felt no blood or slashes. The fox failed to make contact. "That was way too close for comfort."

He peered back at her and snarled. "You alright?"

She rose, brushed herself off, and spoke with strength and conviction. "I am fine. Just startled." She returned to her question. "The 'blood' part of its name must be for its fangs then? Is it vampiric?"

"It is vampiric, but it only feeds on small animals—especially rabbits. Can't get enough rabbit, as a matter of fact. When threatened, it can sometimes release a deadly toxin through its claws." He jerked his stubby thumb at the fox. "There is more to its shadow name, though."

Avalynn raised her brows. "Really? Like what?"

"Watch." He draped a heavy black cloth over half of the crate. The sun-blocking fabric created a dark space. The fox slunk into the crate's corner, hissed, and then disappeared.

Her eyes widened, and her mouth dropped open. "Sun, Moon, and Stars. It is gone—vanished."

"Not gone, but vanished into the dark." He pulled the cloth off. With the sun shining down, it popped back into view. "And here it is again."

"Unbelievable." The fox blended into the shadows. She scratched her head, still staring at the creature. "How do I hunt a fox that disappears?" That created a larger challenge than usual, especially in the forest with all the trees.

He backed away and lifted his palms. "I have said all I can." He tilted his head sideways. "But I have said enough to give you the answer." He grinned and winked. "If you are smart enough, that is."

Smart enough? *Pfft.* Kragar knew better, and so did she. But what was the answer? She replayed their conversation. Fangs. Shadows. Rabbits. She found no answer. She would have to think about it later.

"Come now." He waved for her to follow. "We have more to discuss."

They walked to the far end of the green space. Flags furled showing the wind's direction. Stacks of hay bales served as a barrier while boards were erected for archery practice. Large parchments replaced the usual diamond-shaped targets. Faces were painted on each one.

"These are your competition," Kragar said.

She rubbed her hands together in short strokes while scanning the competitors' faces. "Most excellent, Master Kragar."

He started at the far right with a drawing of Avalynn. The spot-on likeness pleased her. Long jet-black hair. Blue eyes. The artist captured her confidence by showing her chin slightly raised. "This is you."

"Really?" She feigned surprise, then put her hand on her hip. "I think I know myself."

Kragar did not flinch or grin. "Your strength is aiming, and everyone knows that. Your weakness?"

She swallowed. Weakness? She possessed none. First in line to the throne, she did not like hearing such nonsense. Kragar remained by her drawing with his arms crossed. She tossed him the easy answer. "I suppose my weakness is confidence?"

No response. He wore a disapproving expression and continued to the next drawing. She added weakness to her mental checklist of things to figure out, right under Shadowblood Fox and the mysterious note.

"Who is this?" Kragar pointed at the second drawing.

She recognized the long, cherry-red hair and green eyes. "Selene Baffin from Sand Bluff. Her father is the steward there." They went to a courting training session once when they were young maidens and did *not* get along. "I made her cry when we were little."

He howled. "Good girl. She is a displeasure, that one." He pointed at the picture. "Her strength is climbing. Her weakness is aiming. She cannot shoot a center point if her bloodline depended on it."

"Really? How did she qualify for the hunt then?"

"Her father, that is how." Kragar snorted. He moved to the next drawing. "And this is...?"

"Eiric Lind from Cuesta. His uncle is the steward there." His striking, long silver hair and violet eyes made all the maidens go weak in the knees. Not Avalynn. The dim and full of himself fae annoyed her. She couldn't stand his company and would've rather had a conversation with a dead plant.

"Correct. His strength is aiming, too. Yet, water remains his weakness."

No way. She laughed. "Water? Seriously?" She supposed the loser Eiric could not swim.

He tapped the portrait. "Put Eiric Lind in deep water, and he will sink to the bottom like that rock in your hand."

She tossed the forgotten rock and motioned to the next hunter. "That's Finnian Brunt from High Meadow." Long brown hair, green eyes. Nice enough and from a good family. His father acted as steward of High Meadow since one had not been officially named after the Kanes were wiped out. He would be a formidable opponent.

"Finnian is known for strength and stamina, but he is slower than an ocean turtle."

"Interesting." She thought for sure his lack of speed would favor her in the hunt.

He moved on with a raised brow and motioned to the next parchment. "Last but most certainly not least." He shrugged. "Or maybe least. We will not know until the hunters arrive."

The final drawing contained no portrait. On the large parchment, Kragar had painted a red "X" from corner to corner. She inched forward and lowered her voice. "The Sublander." Per her father's orders, the last place finisher and winner of the death penalty prize.

Kragar folded his arms. "Late edition. I have no information on him. But rumors have swirled like the desert's dust."

She locked eyes with the Master of the Blade. "What do the rumors speak of?"

He moved in and lowered his voice. "About him being more than a mere Sublander."

"More than a lowborn?" That wasn't possible. If he was more she would have known.

"Aye. Someone with innate gifts and powers who will change Faevenly forever. A rumor that is not spoken of in the palace, but one which I feel I should mention to you."

A Sublander with gifts? Powers? Change her Faevenly kingdom? She huffed, knowing that the person who would change the kingdom was Avalynn Stromm, not some lowly Sublander. "Yeah, I do not think so."

His jawline hardened. He pointed at Avalynn and stared through her fae princess soul. "That is why you must succeed." His eyes narrowed and filled with blackness. He dropped his voice from tenor to bass and began chanting a dark tune. *Sublander must die... Sublander must die...*

CHAPTER FIVE

The Great Shimmer War ended swiftly, and humans were branded as enemies.

Over the next two days, Mateo watched the landscape morph from barren and rocky to green and flourishing. Rolling fields of blue and purple and blooming flowers of pink and white carpeted the landscape. Ripened red and gold fruit hung from trees and dangled from bushes. No longer in the dying Sublands, the air teemed with a sense of renewal. Mateo's destiny lay ahead.

The carriage driver shouted, "The palace is in sight!"

Mateo's nerves activated as those lightning bugs swarmed his stomach. His head rested against the window. He soaked in his first sight of a real-life palace. Set against a backdrop of rolling hills and lush forests, he spotted the ivory and gold turrets and spires of Stromm Palace. It glistened like a dream.

"A grand sight," Lady Verona uttered.

Mateo tore his eyes away. "There is nothing grand about it." He gripped his knees. "More like a hideous display of power and wealth." The palace could have housed the entire Sublands.

The road of trampled dirt and packed gravel converged with another. Ahead rolled two more carriages, and behind filed in another.

Lady Verona folded her long hands on her lap. "Excellent. Right on time."

The palace loomed closer, and the carriages drew nearer. In front traveled the carriage for House Baffin of Sand Bluff. Their white banner with gold lettering flapped in the wind. It featured the flower, a bluebonnet, representing their province. Above the bluebonnet a large "B" was painted in black. Following House Baffin rolled the fancy carriage for House Lind of Cuesta. Their banner featured elk antlers with an "L" painted in red. Behind House Cuesta traveled the carriage for House Brunt of High Meadow. A sprawling oak tree covered their banner with a white painted "B."

The witch's words from earlier lingered, refusing to leave him alone. His last name crept up everywhere he looked. If Mateo and the Sublands had a banner, it would have been brown and the symbol would have been a red rock. His letter would be a "V" for Vela, not an "S" for Strong.

The carriages came closer to the palace, with people lined up on both sides of the road. They cheered and hollered like back in the Sublands, tossing flowers and ribbons. They waved the Summit Range banner with its mountain peak and tree-lined forest. A gold "S" covered the banner from top to bottom. They celebrated their own, not any others. Especially not the Sublands.

A Stromm palace guard with an emblem on his coat banged on the carriage's door. "Stop! Move aside!"

Mateo craned his neck. "What is happening?" The Sand Bluff and Cuesta carriages moved forward while theirs stopped, allowing the High Meadow carriage to whip around and pass them. "Why are they moving in front of us?"

Lady Verona's jaw tightened. "They are putting us in *their* preferred order." With lips pursed, she gritted her teeth. "With the Sublands last."

"They hate us." Mateo seethed at the second-class citizen treatment. No wonder the Sublands had to make a deal to get into the hunt—they weren't wanted here.

Rhyka raised her voice. "We are the lowest of the low." She quirked a brow. "For now."

On that one thing, he agreed with the witch.

The carriages continued toward the palace in their new order. The closer to the palace, the more people gathered, and the din grew louder. Hollering, boos, and hisses blared toward Mateo and his carriage. *Sublander scum! No lowborns!* Spit flew, and balled fists banged the carriage. Mateo had never felt more unwelcome. Highborns had no idea the manner and respect with which visitors should be treated. Anger boiled inside of him. He would have speared them all—every single Stromm supporter. They deserved nothing less for their insolence.

Lady Verona nudged his knee. "Pay them no attention."

The carriages rolled up to the palace's opened gates. The entryway soared to impressive heights. Pure ivory. Gilded filigree. The carriages continued in a circular path around spraying fountains, manicured lawns, and flowering bushes.

A Stromm palace guard yelled, "Halt!"

Shoulders back, Lady Verona's chin raised higher than normal. "Keep your head high at all times. Let us show them the true nature of Sublanders."

Mateo's eyes narrowed. He would stare down each competitor. Especially Engrendorn of House Stromm, the soon-to-be last place finisher. He would be certain to fall first if Mateo had anything to say about it.

THE
CEREMONIES

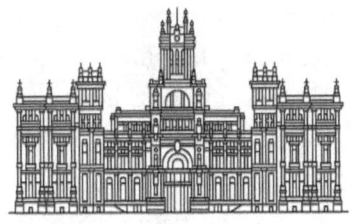

CHAPTER SIX

The Strongs, the ruling house of Faevenly, used a glamour to erase the war from human memory. They then stored every portal on Torch Lake and forbade their use henceforth.

A valynn paced the second-story library. The smell of parchment and leather filled the room. Excitement and nervousness over the arrival of the carriages cascaded through her. She kept her focus down, on the vines and leaves on the gold and red carpet beneath her boots. Not knowing what to do with her hands, she wrung them together. "Any sign of them?"

Lily perched on the seat of the large rectangular window. She parted the purple silk drapes and peered out. "Not yet."

Pulling and cracking her fingers, she again paced about the room. She did not care how the other hunters would respond when they found out she'd replaced Engrendorn. Her mind was fixed on the Sublander. Would he be cunning like Father? Strong like Kragar? Handsome like the dead Engrendorn? She needed to know as much as possible about the one that would face last place.

Lily gasped and flashed Avalynn a wide grin. "The guards are opening the gates."

"Finally." She opened the purple drapes a bit more and locked her chin on Lily's dainty shoulder. "Let us see what we are dealing with, little princess." She would learn what she needed and then teach her little sister a few things about being a royal.

The bright sun bounced off the first three intricately carved carriages. Their richly painted banners flapped in the wind. She did not care about those. Her gaze zipped to the last carriage. Plain brown. No banner. Hideous—a wonder it had made it to Summit Range in one piece. "Look at *that* thing."

"Eww." Lily looked up with a scrunched nose. "Is that ugly thing the Sublander's?"

"I believe so." She wasn't sure what she had expected. But whatever horrible thing fell into the pit of her mind's eye, this was it. "They are Sublanders, after all." Lowborn losers without a decent carriage in which to travel and roam the countryside.

"I suppose it smells like a goblin's den in there."

She kissed her sister's soft cheek and chuckled. "I *suppose* you are right." She had heard the Sublanders carried a certain awful smell of rubbish and rotten fruit perfume.

The brown carriage stopped. A tall woman dressed in copper pants with a copper shirt and long, dark braided hair stepped out. Next came a woman in brown with a black cloak. Her red hair flamed like a forest fire.

"Which one is the hunter?" Lily leaned forward and squinted.

Avalynn kept her focus on the carriage. She spotted movement within. "There is someone else." Here comes the goblin. The red X on Kragar's parchment. But, a tall, slender, and flawless fae hopped out. A small gasp escaped her lips. He wore black pants with a silver shirt. Two strands of sleek black braids framed his face. The rest of his hair hung past his shoulders. Full lips, chiseled high cheekbones, and a perfectly pointed nose—he did not look like any lowborn she had ever seen.

Lily glanced over her shoulder with widened eyes and an open mouth. "Who is that?"

Avalynn bit her bottom lip and swallowed. "I think..." He moved with grace. He strode with royal confidence. "That might be..." Heat rose in her cheeks. Her heart thumped. "It could be the Sublander."

Lily's long lashes fluttered. She swung her head back around. Her eyes sparkled with childlike wonder. "If he came from royalty, he could court me."

"Oh, come on now, Lily." She furrowed her brow. "You must remember, as a princess in line for the throne, that looks are deceiving. He is a lowborn and a Sublander. The beauty of our enemies does not change what we must do. And I *must* defeat him." He must come in last place.

"Ok. Fine." Lily hopped from her perch and took Avalynn's hand. "Let's go see him up close. You have to be there for the processional. But if you are not up to it, perhaps I could take your place."

"You?" Avalynn chortled as they hurried along the empty corridor. "You would not stop looking at the Sublander."

They trotted down the stairs. Avalynn glanced at a full-length mirror at the landing. How did she look? Black velvet pants with embroidered vines along the sides. A fitted purple shirt with pearlized buttons down the back and matching pearl cuffs. She regretted not wearing a dress or something with a plunging neckline. She huffed and pushed the notion aside. Why should she care what that Sublander thought? She grunted under her breath. He did not matter. She had no need to invest any further thought in a dead hunter walking.

Rounding the landing's corner, Maid Nia nearly collided with them. "There you are!" She raised her brows. "Where have you been? The hunters have arrived and checked in. It is time for the presentation to the High King and High Queen." She took Lily's hand. "I will take the little one. You take your place with the hunters. Hurry."

"Sorry, Nia." Avalynn smoothed her long dark hair with her shaky hands. "I am right behind you."

Her stomach twisted into a knot as Nia and Lily disappeared from view. Why was she so flustered? She drew her shoulders back and held her head high. Resting her hand over her heart, she drew in a deep breath. She knew the answer—because the Sublander was beautiful, that was why.

She neared the vestibule. Strumming harps and light chatter drifted her way. The smell of gardenias and roses filled her nose. She needed to heed her own advice. His looks didn't matter. Not one bit. She was the Stromm hunter. Her task was not to know or understand the

Sublander. Her task dictated that she follow her father's command and Kragar's warning.

The Sublander must die.

Avalynn entered the vestibule for the procession. A throng crowded the wide-open and tall space. Harpists played at every corner. Selene, Eiric, and Finnian gathered in the middle but kept their distance from one another. They had no idea she would be joining them.

She scanned the faces in the crowd and quickly found the Sublander. He and his group stood in the far corner of the room, away from everyone. His eyes looked downward as if he studied the marble floor with its flecks of inlaid gold. His eyes then hit the walls with their intricate wood-carved patterns. He ran his finger over the smooth, detailed surface. He looked like a kelpie out of water—so out of place. Making sure he finished last would be no problem. Until that time, she would not mind keeping an eye on him, which would be the easiest part of all.

The heavy double doors to the receiving room opened. The music stopped. Two doormen stepped aside, and Maid Nia came forward. Her pure and elegant voice filled the room. "The escorts and dignitaries may enter. The hunters will line up in the same order they arrived."

The music started again, and the scene inside

bustled. Avalynn turned her attention back to the Sublander. This time, he was not looking around. This time, his steely gray eyes were locked on her. Their gazes met. Smoldering heat oozed all around him. A flush worked its way up her cheeks as a wave of desire raced through her. She quickly turned away, her breath catching in her throat. *Oh my.* She placed her hand on her chest, calming her beating heart. Forget his looks. Remember his station. He was nothing more than a lowborn, and she had a job to do.

"Princess Avalynn." Selene approached, her voice syrupy sweet though her eyes revealed a hint of irritation as they narrowed at the corners. "So lovely to see you."

She nodded, not wanting her or anyone else to know how she had reacted to the Sublander. She raised her chin high. "Selene."

"Princess Avalynn," Eiric and Finnian said at the same time, bumping elbows as they bowed before her.

"Eiric, Finnian," she replied without making eye contact.

The hunters shuffled about and began moving into a line. Selene, then Eiric, then Finnian. The Sublander stayed at the rear. Of course. Avalynn took her place at the front.

"Where is Engrendorn?" asked Finnian. As a Stromm and first in line to the crown, she owed him and the others no explanations. The sooner they accepted that, the better. "I am the hunter for House Stromm."

A trumpet blared, and a string of violins joined. She readied herself to make her entry when the Sublander's shoulder brushed against hers. He zipped past, and walked into the receiving room first. "What the…"

Avalynn's mouth fell open. Her hands balled into fists at her sides. A Sublander? Leading the procession? She pushed away the fact that he smelled like delicious spicy vanilla and sandalwood as she shot daggers with her eyes through the back of his neck and quickly sifted through her options. Make a scene, stop the procession, and force him to the back. He cut in front of Avalynn Stromm after all. Or, march forward now and make him pay later. With the room filled with onlookers, she opted for the second choice. She would have to put him in his place later.

The escorts and other invited guests parted, forming a center walkway for the hunters. One after the other, they made their way to the end of the room where her mother and father sat on their day thrones fashioned from Stardust Oak, the sparkling wood. They wore coordinating purple and black like her. A show of force and royalty. Ceremonial crowns of ivory, gold-dipped vines, and leaves with crystal accents adorned their regal heads.

Master Kragar stood behind her mother. Avalynn paused a step when her gaze landed on Raelor the witch who loomed behind her father. His long white hair hung loose. He wore all black, matching the molten black staff in his hand. His eyes sparkled like diamonds as they drifted across the faces of the hunters. She swallowed. She had not anticipated seeing him, but then she supposed it made sense. The hunt was a grand event. Not to mention the addition of a Sublander.

The hunters neared. Her father's nostrils flared while

her mother's brow raised. They glanced at each other as if they did not understand why Avalynn was not first in line. Biting the inside of her cheek, she buried the impulse to put the Sublander where he belonged right then and there.

Master Kragar stepped forward. He guided the hunters to their designated positions. The Sublander moved into place, and she and the others filed in. The room fell silent. She took deep breaths through clenched teeth as she managed the fiery emotions raging inside. Looks be damned. The Sublander was going down.

Her father rose and clutched the hilt of the dagger at his waist. His commanding voice filled the room. "Welcome dignitaries, escorts, and hunters. The High Queen and I open Stromm Palace to you for the Tenth Summit Range Hunt."

Claps and cheers broke out. He scanned the crowd, accepting the praise, before his penetrating green eyes stopped on the Sublander. "Each hunter will step forward and announce themselves, beginning with House Stromm and ending with the Sublands." He drew out the word 'Sublands' like he had unleashed a deadly disease.

She smirked and side-eyed the Sublander, who'd been put in his proper position by her father. And in front of everyone. Served him right.

She stepped forward, knocking him with her shoulder, and bowed to the throne she would sit on one day. "I am Avalynn Stromm, and I am honored to compete for House Stromm."

She stepped back, and the other hunters followed

suit. Paying them no attention, she waited for the Sublander's announcement. When his turn came, a different kind of silence settled in the room. Strained and defensive—as if all of Faevenly paused for a public beheading.

He stepped forward with a long stride. His shoulders back. His dark hair was smooth, shiny, and perfect. "I am Mateo Vela, the Sublands' hunter. I will be honored to win first place at this year's hunt."

Gasps rang out in waves. Someone in the back of the room hollered. Her father whipped his cloak behind his back. He growled to his witch, "Put him in his place."

A sinister smile spread across Raelor's pale face as he swooped in. He flung out his arm and stretched out his fingers. He pointed at the Sublander, then commanded in a low and gravelly tone, "**Move to your proper place**."

The Sublander clutched his neck. Choking sounds sputtered from his lowborn mouth as Raelor's compel controlled him. His right leg stepped forward with a jerk, followed by his left. Avalynn stayed still lest the witch's command somehow spread to her. She kept her attention on the tuft of red hair on top of Kragar's head as the strain from the Sublander's throat echoed through the room in spurts and and grunts as his boots skidded across the marble floors with each involuntary movement to the back of the line.

When he was in place, silence settled in like a candle being snuffed. Not even a breath from the crowd could be heard. The witch lowered his hand and retook his position behind her father. Raelor was needed after all.

The High King nodded, then returned to his announcements as if nothing had happened. "This year, in addition to the inclusion of the Sublands, a new penalty of death for last place has been instituted." A wicked grin spread across his face. "Along with the immediate banishment of the last place finisher's province."

Whispers broke out. Avalynn's stomach turned. She knew of the death penalty for last place, but banishment of an entire province? Even by her father's cruel standards, that seemed extreme. She would never rule her kingdom that way. Was there something more going on she did not know? Was she being played for a fool? A daughter would not mind. A future queen could not allow that.

With a swish of his cloak, her father returned to his throne.

She wished she could look down the line at the Sublander to see his expression. But she did not dare. What did he think about the newest penalty? What did the others think? Not only did the Sublander face death, but his people were doomed to banishment before the hunt began.

Master Kragar withdrew his axe from his sheath and rested it on his shoulder as he moved forward. "At the crown's pleasure, I have the duty and honor of announcing the prey in this year's Summit Range Hunt." He held out his thick hand to calm the cheering. "The untamed, dangerous, and cunning game this year is the Shadowblood Fox." Oohs and aahs filled the room. "Each hunter will be allowed to view the animals tomorrow. All rules and procedures will be explained at that time as well." Master Kragar moved his axe to his other shoulder and then stepped back.

The High Queen rose, her elegant fingers pushing off the armrest with the slightest touch as if guided by the gentlest breeze. Her dark hair cascaded down her back like an ocean's wave. She smiled in her benevolent and caring way. "My distinguished guests and honored hunters, as you can see, much has gone into the preparations for this year's hunt." Her neck arched with swan-like grace, accentuating her poise. "After tomorrow's viewing of the prey and review of the hunt's rules, we will have the Gala of the Hunter's Moon." She folded her hands together. "And then, of course, the next morning will be the hunt."

More clapping rang out, and the High Queen waited for the quiet to return. "Each hunter will be assigned an attendant at the end of today's celebration. We hope everyone feels welcome. Food and drink will now be served."

Music filled the space, and everyone started buzzing. Avalynn spun on her heels, ready to confront the Sublander for entering ahead of her, but he walked away briskly. She marched toward him, lunged, and grabbed his arm. Her palm tingled from his touch, his arousing scent made her knees weak, and a sea of goosebumps erupted all over her body. She swallowed, dropped his arm, and raised her chin. *Stop thinking about him like that. He is a lowborn.* "I have no idea who you think you are. But you will not be winning anything."

"Who do I think I am?" He stepped closer and looked

her up and then down. He appeared completely unfazed to be standing in front of a princess from House Stromm. The arrogance. "I am Mateo Vela of the Sublands. Get that straight, princess."

CHAPTER SEVEN

Over time, there came to be twin princesses in the Strong family—ambitious Princess Malena and curious Princess Celyse... Celyse is your grandmother.

His hand shot to the spot where Avalynn Stromm had touched him. The connection sent a wave of something inside of him he hadn't felt before and wasn't expecting. But anger quickly erased all that.

Rubbing her away, he squeezed his hands together as he marched out of the receiving room. Her father had challenged him, his witch had compelled him, and the princess had warned him.

He sensed a pressure so strong it might have shattered every bone in his hands. Stinging pulses shot through his arms. He would have sent those pulses into the king's face if he could've.

How dare his Highness! In front of everyone, the king ordered that witch to spell him and drag him to the back of the line. And how dare that wretched Princess Avalynn! *She* threatened *him*? Please. As if she or her father could have kept him down. And to think that

Rhyka thought he would in any way be linked to her. Never in an eon would that happen.

He swung his arms as he crossed the vestibule floor. The widened eyes of the doormen spotted him. They scrambled into place. Uh-uh-uh... With a series of grunts, they heaved the thick and dense palace doors open.

Verona hissed behind him. "Mateo, stop." Her padded boots struck the floor in short strides. "Now."

He wasn't stopping. If she had the key to victory in the hunt, he would have kept going. He needed to exit that cursed place no matter who or what followed.

The cool night air soothed his face like a refreshing splash after a hard run. The comforting scents of earth and fauna erased the palace's garish and powdery perfumes. Where the crushed granite met the grass, he stopped. The nearly full orange moon filled the night sky and lit up the grounds with a radiant glow.

Verona caught up to him. "Have you lost your mind?" Quick bursts of vapor billowed from her mouth. "Challenging the king like that?"

"He had it coming." The High King had no right to order his witch to compel him like that.

"Maybe so. But we are who we are—Sublanders." She rubbed her forehead as if they had no choice. "We have to play our role until you get in that hunt." She leaned in and whispered, "They will remove you before it starts if you pull a trick like that again." Her eyebrows raised the length of her forehead. "Or send you to the dungeons. You are lucky that witch did not end you on the spot."

Rhyka drew near, her presence adding another level of frustration. "Foolish boy."

"I am no fool. I am mad. You are afraid of them, but I am not." Lady Verona had her limitations as the steward of the Sublands, but he did not have those same binds. "They have no power over me except that which I give them." As long as Mateo drew breath, no Stromm would ever wield power over any child of Manny Vela.

"Enough with that," Rhyka warned. "What did Princess Avalynn say to you?"

"Nothing important." Her perfectly formed lips, the color of red rose petals, sprang to mind. He pushed the visual aside.

Rhyka clutched his arm. "What did she say?" The witch shook him as if he were a child.

He jerked his arm away. "All the princess said was 'you will not win anything.'"

Lady Verona exchanged glances with Rhyka. She squinted and then whispered, "The Stromms are up to something."

"With Raelor's aid, no less," Rhyka replied.

Mateo opened his palms. "Of course, they are up to something. First, Engrendorn was the hunter, and now the Stromm heir is? How does that even make sense?" The Stromms played by their own rules.

Lady Verona looked at Rhyka. "We will find out."

He shook his head. "It doesn't even matter." His father and sister needed those healing seeds, so did little Poppy, and so did the rest of the Sublands. He was not going to let them down. "They can cheat all they want. But they still have to release those foxes. And when they do, they will figure out a thing or two about me...like I do not lose."

"Ahem, excuse me, honored guests?" It was the petite woman who had ushered them into the receiving room.

Lady Verona faced the maidservant while Mateo composed himself.

The maiden tipped her head. "I am Maid Nia, your assigned attendant while you are at the palace. I would be honored to show you to your rooms. That is, if you are finished with the evening's festivities. Your things have already been delivered."

"That would be splendid." Lady Verona nodded. "Thank you."

Maid Nia motioned with her arm. "I will lead you around the exterior of the palace to the guest rooms at the rear. It is a shorter walk this way." She took a step. "Please, follow me."

Despite the bright moon illuminating the gravel pathway, lighted orbs dotted the path. Round. Shimmery. Hazy around the edges. "We don't have these in the Sublands," Mateo muttered, as if the glowing spheres could hear him. "How do they work?"

"The magic of our gnomes," Maid Nia explained. "They maintain the grounds and the orbs, both outside and inside the palace."

Mateo studied the shrubs and trees lining the path. "Are the gnomes here now?"

"They keep hidden." Her soft steps kept a steady pace. "I have never seen one myself."

The obscene luxuries of this place...while back home, Sublanders struggled. His family and so many others could benefit from this type of wealth. They could have plenty of healing seeds, food, fabric, and building materials. Winning the hunt would elevate the Sublands in countless ways. With this level of wealth, his mother might even have still been alive today.

The maid stopped at the palace's rear and presented a simple door. No carvings, no adornments, only plain thick wood—perfect for a Sublander. The hinges creaked as a doorman opened the entrance. Maid Nia started up the winding staircase. "This wing of the palace is perfect for privacy and relaxation." Her flowing white dress settled as she reached the second-floor landing. "On this floor, we have a library along with three bedchambers. Each has a washroom. On the third floor, you will find a fourth chamber, also with its own washroom. All meals will be provided in the receiving room, where we were earlier, and—"

"I will take the third floor." Mateo did not need to hear any more. His foot hit the step, and he turned to the maid. "What is my schedule for tomorrow?"

"When the sun is at its peak, all hunters will meet in the training circle in the rear of the garden. The gala follows in the evening." She raised a finger. "Oh, and please do not roam the grounds at night. It is strictly prohibited."

He bowed his head to her. "Thank you." He met Lady Verona's eyes. "See you tomorrow."

Despite the plain wooden door at the entry of the wing, the guest room was as grotesquely opulent as the rest of the palace. Gold flecks dotted the floor. Richly carved wood covered the walls. Mateo pressed his forehead against the door with a bang. Was there any place here that was not dripping in wealth? The Stromms did not deserve to even breathe.

Floral perfume wafted through the dense air. Like a ray of light, her image flashed in his mind. Avalynn Stromm. He pushed it away, then searched for the sweet aroma's source. He found an arrangement of roses and lilies on the stone table by the opened window. He strode over, snatched up the vase, and dumped it outside the window.

His hand moved to the spot where she'd touched him. It lingered like a hot metal brand, and her face sprang to his mind. Those ocean-blue eyes. That soft cream skin. Those tight-fitting—

"Stop!" Mateo growled and rubbed that spot—her spot—off his arm. She was a Stromm, nothing more. An ice princess who only cared about her station. He must focus on winning the hunt, not her hand.

He quickly assessed the bedchamber. A fireplace, a sitting chair, a wardrobe, and an obscenely spacious four-poster bed. The attached washroom housed a wash basin mounted on a counter and a sizable tub, all with the same details as the rest of the space. His entire family and four others could've made their home inside this one room.

He tossed his bag on the cot, sifted through his stuff, and found nothing missing. He removed the onyx dagger his father gave him at age eleven, his mother's treasured scarf, and his father's cross. He sheathed the dagger at his waist, sat on the window seat's edge, and rubbed his forehead. Everything was on fire inside Mateo. He needed a quick run to clear his mind. Like his nightly jaunts to Spirit Butte in the Sublands, he needed to get away. He did not belong here in Stromm Palace.

His eyes adjusted to the moonlight. He studied the overly manicured bushes and the needlessly spraying fountains. His stare drifted beyond the bountiful grounds. It landed on the dark and wild forest of Summit Range and the base of the blue mountains.

The hunt.

His heart raced as he scanned the forest shadows. He spotted movement...a white creature. His eyes narrowed. A horse pranced and played alone. He smiled, having never seen such a magnificent creature. He needed a closer view. Maid Nia had declared roaming the grounds forbidden, so he would have to sneak out.

He peered over the window's edge. A vine-filled lattice reached his room. Easy. He scanned the path to the forest and identified several pockets of darkness. Again, easy. He rubbed his hands together in quiet anticipation. Time to have some fun. Maybe even gain an advantage from a secret hike through the Summit Range.

Nobody would ever know.

Avalynn gulped her gala wine and threw the glass into the fireplace. How dare he! The Sublander had challenged her and her father. Good thing he left early. Making sure he came in last would be her pleasure. And to think...she had begun feeling sympathetic toward him and his lowborn people.

Eiric, Finnian, and Selene approached. Eiric crossed his arms. He glanced in the direction the Sublander had gone. "Are we teaming up to make sure the Sublander scum comes in last place?"

Selene handed Avalynn a fresh drink and sipped her own. "Walking in and passing us up? As if he was not a dreaded lowborn?" She raised her glass and took another sip. "Nothing would please me more."

Finnian nodded. "Me too. The lowborn must go."

Form an alliance with her competition? The Sublander guaranteed last place? It would make her job much easier. She pictured his pretty yet defeated face— last place, death penalty, the end of him and the Sublands. She was game for such an endeavor. Her father would be pleased. "He has no idea what is coming."

Maid Nia tapped the back of her arm. "Excuse me, my lady. The attendants are escorting the hunters to their bedchambers now."

A team of maidservants approached. Selene leaned into the group and raised a glass. "Down with the Sublander."

Everyone nodded, then separated.

After the obligatory goodnight to her parents who were entertaining dignitaries, Avalynn followed Nia from the room and up the stairs. "Can you believe that Sublander?" She huffed with each step. "Mateo Vela. A horrid name for a horrid lowborn."

Nia shook her head. "Perhaps he reacts to removal from his element." She slowed her quick step. "Like a fawn that never leaves the den." Her tone softened to a feather's tickle. "His people suffer greatly."

The princess wrinkled her nose. "If they suffer, it is on them. They have violated too many laws to deserve leniency." Her sympathy failed as it applied to the Sublands. Especially now.

Nia reached for Avalynn's bedchamber door. "Your loyalty allows the king to speak through you." She tilted her head. "But what do *you* think?" She tucked a strand of Avalynn's hair behind her ear and then tapped her chest. "What is inside *your* heart?"

Her heart? As if that mattered. Her duty and her heart were two strange ships that passed in the black night. If she went to the bottom of the sea, it would be for duty. Especially after the Sublander's defiant display in front of everyone. She pulled her strand of hair back to where it was. "Duty is my *only* path."

CHAPTER EIGHT

Princess Celyse found a shimmer portal and peeked at the human realm, where she met Julio Avila... He is your grandfather.

Avalynn paced her room. Her father tasked her. The Sublander challenged her. Now Nia wanted her to think about her heart? Perhaps she could've added twelve more things to put on the list.

She fell face down on her pillow-littered bed. Her thoughts scattered every which way while she pictured Mateo. Eyes like a tempest sky. Hair, black as night. Beautiful, arrogant, infuriating...all things she was not expecting. She rolled over, grabbed her feather pillow, and slammed it against her face. *Stop thinking about him. Stop, stop, stop. Focus on the hunt.*

Whoosh.

She sat up. Her glance found a plain white envelope on the floor. She hopped off her bed, rushed over, and flung open the door. No one was there. Her eyes darted one way and then the other. "Hello?" The empty corridor echoed.

She returned inside and with a quick step, her hand swooped up the envelope. She pulled out the handwritten note.

Be brave, for a new path is on the horizon.

Another mysterious message. She rubbed her forehead, then pinched between her eyes. Who was doing this? She set aside the envelope and note. Her hand searched under the mattress and found the previous one.

Trust your instincts, not your past.

She placed them side by side. Same parchment. Same simple yet elegant black lettering. She raised both to her nose. Same woodsy, earthy scent. It wouldn't require an inquiry to learn they came from the same person. But *who* slipped these under her door? And why?

With all the excitement, she forgot to tell Nia about the first letter. Now she had two to tell her about. She shoved them under the mattress, walked over to the window, and sat on the windowseat. A gentle breeze tickled her cheek.

Trust her *instincts*? She already did that. How was the *past* pertinent? *Be brave*? She already was. Since birth, nothing scared or got the best of her. Yet, the reference to her new path troubled her most. Surely, it meant the hunt.

Avalynn gazed outside from her perch on the window seat. The large moon glowed, and the night stars glistened. She pulled her legs up to her chest. Her arms wrapped around her knees when movement in the bushes below caught her eye. Somebody was violating the rules of Stromm Palace.

She leaned forward and studied the shadows. A tall

figure crept along the near-darkness, heading toward the back of the gardens. Her gaze followed the creeper along the path, then sped past, wondering where the person was headed—bushes, trees, fountains, benches. Her gaze stopped on the edge of the forest. There it stood—her beautiful white Enbarr—the one she had ridden only a few nights ago.

Avalynn's heart raced. The creeper... Her Enbarr...

She snatched her bow. She flicked an arrow from her quiver. Her aim fixed on the creeper. She pulled the string back. And then the forest darkened.

Thunderation.

She leaned out the window and glanced up. A cloud was passing over the moon, hiding her target. She lowered her weapon and waited for the slow-moving mist to finish its course. But the creeper would surely reach her Enbarr first. She had no time to waste. Her Enbarr needed her protection.

She snatched her black cloak. Quiver at her back, bow slung over her shoulder, she descended the lattice with ease. She darted across the gardens, taking the same dark path as the housebreaker. She knew all visitors were forbidden from roaming the grounds at night. What fool would have violated such a royal directive?

Dawning realization filtered through her. She paused her step and furrowed her brow. She knew the exact fool —the Sublander. He stepped in front of her for the procession. He declared himself the hunt winner. Well, his luck had run out tonight. If he touched her Enbarr, he would wear an arrow for a hat.

She picked up her pace. She slipped the bow off her

shoulder and unsheathed an arrow. He was not getting anywhere near her Enbarr. Her heart thumped. Her muscles tensed. With each stride, she exhaled bursts of warm vapor into the chilly night. She was gaining on him. Soon, he would fall at her feet.

As the perfectly manicured gardens slipped past, she crossed into the wild area where tangled undergrowth and gnarled roots reached out to claim the path. Moonlight began filtering in from above. Finally, she could take the shot.

She slowed. She nocked her arrow. She pulled back the string. Her aim narrowed on the space between the Sublander's shoulders, then quickly redirected to his hand. She could not end him there and then. He still needed to compete in the hunt so he could take last. Her father still required appeasement. Worse yet, killing the Sublander would signal to her father that she, too, had violated the rules.

She let out a long breath, her hand keeping the string taut. As she was about to release her weapon, the Sublander spun and caught her eye. He crouched like a black panther with his dagger over his head, ready to unleash.

A standoff in the Summit Range forest. It came down to her or him. Her arrow versus his dagger. Avalynn, the bold Stromm princess and Mateo, the mysterious Sublander.

BRAYYY!

An urgent whinny filled the air. Hooves thundered. The gorgeous Enbarr galloped between them, skidded to a halt, and reared up on its hind legs like a steed possessed. That silver mane sparkled in the moonlight. Its lavender eyes widened, ears pricked forward, and nostrils flared. *BRAYYY!*

Avalynn stumbled and fell on her backside, awestruck at the display. "Okay, okay!" She lowered her weapon. "I see what you are doing."

The magical Enbarr continued stamping and stayed between her and Mateo, snorting and whinnying. From the ground, she saw Mateo, still on his feet, his dagger in hand. She said the only thing that made sense. "It wants you to put your weapon away."

Mateo's brows shot up. "Are you jesting?"

"No, I am not. Now, do as you are told, Sublander."

He muttered, then raised his dagger in a slow show of compliance. "I am sheathing my weapon now." He slid it in place at his waist. "There."

The Enbarr stilled. After a satisfying snort, it sauntered to a nearby cluster of clover and started grazing. Her tail flicked innocently as if she had not charged between them.

Mateo glanced at the Enbarr, as if worried it might stampede him. He approached Avalynn with an outstretched hand. "Let me help you."

She swatted him away. "I do not need your help, Sublander."

He furrowed his brows and stepped back. "I have a name. It is Mateo. Mateo Vela."

She rose and dusted herself off. "You are not allowed out here at night, Mateo Vela, lowborn of the Sublands. It is forbidden. You should know this." His lowborn brain had probably already forgotten.

He tilted his head and huffed. "*You* are out here."

Her pulse quickened. She gritted her teeth. She rested her hand on her bow, ready to jerk it into firing position. "Hold your tongue. I am the future High Queen. These are *my* lands." The lowborn needed a lesson in respect.

"Oh, I know who you are, ice princess." His hand wrapped around the dagger's hilt. "And I know where I stand...in unwelcoming Stromm land."

"What did you call me?" She clutched her bow and grabbed an arrow. She knew of this nickname, but hearing it spoken ignited a wildfire within her. He had no idea with whom he dealt.

He stepped forward and jerked his chin. "You heard me."

The Enbarr snorted. It pawed at the ground and backed up between Avalynn and Mateo. It shook her head and let out a low bray.

"Not now," she hissed to the creature, moving to the other side of the beast and coming face-to-face with the Sublander.

Mateo crossed his arms, and a small, irritating smile tugged at the corner of his lips. "Even your horse knows you are acting ridiculous."

Every word out of the Sublander's mouth vibrated her insides and dug his last place grave deeper. "Name-calling will get you nowhere, Sublander. And it is no horse. It is an Enbarr! It does not belong to me but to the Sun, Moon, and Stars. A magical beast that transports people to the Passing Place and can only be ridden by the purest of hearts." That excluded him and his people in the Sublands.

A look of wonder spread across his face. "This is an Enbarr?"

The magnificent creature stamped her hooves. Its mane hung long and flowy. Those long lashes curled at the edges. While on the petite side, it still possessed the typical long legs and slender body. By the light of the bright moon, Avalynn saw the purple tint in the Enbarr's wise eyes. "You have never seen one?"

He approached the beast with slow steps. "I have not. We do not have much magic in the Sublands." He stretched out his hand. "May I touch it?"

"Sure. If it wants you to, that is. It might bite your hand off." Visions of the Enbarr attacking the Sublander brought a smile to her lips. It would serve him right.

He cocked a brow. "Now you jest with me."

She shrugged. "I am not jesting. It is up to the Enbarr if it allows your lowborn touch." If it were up to her, he would lose an arm.

He clenched his teeth. "Enough with calling me lowborn and Sublander." He double-tapped his fist over his heart. "I am Mateo Vela. A fae and a hunter like any other. My bloodline belongs here as much as any other bloodline." He raised his voice. "I share this land with you!"

She swallowed. Pain etched across his perfect face, his features tightening as if he carried the weight of a thousand crushed souls on his shoulders. Despite her softening heart, he was still lowborn, a Sublander, and she had a job to do. Despite all that, she wanted to say something to him but could not find any words for Mateo Vela from the Sublands...except that he was unexpected.

The Enbarr moved closer and nudged Avalynn. She stroked the beast's silky soft muzzle and cleared her throat. "You can touch it. The creature will not hurt you." There'd be no harm in letting the lowborn touch something so magnificent.

"I've changed my mind." Mateo shoved his hands in his pockets and started back to the palace. "Nice to meet you, future queen, current princess, Avalynn."

Her jumbled thoughts left her speechless. He and his kind were beneath her. They caused anguish and turmoil in Faevenly for as long as she had lived. Even before. Still, he had a point. They did share the land. Not Summit Range land, but Faevenly land.

With her head resting against the Enbarr's glimmering mane, she watched Mateo walk into the dark shadows. With no further light from the moon or stars, he slowly disappeared from Avalynn's view. Her heart twinged with a deep ache. She could not understand why.

Avalynn scaled back up the lattice. She plopped into her room. Her feet hit the floor, and a knock sounded at the door. She froze, bow in hand, and boots covered in grass and mud. If it was her father, she would as soon leap back out the window. "Who is it?"

"My lady, it is me."

Whew! She exhaled and opened the door. She needed her faithful maid servant and friend now more than ever. "Oh, Nia." Finally, someone she trusted.

Nia held a tray with oils and a glass of orange-tinted water. She looked at Avalynn's cloak, bow, and boots, then hurried inside and closed the door. "My lady, what have you been doing?"

"Let me show you." She tossed her things on the floor, then went to her bed and shoved her hand under her mattress. She rooted around, grunting, and then pulled out the plain white envelopes. "I meant to show you these earlier."

Nia set the silver tray on the table. "Oh my." She placed her delicate fingers over her mouth. "What are those?"

"Notes. Someone slipped them under my door. On two separate occasions." Avalynn pulled out the parchments and set them side by side. She folded her arms while Nia read them aloud.

"Words of guidance?" Nia asked.

"I guess." Avalynn shrugged with a sigh. "I wish I knew." She stuffed the notes back in the envelopes and returned them to their hiding spot. She sat on the edge of her bed, silent for a few seconds, sifting through her thoughts of Mateo and the Enbarr. He didn't seem so lowborn to her.

"Nia, can I ask you something?" Her tone was soft and low.

"Anything, my lady."

"Why do we hate the Sublanders?" She clasped her hands in her lap. "I know what I was taught about our realm and the human realm living peacefully until the humans wanted to take over. I know all about the Great Shimmer War and how our realms separated and then later how the Strongs committed atrocities against the humans." She played with her fingers. "But after all that, the Strongs united with the Sublanders, right? And if they united, then why do we still hate them?" The story made sense, but the resulting outcomes did not.

"They did unite. It was Queen Celyse who fell in love with a human. Then later, their daughter, Princess Gabriela, fell in love with a half-human, half-fae Sublander. But those love affairs did not change the hearts of the fae purists."

"But why? I do not understand."

"Who can know the reason why hate lingers?" Nia placed her head against Avalynn's shoulder. "Or why some think they are superior to others? I suppose it could be the inability to let go and move forward. Or the fear of history repeating itself. But there is one thing I have learned in all my years in this glorious realm. There is great power in asking these questions." She took Avalynn's hand and squeezed. "Great love in forgiveness, in pushing the pain away and looking forward to the future with clear eyes and open hearts."

Avalynn's chin quivered, and she could not explain it. "I saw the Sublander tonight. Out in the forest." She could not believe she told this to anyone, but she could trust Nia.

"You did?" Nia stayed calm, as Avalynn expected.

"I did."

"And?"

"There was no brightness in his eyes. Only pain." The silence in the room thickened as Avalynn's heart grew heavy.

Nia rubbed her arm. "I am sorry, my lady."

She scooted closer to Nia, feeling the comfort from her friend. "I am too."

CHAPTER NINE

When the courting season approached, Celyse hid her portal and ignored Julio, choosing duty over heart.

Everything about Mateo's bed felt wrong. The plump feather mattress beneath him smothered his body like quicksand. The soft silk sheets over him clung to him like chilled water. He flung his covers off with a grunt. Sitting on the bed's edge, he missed the stone rocky floors of his room. He yearned for the thin cotton blanket fashioned from cheap threads that reminded him of his life and that place he called home. Swaddled in luxury in Stromm Palace, he would have passed for an entombed yet villainous god. Lirien and Gareth would have laughed at him for a lifetime and called him Your Highness.

Gleaming moonlight streamed through the open window. The soft light brightened a large spot on the floor. Stormshroud should be there, curled up, paws twitching. He'd been caring for her since that night he and his father found her. So small and frail, he'd bundled her up as soon as they got home. He used a cloth to drip water into her mouth. For food, he crushed insects into a paste and fed her small portions. She whimpered at night, and he was never sure if it was due to missing her pack or just being so small. But every time he wrapped her in his arms and held her to his chest, she stopped.

Was she okay? What about his father and little Flori-ana? He prayed to the Sun, Moon, and Stars that her sweet heart still struck a beat. She had to be alive. He was not about to let another loved one leave him. His mother would have been proud of him and his quest for the benefit of the Sublands.

He rubbed his face, forcing away his worries for his family. He needed to focus. Today he would see the prey for the hunt and later attend the dreaded ball. He would size up the competition there. Tomorrow he would hunt. The hours could not pass quickly enough.

He paced the room. His legs tingled and ached unless he moved. His mind raced with the day's upcoming events. When the sun shone bright enough to wake up the palace, he dressed in his green pants. He put his black shirt on inside out and his brown boots on the wrong feet. He slowed down. He needed to relax. With everything on the right way, he sheathed his dagger at his waist and then made his way to the receiving room for breakfast.

He was the first one there. The ice princess was prob-ably still asleep in her bedchamber. Or maybe she was eating golden flakes for breakfast with the High King and High Queen. Either way, she was sure to be surrounded by servants. He stifled a growl. *Stop thinking about her. She is your natural enemy by birth and by the rules of the hunt.*

Maid Nia approached him with a quick stride. She was wearing the same outfit as the day before, all-white maidservant attire. But today, she wore a yellow ribbon in her hair instead of the blue one.

"Good morning. I see you are an early riser." Her head tipped, and she glanced over his left shoulder. "Will your party be joining you?"

"They may later. Right now, it is only me. Thank you." Though he knew he could not escape them all day, he wanted to be away from the manipulative mouths of Lady Verona and Rhyka for as long as possible.

"That is fine. The food has been prepared. You may help yourself." Maid Nia motioned to a row of tables along the back wall filled with generous helpings of eggs, cheeses, fruits, and warm breads. The aroma of dripping butter and crushed garlic on that bread made his stomach grumble like Stormshroud's before devouring a desert rat. This spread would've fed a hundred Sublanders.

He loaded his plate and sat at the room's far end. After a few bites, the other hunters strolled in. First, Finnian, and then Eiric, followed by Selene. They served themselves and then sat together. Now and again, Selene glanced his way and then smirked with her paper-thin lips. No doubt the other hunters plotted against him. They should have held up a sign. "Us Against Him." Who cared? He didn't want to ally himself with those highborn losers anyway.

Would the ice princess join their devious designs? Probably. Highborn scum always stuck together. He'd have to wait and see to know for sure.

After his last bite, he searched for an empty basin or

other receptacle for his dirty dishes. Nia scurried over. "I will take that for you."

Of course, she would. "Thank you."

"You are welcome. When you are ready, I will show you to the training circle in the garden, where Master Kragar will meet you later."

He did not need an escort. "No, thank you. I think I can find it myself." In the night, Mateo had passed a large grassy circular area set up for archery practice, so he knew where to go.

She half bowed to him. "Very well. Enjoy your day, then."

He made his way toward the exit and passed the other hunters. "Lowborn scum," a male voice hissed.

Mateo froze. He slowly turned around. "Which one of you highborn leeches said that?" He hoped someone would answer. He was more than ready to let out his frustration.

Selene's eyes grew wide. The other two hunters crossed their arms and remained silent.

He patted the dagger sheathed at his side. "Cowards." Of course, the highborn would not back up his words with actions. Mateo began walking away when a chair slid across the floor with a screech.

Eiric rose with his chest puffed out. "There are no cowards at my table, lowborn."

He smiled and sauntered over. Today was his lucky day. He got up in the highborn's smug face. "I think there are." He jammed his finger against Eiric's chest and pushed. "And you are the biggest one."

The silver-haired hunter swung. Mateo sidestepped

in a flash, backhanding Eiric with a punch to the nose, sending a spray of garnet-red blood into the air.

Mateo smirked. "Hey, we bleed the same color."

Finnian sprang to his feet. Mateo readied himself to face the beefy hunter when Eiric hurled a chair against his back, allowing Finnian to double-punch him in the face. Mateo spun, chairs flying. He landed on Selene, who grabbed her fork and stabbed at his hand. He pulled away in the nick of time.

"Too slow," he sneered.

Pushing himself away from her, Mateo spat out a wad of blood. He eyed Eiric and Finnian. Two against one—no problem. He could take them. He charged when someone grabbed the back of his shirt and yanked him to a halt.

"Enough!" Master Kragar's booming voice filled the room. "No fighting in the palace!"

Mateo backed away, hands in the air. "I was not fighting." He glanced at Eiric, who was holding his nose. "Only making friends. Right?"

"Out!" Master Kragar yelled. He jerked his thick thumb toward the exit and shook his head. "If you are finished with your nourishment, Sublander, then take your leave."

"My name is Mateo." He wiped his mouth with the back of his hand, staring down at the dwarf. "Mateo Vela of the Sublands." The dwarf should have learned the name by now.

Kragar's lip curled. "Out of here before it is too late for you."

Mateo eyed the hunters. Adding Kragar to the mix

would make for terrible odds. He'd have to settle the fight with Eiric and Finnian during the hunt. As for Kragar, he made a mental note...maybe another time.

Mateo tipped his head. "See you all later, then."

Avalynn's door burst open as she gathered up her boots, and Lily dashed in. The young princess wore a bright, shining face. Her eyes sparkling. "Mateo got in a fight."

"What? With whom?" Avalynn asked, her mind jumbled at the surprising news.

"The other hunters."

She sat on the bed's edge and slipped her tall black boot over her black pants. She was still processing what her little sister had said.

Nia swept through the doorway next, dressed in white. Her slippers flitted across the floor. Her eyes shimmered. "My lady—"

Avalynn finished the maid's thought. "The Sublander was in a fight, I know."

"Did you see it? Were you there?" Lily tugged at Nia's flowing skirt.

"I was, little princess." Nia bent at the waist and raised her brows. "It was during breakfast. Eiric swung at the Sublander—"

"Did he get Mateo?"

"No, little princess. The Sublander sidestepped Eiric and then hit his nose. Blood spurted."

Lily gasped. "Oh. I bet that hurt."

Avalynn laced her boot. "I wonder what they said to him."

"You think the Sublander was provoked?" Nia asked.

"I do." Lily piped in. "He is way too lovely. A lovely person like him would never start a fight."

Avalynn embraced Lily by the shoulders. "What did I tell you about looks not mattering?"

"I think maybe for Mateo Vela, they should matter." Lily chuckled, then broke away from Avalynn's grasp.

"Looks aside..." Nia nodded her head. "The Sublander is out of his element. I doubt he would have started anything."

"He is exactly the sort of person who would start something." Avalynn grabbed her boot. "You saw what he did at the procession, Nia."

"What happened after the Sublander hit Eiric in the nose?" Lily lay on Avalynn's bed and rested her hands under her chin. "Tell me everything."

Nia continued. "Well, after the Sublander hit Eiric, he readied himself for Finnian. But then Eiric threw a chair at his back, allowing Finnian to strike the Sublander when he was not looking."

Lily slammed her hands over her mouth. "Please tell me he did not bleed and that he is still beautiful!"

"He did not bleed."

Lily sighed with relief. "Good. That was not fair of Finnian!"

"Life is not always fair, Lily," Avalynn reminded her sister for the thousandth time. She finished lacing her boot and started on the other. Suddenly, her task to make sure the Sublander came in last seemed more difficult than she'd once thought. Good thing she had the others to help her. She would need to solidify their alliance at the training circle. Maybe even come up with a plan.

She rose and threaded her black belt between the loops. She straightened the collar of her purple shirt. "How do I look?"

Lily smiled. "Beautiful and strong."

Avalynn knelt and pushed Lily's long silver hair behind her sharply pointed ears. "More so than the Sublander, little sister?"

"Of course, my future queen. None in this land can outshine my big sister."

"Most definitely." Nia picked up the silver tray from the bedside table. It held delicate crystal vials. "All you need to complete your look is your oils. I have two for you to choose from." She pointed to a pink one. "This one features rose and geranium." Then she pointed to a green one. "This is a blend of amber and jasmine."

"Pink, pink," Lily encouraged as she clutched her chest. "It is so romantic."

Romantic? Did Avalynn want to be romantic with Mateo? Her hand hovered in midair. She and Mateo shared opposing destinies. She needed to remember that. She snatched the green vial. "This one is perfect."

"Boring." Lily scrunched her nose.

"I am preparing for a hunt, little princess. Not a courting season." Avalynn dabbed the oil on her wrists. With a slight turn, she ran her finger down her neck, spending extra time with the oil between her bosom. If she came in close contact with Mateo, it would not hurt to smell her best.

Avalynn saw three crates upon her arrival at the training circle. They were set out in a triangular shape around the grassy area. Mateo bent over one crate by himself, peering at the Shadowblood foxes inside. From her vantage point, she could see a bandage near his right eye and signs of a swollen lip. Selene and Eiric stood together at another crate. Eiric sported a bandage across the bridge of his nose. Finnian appeared unscathed and stood alone at the third.

The bright sun made it easy to see the sleek black fur of the foxes inside. Another scan of the setup showed no coverings around. Nobody but her would know of their disappearing abilities. *Good.* Alliance or not, she would keep that strategic piece of information to herself. The others would find out in their own time and in their own way.

She walked past Mateo and stopped next to Finnian, who bowed. "Princess Avalynn."

"Finnian."

She kept an eye on Mateo without directly looking at him. Finnian inched closer. He lowered his voice to a whisper. "Are you still with us?"

She watched Mateo study the foxes. His face hovered close to the bars, without a care for the danger within. That fool had no idea what he was dealing with. "Yes. I am in," she said.

Boots stamping, arms swinging, and axe clanking, Master Kragar trudged in. His long, curly red hair was braided down his back. He stopped in the middle of the triangle. He drew his axe from the sheath and began using the weapon as a pointer. "In these crates are the Shadowblood foxes you will be hunting. One for each of you. The task is simple. Capture the buggers and bring them dead or alive to the spot where you will set out in the morning." He jerked his axe toward the palace. "Over there."

He paced in a circular motion. "Each fox is magicked so that when it is captured, a signal will be sent into the air for all to see." He threw his axe into the ground. It landed with a thud. He cupped his hands in front of his stocky chest. "The forest has also been magicked, creating a boundaried hunting area designed to keep the prey somewhat contained. The magic will keep them within that boundary." A mischievous grin spread across his ruddy face. "It will not harm you if you touch it, but it will sting...only a bit."

He slammed his hand around his axe and yanked it out of the grass. "There will be no killing of each other. No exceptions. Though if you die by other means, then you die by other means." He spit over his shoulder. "You are allowed one weapon of your choosing. Makes no matter to me or anyone else what it is. You will also receive a prepared satchel to take with you."

Kragar's face turned cold. He dropped his voice low. "The final hunter to cross the finish line loses the hunt and his or her life, followed by the banishment of that loser's province. By decree of the High King and High Queen. Let it be so."

Master Kragar let his words sink in for a moment, his

stare fixing on each hunter in turn. When he got to Avalynn, she detected a sorrowful sentiment in his hunter-green eyes. Did he think she would lose? She did not like his look at all.

He tossed his axe from one hand to the other. "The Gala of the Hunter's Moon will take place at nightfall in the Grand Ballroom." He pointed his axe at Mateo. "There will be no fighting." He leveled the Sublander with a warning look before circling back to Eiric. "Not during the gala and not after. You all are guests and will act with respect to your hosts." He rested his axe on his shoulder. "You all have lots of prettying up to do for tonight's big shindig." He burst out laughing and shouted, "Now get out of here!"

Without so much as looking at Avalynn, Mateo spun on his heels and left the training circle. He carried himself as if he were the most skilled fighter in all of Faevenly, from royal lineage, and not a lowborn.

"I would rather kill that lowborn than try to beat him," Eiric seethed as he and Selene joined her and Finnian. "The rules be damned."

Selene shrugged. "Perhaps an arrow could accidentally miss its mark and land in his pretty eye. That would put him in last place."

"Kill him? And risk the wrath of the High King and his witch?" Finnian's eyes stopped blinking. "I would not want their punishment."

Their idle, useless, and cowardly words floated in one of Avalynn's ears and jetted out the other. She needed the best to manage and defeat Mateo, the Sublander. Her task required a way for him to come in last while she came in first. The other hunters combined couldn't beat him even if he slept. She must not rest her fate on them. She needed to partner with somebody who could match the Sublander.

A wild answer presented itself like a flash of steam from the Enbarr's muzzle.

Form an alliance with the brash Sublander. Convince him like only she could that she wanted to work together. Then, at the last moment of truth, sabotage him. He would never know what hit him. She would prevail, make her father proud, and solidify her place as the future queen of Faevenly.

CHAPTER TEN

Celyse later learned of a threat to humans involving the shimmers. Using her own, she crossed into the human realm, seeking Julio's help in unraveling the mystery.

Avalynn entered her bedchamber to bustling activity. On the left side, Nia fidgeted with a row of floor-length gowns hanging from fixed golden hooks. On the right, three petite maidservants tinkered with crystal vials and porcelain jars on the mahogany vanity. They were dressed in all-white with flowers and leaves in their short-cropped brown hair.

"My lady." Nia scurried over. "Time for you to get ready for tonight's gala. Where have you been?"

After the training circle, she'd wandered the gardens for a bit, clearing her mind and thinking. Mostly, about Mateo. "I was getting myself ready for the hunt."

Nia pulled Avalynn into the marble washroom. "Well, now is the time to get the rest of you ready. You must look your best tonight." She handed Avalynn a soft white towel. "Hurry with your bath. The other maidservants and I will prepare your things."

One step inside the washroom and the aroma of fresh

flowers filled Avalynn's face like a breath of fresh air on the first day of spring, but magnified. She spied the source right away. A tub filled with lapping clear water covered in curling red and pink rose petals with sprigs of white jasmine scattered throughout. Although she had not attended a gala lately, this was too much. Lily, the little romantic, must have gotten to Nia.

She set her fluffy towel aside, undressed, and slipped into the tub. She submerged herself fully in the warm water. Tingling shivers raced throughout her tired system. She held her breath and stayed there, feeling energized with each ripple against her skin.

She opened her eyes underwater. Light danced and shimmered through the water's surface, blurring the red and pink hues so she could barely make out her family crest on the ceiling. The mural of mountain peaks, trees, and the gold-painted S resembled a messy stain.

She broke the surface with a sputter, then flicked the petals from atop her head. Eyeing the mural now, every painted brush stroke and scenic element looked perfect, in true House Stromm fashion.

But what to do about Mateo? She brought her nose closer to the roses. Smelling 'romantic' like Lily suggested earlier could benefit her. She plucked the oils from the tub's edge and began washing. Perhaps the Sublander would be enticed by her scent and fall for her fake alliance, especially since their unscheduled rendezvous in the forest left them nearly ending each other. She had a lot of work to do in order to earn his trust.

Rinsing the oils, her head dipped underwater. She ran her fingers through her long hair and focused on the blurred crest again. Maybe a gown with a plunging neckline would help the Sublander along. That should do it. He would fall under her spell. She would own the Sublander's heart as well as his head. The plan was perfect.

She hurried out of the tub, dried off, and pulled on her robe. With no time to waste, she entered her bedchamber to find Nia still fidgeting with the gowns. "Ah, there you are, looking fresh and smelling like the loveliest garden."

"Thanks to you and your petals." Avalynn raised a teasing brow. "How many rose bushes were violated for my pleasure?" It must've been a hundred or more.

Nia smirked. "Just enough." She held up one of the gowns. It hit the floor in a dazzling tuft of green with half sleeves and a scoop neckline. "How do you like this one?"

"Pretty color, but I would like to see the others." The neckline was all wrong. It did not plunge, and she needed that plunge for Mateo.

Nia placed the green gown back on the hook. "What about this?" She showed her a deep gold sheath with a high neckline.

Avalynn shook her head. Her maidservant went in the wrong direction. She would need to be more specific. "I was hoping for something more..." She cleared her throat and circled her hands in front of her bosom. "Provocative?"

The younger maidservants giggled and clanked the vials that nearly spilled from their hands. Nia's mouth dropped open, and her eyes widened. "Oh! Well, if that is your desire, then I know just the one." With a twinkle in her eye, Nia held up a deep purple strapless gown. Lace with crystal accents adorned the plunging bodice, then cascaded down the voluminous skirt that sparkled like a regal sky at sunset. "Like this one, my lady?"

With a swallow, Avalynn nodded. The front plunged so deep she thought her parts would fall out. "Yes, like that." But then she glanced down at her figure, second-guessing her decision. Flat chest. Few curves. Would she even look good in that? "Um..." A nervous chuckle escaped her lips. "Maybe that is not enough top-half material for me."

"Nonsense." Nia hung the dress. "You will shine like never before, and so will"—she moved her hands in front of her chest like Avalynn had—"these."

This time, all of the maids burst out laughing, even Avalynn. Nia took her hand and led her to the vanity. "Let the maids apply your paints and fix your hair. The dress will come last."

With a smile she nodded. "I am in your trust." She knew they would work their hardest to make sure she looked perfect.

The dainty maidservants got busy. Using the pads of their delicate fingers, they applied hues of bronze and rose to her cheeks, blending the shades together as they accentuated her high cheekbones. When they finished, they moved to her eyes, coloring the lids with deep purples and browns. Next, they lengthened her lashes with a thick black pigment. Lastly, they painted her lips with a soft pink gloss that smelled like the sweetest nectar.

With her face the way they wanted, they moved to

her thick dark hair. Brushing and braiding, they swept Avalynn's locks up in the front, allowing delicate wisps to frame her face. The rest hung down the back in waves. With everything perfectly smooth and shiny, the team stepped away.

Placing her hands on Avalynn's shoulders, Nia stopped her before she could turn to look. "Not yet. Your dress first."

Nia and the maidservants set the frock on the ground. Avalynn stepped into place. Pulling it up, they fastened the crystal studs along the back. When finished, they moved aside.

Nia beamed with pride. "You may look now."

When Avalynn saw her reflection in the mirror, she blinked. She had been to many galas, balls, and other royal events, primped from head to toe. But today's session left her speechless. Her rough edges were polished, her features highlighted in all the right places. The colors on her cheeks and eyelids were rich and elegant. Her hair belonged on the head of a goddess. Her fingers rolled lightly down her cleavage, marveling at what she did not even realize she had. "You all have outdone yourselves."

Nia took the finishing piece from the vanity—a platinum tiara with crystals, pearls, and gold-dipped leaves. She nestled it in Avalynn's thick dark hair and stepped back. "There she is." Nia and the others bowed. "Our queen."

Down the corridor she went, her insides rattling like a clanging bell. As she neared the grand staircase, her ears filled with the violins' soft strumming. What would Mateo think of her gown? Or her lips? An opus of fragrant florals tickled her nose. Would he even notice her? After the careful selection of her gown and all the work her attendants had done, he had better. Unless she had missed her mark, he would not be able to resist her.

Rounding the staircase's landing, she nearly collided with Eiric. The bandage across his nose was gone, more than likely due to the palace healer providing him with salve from the Green Falls. His eyes darted to her neckline like a ravenous hawk before settling on her face.

"Avalynn. Princess." He cleared his throat and bowed. "You are most lovely tonight. It would be my honor to escort you into the ballroom."

Oh, this was good. Courtiers always desired what they could not have. She smiled, knowing Mateo would surely be no different. "That would be lovely, Eiric." She took his outstretched hand, and together they made their entry into the ballroom.

The scene unfolded in opulence—a symphony of sights and sounds of the most royal and privileged dignitaries in all of Faevenly. Ornate vases of gold and silver showcased the garden's roses, gardenias, and lilies. Gilded arches and towering columns adorned with intricately carved flowers and leaves lined each side of the space. Circular tables with the finest white linens, perfectly polished silverware, gold-edged plates, and dazzling centerpieces dotted the outer edges of the dance floor. Sparkling crystal chandeliers lit by purple-hued candles and floating orbs dotted the celestial heights. They cast a warm glow on the polished marble floor.

The string quartet played, accompanying the festive chatter that filled the air. Magnificent ball gowns rustled, and the dancers' rhythmic tapping became lost in the evening's splendor.

Eiric wasted no time. "I would be honored to have your first dance, my princess."

Walking in with Eiric? Sure. No problem. But giving him the first dance? No way. Scrambling for a reply, she spotted Lily on the room's other side. Nearby stood Mateo, in the corner by himself, wearing black pants, a white shirt, and a long black coat. Hands in his pockets, he turned away from the festivities and stared through the streak-free windows along the back wall. This was her opportunity, and she pounced.

"Oh..." She waved at Lily while she glanced at Eiric. "I see my little sister and must speak with her. Perhaps another time."

His shoulders slumped, and then he bowed. "Of course. I will look for you later, then."

She left Eiric while his last words lingered, working her way through the buzzing crowd. Her true target, Mateo, must have sensed her approach. His neck slowly swiveled. He turned and faced her. A subtle catch in her breath betrayed the impact of being so close to him.

"Hello, Mateo," she said, breathless. His lip was stitched, and he wore a bandage near his eye, yet he was still striking. Maybe even more so.

"Princess." He nodded and kept his steely eyes on

hers, not bothered by her strategically selected gown. "What insults would you choose for me this evening?"

She had several in mind, none of which advanced her goal—teaming up with him. She settled for a demure smile. "No insults. Quite the opposite." She straightened her shoulders and showed off her gown's seductive cut. Why was he not daring even a peek? "I came to offer my apologies." She paused for a reaction. He gave none. "And, my first dance."

Never in a thousand lifetimes would she have dreamed of asking a Sublander to dance. Looks be damned, he was not worthy. Worse, he was taking too long to reply. Heat surged through her cheeks at his silent refusal. "Forget it." Pompous little lowborn.

She spun on her heels. But then he grabbed her arm. The touch sent a shiver down her spine, igniting a fire that blazed within her. A fire she desperately tried to ignore whenever he was near. She turned to face him, and their eyes locked. For a heartbeat, the world around them ceased to exist. It was just her and him and their magnetic pull. She had never felt this way around another.

He stepped back, releasing her arm, but the link lingered like an invisible thread between them. "I would like that...very much..." He swallowed hard in the electrified silence and bowed his head, as if forcing himself to contain the intensity of the moment. "But...I do not know how to dance and would not want to embarrass you."

Now that was unexpected. A touch of sympathy for the Sublander gathered inside of her. Had she been reading him all wrong? She closed the gap between them.

"I can show you." With a finger, she lifted his chin. "It is easy. I will help you."

The music switched from an upbeat tune to a soft ballad.

She held out her royal hand. He looked down, as if considering his next move, and then took her hand with a surprisingly gentle touch. A flutter of wings swirled in her stomach, her heart racing as she led him to the middle area with the other dancers.

"Your left hand holds my right, like this." She held her right arm up and hand open, and he wrapped his fingers around hers. With that position secured, she went on. "Your right hand will stay on my back, guiding me through the dance while my left one rests on your shoulder." They stayed still in the dancing position, eyes locked, desire building, before moving in the same circular pattern as the other guests.

His steps were fluid, his movements graceful like he had danced at royal functions his entire lowborn life. She quirked a brow. "Are you sure this is your first time?"

He scanned the crowd and then returned his attention to her. "I am sure."

"You are a natural, then." Their eyes remained fixed, his with an unsettling intensity. Did he have another expression? Not that she minded that one too much. It belonged to her, and she wanted it.

He cleared his throat. "This is most decidedly not natural for me."

"This is not entirely natural for me either." She gazed into those steely gray eyes. Like a strong magnet, they would never lose their pull. She should look away and prevent him from becoming anything more than a Sublander and last place finisher. But right then, she did not want to. Her mind, body, and spirit said the same thing. Keep looking. Never turn away.

"You dance as if it is natural for you."

She forced her attention back to their steps. "I have been to many of these things, but I much prefer my feet in the grass, face in the sun, and being outdoors in the forest hunting, practicing archery…"

"Or riding your Enbarr?"

She smiled. "Or that." He remembered. His thought process matched hers. They were of one mind for the moment.

The Enbarr stopped them from ending one another. It forced them to lower their weapons. What would the creature think if it knew they were dancing together? Something told her it would surely be pleased. But the Enbarr had no idea who Mateo was and what Avalynn must do—a task she could neither ignore nor forget.

The music continued, and she needed her deal done before the song ended and another began. There was no better time than the present. "Tomorrow will be my first time competing in the hunt."

His brow twitched slightly, as if concerned by her sudden change of conversation. "Mine as well." He moistened his lips. "But you already know that."

She angled her head upward and stared at his barely open mouth and slightly parted, wet lips. Did he notice her gloss? Did he smell the sweet nectar and desire a taste? A charged pause hung in the air between them; an unspoken invitation lingered. She needed to focus on her mission. Their kiss could never exist. She cleared her throat. Her plan was all that mattered. "I wonder, Mateo, if we should somehow work together."

His brows bunched in the middle. He paused his steps before falling back into a steady rhythm. "Why would we do that?"

Why? Sun, Moon, and Stars. She actually needed a reason? She stepped closer and lowered her voice. "Because the other provinces are...how shall I say it...not worthy."

"How so?"

"It is nothing that needs explaining." They were unworthy compared to her. Her statement was true. But she could not tell him that.

His hand remained on her waist. When he spun her, he touched her all the way around, sending tingles everywhere. When they faced each other again, he agreed to her proposition. "Fine. How do you propose we work together?"

"Good question." His defenses had dropped. He fell for it. "I am not sure. But I propose we stay together and look for ways to help one another."

He stepped closer, leaned in, and whispered, "If working together means I win, then that is acceptable."

Of course, the Sublander would say that. "We shall see." She needed to play along.

Words fell away as the dance took them. The rhythm ebbed and flowed between them, each movement as intimate and perfect as the rise and fall of waves. No one else found space in her mind. It belonged to Mateo. He flooded her senses like a gentle ocean breeze. Those intense eyes, that long, sleek hair, his lean and muscular frame. The perfect blend of spice and vanilla and sandalwood that made her head spin. Best of all, his firm yet gentle touch. She would let him touch her all over if she could.

The ballroom faded as she drifted closer to Mateo. The timeless gap between them disappeared. His eyes searched her face before finally drifting to her chest, roaming her curves with longing and desire. Should she move back? Or stay in this endlessly pleasing pose forever, letting him have her with his eyes?

The enduring ballad ended. Another song began, but they remained as they were, eyes locked. A symphony of emotions swirled within her—desire, anticipation, and vulnerability. Feelings she had never experienced before, and most certainly did not expect. Especially from a Sublander.

She ignored the hand that tapped her shoulder. The tapping continued, softer at first and then harder. The words finally sunk in. "Princess, may I have the next dance?"

She turned to see Eiric's eyes boring a hole through Mateo. Eiric had no claim over her, though he sure acted like he did. Before she could decline his request, Mateo dropped her hand. He released her waist. "Thank you for the dance." His head tipped, and then he bowed. "It was my privilege to learn from a princess."

CHAPTER ELEVEN

Celyse, Julio, and Julio's best friend, Manny Vela, discovered one of the royal families was manipulating the shimmers in a way that would harm humans forever.

Mateo couldn't leave the gaudy ballroom fast enough. Filled with wealth and oozing with opulence, it was no place for him. The sneers and side glances from the crowd confirmed it. Grabbing two glasses of bubbling drink from a silver tray, he downed the liquid as he exited the palace and marched to the wing where he was staying. Tossing the empty glasses in the shrubs, he bounded up the stairs, taking two steps at a time, and headed toward his bedchamber.

When Avalynn had entered the ballroom, she appeared like sunlight filling a room, dazzling. Smooth, flawless skin and long, lustrous midnight hair. He had taken in every inch of her face, neck, and shoulders until settling on where his eyes did not belong. But then he noticed Eiric Lind of Cuesta holding her hand.

He had no claim or right to the princess. Who cared that she walked in with Eiric? He did, that's who, and he could not help himself.

He had turned away, but it only took her two minutes before she was batting her eyelashes in front of him, asking him for a dance. He knew she was playing a game, but went along. And then she suggested an alliance. She must have thought him a fool. He would never believe that she truly wanted to work with him, a lowborn. As if he would trust the highborn ice princess at all. He knew better.

But then something else happened... Something odd and entirely out of his control...like the force of the moon toward the shining sun. With each movement, an unspoken attraction found them. Everything about her pulled him toward her. Her floral scent, her magnetic touch, and her sweet breath. He could have kissed her in that moment, even if it meant being struck down by the Stromm witch. He would have dared it. But Eiric tapping her shoulder took that away.

Good thing because it wasn't real.

He flung the bedchamber door open when a hand clutched his arm and pulled him in. Rhyka stood next to Lady Verona. She slammed the door behind him.

"What is the meaning of this?" He snatched his arm back and moved away. They were dressed in formal gala attire. Verona in a simple red sheath dress. Rhyka in all black, her flaming hair standing out like a fire in the night. "Why are you in my bedchamber?"

Rhyka pulled back and pressed her finger against her lips. "Lower your voice. Who knows what ears are near."

Lady Verona stepped forward. "We have received a raven from home." Her tone hit a serious note. "A message from Camilla."

Mateo's concern soared as his stomach dropped. "What message? Is it my family?"

"Poppy has fallen into the Dragon Bellow slumber." Verona exhaled a long breath. "Manny and Floriana are still conscious but slipping fast."

A chill raced down his spine. Few survived the deadly slumber. Could little Poppy? The world around him blurred. His family was 'slipping fast.' He had no choice but to win the hunt. A heavy and unfair hand gripped his heart. The need for the healing seeds reached a critical point. He had to win and save his family and the Sublands. He lowered himself onto the edge of his bed but couldn't speak.

Rhyka stepped closer. "With the hunt tomorrow, the hour is nigh for me to finish what I began in the carriage. About your destiny. About the Strong blood running through your veins." Her diamond eyes flashed with urgency. "Are you ready now?"

A venomous swirl churned in Mateo's stomach. *Ready?* He would do anything to save his sister and father and Poppy. "Of course, I'm ready."

"Good." Rhyka motioned him to sit on the edge of the bed then stepped closer. "This will not hurt." She placed her cool palm against his forehead. His ears fell silent as if stuffed with straw. Feeling suddenly weightless, his vision tunneled to black. His body lost all sense of self as he drifted into nothingness. Within seconds, his feet hit solid ground.

"Open your eyes," Rhyka whispered from within his head. "Go on."

Mateo cracked open his eyelids. No longer in his

palace bedchamber, he stood in a dark, misty place. Rhyka lowered her palm from his head.

"What is this?" He couldn't see anything but a gray blanket of haze. "Where are we?"

"Keep looking." Rhyka stepped aside. The mist around them faded.

He was in a cramped bedchamber. A woman in a purple nightgown lay on the bed. With eyes closed, her white-streaked brown hair plastered against her face. Blood stained the white sheets around her legs. A stocky dwarf dressed in all-white maidservant clothing held a swaddled baby. Tears streaked down her face while the baby wailed. Another small maidservant huddled in the corner.

Mateo's heart skipped a beat. He took two steps back. "What is this?"

"Your birth." Rhyka pointed at the baby. "That is you." She pointed at the lifeless woman on the bed. "That is your mother. Princess Gabriela of Strong Haven. You are the son of Gabriela and Leaf. You are the grandson of Princess Celyse and Lord Julio and the great-grandson of High King Rowan and High Queen Anise. You are the last remaining heir of Strong Haven."

Mateo turned away. He'd heard of those people from history tellings, but he didn't know them. "I am no Strong." He knew who he was. "I am Mateo Vela, son of Manny and Faeryn Vela."

Rhyka's vision continued as the maid shushed the baby, and the infant's wails lessened. He glanced over his shoulder at the scene again. A long, dark staff leaned against a marble table. A tall, dark wooden wardrobe chest with intricate flower and leaf carvings took up one wall. A dressing table with vials of silver and gold took up another. He caught his reflection in a circular, gold-framed mirror. Tall, pointed ears, long dark hair and fair skin. He averted his eyes from the woman on the bed. "I look nothing like her," he seethed between clenched teeth. "I look like my mother, Faeryn Vela."

Rhyka clapped back. "No. You look like the mate to Princess Gabriela, your father, Leaf of the Sublands."

Heat rose in his cheeks. He clenched his fists. The veins inside his hands pulsated. "Get me out of here. Now." He had no reason to stay. He invaded someone's sacred space. That was not his birth.

Rhyka swooshed her arm. The scene dissolved.

A jerk and a tremble and Mateo was back on the edge of his bed. He snapped to his feet and spat on the floor. "Lies." He paced his bedchamber, his insides burning like an inferno. "Why are you showing me lies?"

Lady Verona blocked his path. "She showed you the truth, not lies." She raised a clenched fist and elevated her voice. "And that truth can change everything for our people." Her eyebrows lifted. "It can help you win the hunt and get the reward, including those seeds."

He knew fae could not lie. So how could they be spewing such horrid untruths? "Witchery is allowing these vile tales."

"Listen, boy," Lady Verona threatened. "We are telling you the truth because there is great power within your human witch side." She jabbed her finger against his chest. "And you *must* awaken it."

He stumbled back. *Human witch side?* "You are mad.

Both of you." He had reached his fill of their misconceptions and outright falsehoods. "Perhaps you nipped too much of the High King's grapes?"

Lady Verona sighed and rubbed her forehead. "When I was a young Sublander, about your age..." Her eyes took on a faraway look. "I was part of a ring of protectors whose sole purpose was to protect Princess Gabriela, your mother. At that time she was the last remaining heir of House Strong." She locked eyes with Mateo and lowered her voice. "Manny Vela was part of that ring of protectors."

"My father?" He swallowed a gulp of air. They gained his attention by mentioning Manny.

"The human man who raised you." Verona nodded. "Yes. Manny was with us, along with my brother, Adrius; the ward of the Sublands at the time, Lord Rook; a powerful witch named Lady Sonia; your birth father and fellow Sublander, Lord Leaf; and then, of course, your mother, Princess Gabriela."

Whatever had happened to them might have been awful. But she was wrong about his parentage. Still, he wanted to hear more. "Tell me more about this ring of protectors."

"Our mission was loaded with danger. At one point, we raced through the tunnels under the Strong Haven Palace. Draven the witch and his warriors were on our tail. And then your mother, the princess, she..." Verona closed her eyes. Her lips twitched. "She brought forth a powerful blue light from her body. A surge of power all around her. She brought down the tunnel behind us, and we managed to escape."

Verona took a deep breath and opened her eyes. For the first time he noticed the dark circles and creases across her forehead. "Your mother's power was rare, like nothing I had ever seen before or since. It came from her father, Julio Avila, your grandfather, and their human ancestors before him. Rhyka and I believe the same power lives inside you."

Why would his father, Manny, keep something like this from him? He loved his father with all his heart. "If what you say is true, then why hasn't my father told me this?" He was supposed to believe that Manny had lied to him his entire life? He didn't think so.

"Because he knew the evils that sought to end the Strong bloodline." Verona's gala dress rustled with her movement. "He protects you with his life. He loved Gabriela as his own and stepped in as her sire when her father, Lord Julio, was killed, presumably by the Kanes."

All the deception made Mateo's head spin. Though one thing he knew for certain. None of what they told him would save his family. "There is no power inside of me." They hoped against hope for something that simply did not reside inside him.

Verona pointed her finger at Mateo. "Gabriela's power came to her when she needed it the most. It will be the same for you."

Mateo walked to the open window. A cool breeze brushed his face. The full moon filled the sky. Surely, he was not a Strong. But that voice deep inside of him nagged. It told him that he should consider the possibility. If power resided within him, he knew nothing about it. But perhaps it might help him win the hunt, rescue

Poppy from death's doorstep, heal his father and little sister, and maybe even deliver the Sublands out of the ashes.

And after the grim news from home, he needed to win that hunt.

CHAPTER TWELVE

Celyse, Julio, and Manny, along with allies from the Sublands, stood against this family and their evil witch, Draven.

Violins strummed in Avalynn's head as she waltzed into her bedchamber. She had danced with him— Mateo Vela. Her hand moved to the back of her neck, where he'd touched her. The warmth from his fingers lingered. He had noticed her. She closed her eyes and drew in a deep breath, reliving his steely gray stare roaming her figure. Her heart thumped and ached at the same time, something she had never known or felt before.

He'd accepted her alliance. That would make her task easier. Relieved, she kicked off her satin slippers and then stared into the darkness. From the blackness, it hit her like a blinding light—Mateo would die, and she would be the cause. The thump and the ache in her heart made more sense.

"That was quite the display... You and the Sublander."

She spun and faced the High King. "Father, I did not see you there."

He sat on the white plush chair, facing the empty fireplace. The moonlight from the sitting room's window lit him halfway. His other half blended with the shadows. "Come forth, my daughter."

She linked her hands in front of her and walked toward him. Stepping into the sitting room's space, she waved her fingers, and the fire sprang to life.

His legs were crossed. He held a gold goblet and still wore his gala attire—all silver with gold accents. On his head rested the realm's most formal and luxurious crown. It was adorned with tall antlers, gold vines, pearls, and crystals. She would one day wear that crown. Her rule would exceed any Faevenly had ever known, including his.

"The evening was most splendid, Father." What was he doing here in her room? She and Lily had presented themselves at the formal toast. Other than that, she had not paid him or her mother much heed. "I do pray that you and Mother had a lovely time."

"We did..." He rose and faced the fireplace. His goblet hit the mantle with a clink. "Perhaps not as much as you did."

Oh no. He'd been watching her. She could not let him know she'd become conflicted. A laugh that sounded weaker then she intended escaped her lips. "You know how I love to dance." She would not mention her fake alliance with Mateo. The less she said, the better.

"Yesss, I do know." He held out the 's' for a long beat, sounding like a slithering snake. He smoothed his long coat, tilted his head, and studied her. "Which makes me wonder why *we* did not dance."

"Indeed." Her worries refused to go down with a swallow. "My apologies. Next time?"

"How about now?" He extended his hand. "Who knows if there will be a next time."

A shiver shot down her spine. No next time? "Of course. Whatever pleases you, Father."

He held her with a firm grip. His muscles tensed, and he led her in a small circular pattern. The flames offered little warmth against his ice-cold touch. "Did your mother ever tell you the story of your birth?"

Her birth? "I do not think so." Her mother busied herself with formal events, gowns, and jewels. They had conversed but little throughout her life, let alone about the day of her birth.

"Allow me to share that day with you." His grip around her hand tightened. His touch at her hip pierced her like cold steel. "The High Queen prepared for your entry into this world for months. She had this very room redesigned with the most elegant fabrics, the softest rugs, and the most luxurious paints. As her belly grew, her plans followed. With Raelor's assistance, she knew the exact date you would arrive and invited all the royal maidens to meet you, the heir to House Stromm and future High Queen of Faevenly." He paused, prompting her to speak.

"That all sounds so wonderful." What happened to that lady?

His steps slowed. "It was wonderful...until it was not." His grip tightened further. "You came much earlier than expected. Neither Raelor nor the lady healer were here to assist. Thank the Sun, Moon, and Stars for Nia.

She had just joined us as a maidservant and assisted the High Queen. Nia did all that she could. Still, when you entered the world, the breath of life did not follow."

Avalynn stumbled over her frozen feet. "I was not alive?" She had not been told this before.

"Correct." His chin lifted. "Now, be careful with your steps, my daughter, lest you spoil our dance." He yanked her back into movement, pressing her forward in the same circular pattern. "The High Queen could not bring herself to look upon your lifeless face. Neither could I. So, Maid Nia whisked you away. But fate had superior plans for you. Not two minutes later, your wails rang out. You were brought back to the High Queen, but she had fallen into a fretful state from the trauma of your arrival, a despair that took Lily's birth to break."

Her panic escalated with each turn of the dance. Her hand throbbed from his squeeze. "I wish to stop dancing, Father." Learning she was born dead and then revived had weakened her resolve.

"You wish?" He grabbed her forearms and squeezed with all his might. "Let me tell you what *I* wish." Spit flew from his mouth with each word he hurled at her, his voice reaching new heights with each one. "I wish you had come out of the womb breathing. I wish your High Queen mother had not fallen into despair. I wish for you to do as I command and make sure the Sublander finishes last in the hunt!"

His hold tightened. Avalynn's knees buckled. "Father, stop!" She sank to the floor. Her desire to strike back flared up. But her hands stayed gripped by her aggressor.

He released her with a shove, straightened the collar of his jacket, and then dusted his hands off. "Tomorrow's hunt is critical."

Rising, she rubbed the spot on her arms that he had burned. Her skin parched and reddened. She wanted to scream, throw him to the floor, and claw out his eyeballs. But she possessed no power. Only he did. "I told you. I will not fail."

He snatched the tiara from her head and flung it into the fire. "You are only what I allow, dear daughter. And you are nothing more than a mere hunter." He turned to leave but lingered at the door. He hissed over his shoulder, "You have a wish but no real claim to my throne."

The door closed behind him, and she marched to the mantle. *Monster!* She grabbed his goblet and hurled it into the fire. She sank into the white plush chair and watched as the flames devoured the gold cup and platinum tiara. How dare he lay hands on her!

She cupped her face with her hands. Tears spilled from her eyes. Not alive at birth! And nobody bothered to tell her. She wiped her eyes, noticing the red marks on her forearms. Staring into the flames, the goblet and flaming tiara's molten edges distorted the true treasures within.

But she came back to life. She lived for a reason. The Sun, Moon, and Stars always had a purpose. Her destiny would never be fixed by that man or any other.

Feeling lower than low, her heart needed a friend. Her mind needed answers. She dashed to the door, jerked it open, and hurried down the corridor. Approaching the stairwell to the servants' quarters, a young maidservant bowed. "Princess Avalynn. May I be of assistance?"

"Please tell Nia I need her right away."

"Of course, my lady."

Avalynn paced her bedchamber when Nia entered. "My princess, I apologize for not being here sooner to help with your dress. Your father asked that you not be disturbed."

"I do need help with the dress. But that is not why I summoned you." Avalynn turned, and Nia unsnapped her buttons. She stepped out of the frock, slipped into the robe, and hid her father's red marks along her arms.

Nia gathered the dress. "Is it the Sublander? Mateo?" She hung the used garment on a hook. "I saw you two had a lovely dance."

It was neither Mateo nor the dance. "He is not the problem." She held back the tears, but one escaped and rolled down her cheek. "It is not Mateo. It is me."

"What is it, my princess?" Nia rushed to her side. "I am here."

She wiped her face and stared into the distance at nothing. "I was not alive at birth?"

"My Stars," Nia whispered. "Your father told you."

"He did." Her chin quivered no longer. "Why was I never told?" Father hurt her. Marked her arms. He threatened her and burned her tiara. She wanted answers.

Nia took Avalynn's hands. "The High King compelled me. I was forbidden. But now that you know the truth, that spell is lifted." The maid gently stroked her cheek. "But that moment is not your story. Your story is happening here and now."

Fire logs crackled at the other end of her bedchamber. Avalynn could not see the flames from where she sat. Still, she pictured the precious metals in the fire turning into a molten mess. "Why does Father demand Mateo's death? Why does he desire the banishment of all Sublanders?" Such a bold move did not seem to her to favor the future of Faevenly. Where would balance be found?

Nia said nothing.

"Do you know?" Avalynn readied herself for whatever secrets the maid would spill as her demeanor suggested she knew plenty.

Nia dropped to her knees. She took Avalynn's hand and bowed her head. "There have been whispers of a Sublander with great powers that will usher in a new era in Faevenly." Slowly, Nia's head lifted. "Part fae, part human witch, the Only One will bring peace."

Whispers. As a child, she had heard them but never again. No doubt, they were blocked by her palace and her duty. Now they were returning to her. Even Master Kragar spoke of them when he showed her the Shadowblood foxes. He warned that someone with innate gifts and powers would change Faevenly forever.

Her heart raced. The whisperings meant Mateo. Strong, yet gentle. Graceful like royalty. "He is the one... Mateo." She was sure of it.

Nia nodded. "It is believed so. No one knows for sure. The High King and High Queen do not want that to happen. They deny it all. They fight to preserve what they have."

Darkness encroached as the weight of a thousand shadows fell on her shoulders. "And I have to make sure he comes in last. Kill the bringer of peace for all of Faevenly." *Protect my family and my crown.*

The maid whispered an assent. "As sure as the sun rises and falls, everything will change after the hunt."

"And I will be ready for whatever happens." She had to be. Her future depended on it.

Nia reached into her flowing white dress and withdrew a glass vial with green liquid. Avalynn recognized it right away...healing salve from the Green Falls. "Take this with you into the hunt in case you need it. Keep it hidden. The realm must preserve its princess at any cost."

Avalynn wrapped her hand around the vial and held it tight. She hugged Nia, then said a silent prayer to the Sun, Moon, and Stars that the hunt would not see her needing the salve. Though something inside of her said she would.

CHAPTER THIRTEEN

After many lives were lost, the Sublanders were victorious, and peace returned to Faevenly.

Mateo's hands trembled as he pulled on his dark-green pants. Many counted on him. His little sister Floriana, his father, Gareth's sister Poppy... He shouldered the hope of all Sublanders. Now he had the beautiful yet devious Avalynn Stromm to worry about. *What was she up to?*

He tucked in his long-sleeved black shirt. Would she try to tempt him again? Her face and beautiful smile flashed through his mind. As much as he fancied her figure under that dress...*that* dress. He shook his head, clearing the Avalynn cobwebs—he had a job to do.

In the washroom, he threaded his black belt through the loops and focused on the prey. The Shadowblood Fox, not Avalynn Stromm. Nothing else mattered, not even Lady Verona's and Rhyka's lies about his parents. He pictured the fox in his mind's eye. Sharp claws, dark beady eyes, a strong small body. Catching the creature would be a challenge, but he'd hunted fox before. This one should be no different.

His boots laced, he returned to the main room but stopped dead in his tracks. A white envelope rested on the floor. *Now what?* He scooped it up and pulled out the simple black-inked parchment. *Protect Princess Avalynn.* What in thunderation? He jerked his door open and studied the corridor. Nobody. More games—he was *so* sick of games!

Stepping back into his room, he crushed the note, chunked it against the wall, and then kicked it under the bed. *Protect her?* Not a chance. In order to succeed for his family and the Sublands, he needed to protect himself first. Not her, not anybody else. She was on her own.

He slammed his fists against the mattress. *Focus. No distractions today.* With a steady breath, he surveyed the forsaken bedchamber. Since he might not return, he started shoving his stuff inside his bag. With everything in, the last two items sat on the table near his bed. He added the black scarf his mother made for him. But his touch lingered on the cross. His father, Manny, whittled it. But what if he hadn't? What if... He pushed it aside. *Don't believe their lies.*

He held the cross close. He reminded himself of his father's words. "Faith is a warrior." He kissed the wooden cross, then slipped it deep into his pocket and patted it. "I am a warrior. The prize is mine."

A knock at the door and Maid Nia entered with an air of formality. "Good morning." She scanned the room and noticed his bag. "Your things are packed. Very good. Your bag will be gathered later and placed for safekeeping until after the hunt. Now, I will escort you to the receiving room for your breakfast, your hunt satchel, and your weapon of choice."

He clutched his dagger sheathed at his waist. His father gave it to him when he was young, and he never hunted without it. "I already have my weapon."

With pursed lips, she shook her head. "That is not the custom. Every hunter must choose one from those provided. Weapons from outside the palace are forbidden."

He raised a brow. He had to use one provided by the Stromms? What a load of dung. They probably had a special weapon for the Sublands. One that was faulty and poorly made. "Someone should have mentioned the weapons rule."

"My sincerest apologies." Maid Nia lowered her head. "It is a long custom of the Summit Range Hunt. As a newcomer, I should have mentioned it to you."

Another day at Stromm Palace, another Stromm rule change. Would they want his pants next? "That's fine." He added his dagger to his bag. "What will be my choices?"

"Dagger. Spear. Bow. Now, please." She beckoned him forward. "We have a strict schedule."

Maid Nia led him out of his wing, through the palace, and into the receiving room. Mateo found the room's setup different from before. Guards in full gear lined the room. Tables were set up in the middle. One table contained a spread of fruit and bread. Another had five packed satchels. On the final table nested rows of weapons. Hawkeyed and resolute, Master Kragar guarded the weapons table, axe on his shoulder and at the ready.

Maid Nia faced Mateo. "This is where I leave you. All the blessings of the Sun, Moon, and Stars."

"Thank you."

Now, what was next? He had no idea until Avalynn and the other hunters strolled in. Avoiding eye contact with the princess, he followed their lead and served himself a plate of food. He sat away from them, eyes down, and ate quickly. She didn't matter. Her fake alliance wasn't going to work out for her.

When finished, he moved to the table with the satchels. Along with the other hunters, he grabbed one. It was fashioned from rough wool and didn't weigh much. He resisted opening it for inspection, he could do that later. Swinging the bag over his shoulder, he snuck a glance at Avalynn. Her nose in the air, chin up, and eyes down. He huffed. Ice princess mode. He could not afford the distraction.

At the weapons selection, she picked a bow and arrow set. She slid them into the quiver at her back. No surprise there. He'd heard of her archery skills. Selene chose a spear, as did Eiric and Finnian.

Mateo reached for a dagger and sheathed it at his waist. He would fashion a spear while in the forest—two weapons for one. A privileged highborn wouldn't think of such a thing. In Mateo's mind, it would be their ultimate downfall.

A hush fell over the assembled hunters, and Master Kragar started chanting... *Uh-uh...ohhh!* He lowered his axe. He tapped it in his hand while pacing throughout the group. *Uh-uh...ohhh!*. He planted his feet, raised the axe's flat side, and slammed it atop his head. *Ayyy!* His eyes widened. *Ayyy!* He slammed his head two more times, a drop of blood coming from his scalp. "Now! The moment you have all been waiting for—the hunt!" A wicked glint sparkled in his mad eye. "I will escort you to the far end of the garden. There you will line up and their Majesties, the High King and High Queen will see you off."

He took his place before them and grunted. He perched the blood-stained axe on his shoulder. "We march to the send-off." More drops of blood oozed from his hairline, but he didn't seem to notice. He stroked his lengthy red beard. "Let us go, then. To the hunt!"

THE
HUNT

CHAPTER FOURTEEN

The Sublands' victory hinged on Julio's blue energy power and his innate human witch abilities.

Avalynn focused on a patch of grass in front of her. The tall blades swayed with the gentle breeze. The early morning sun cast a warm glow on the crowd. Despite the warmth, her insides were frozen like ice cubes. She only wanted to be a hunter and win the prize. Now she was trapped inside palace politics, a mysterious prophecy, and a deadly task with Mateo Vela.

Was he really the bringer of peace?

Addressing the crowd, her High King father and High Queen mother stood on a dais above her and the other hunters. Would they notice she did not look them in the eye? Her mother, no. Her father, a definite yes. Like a vulture hoarding its kill, she knew he kept a keen eye on *everything* in his usual way—her, Mateo, the other hunters, the dignitaries. Nothing got past him.

A butterfly fluttered and skirted a cluster of white daisies. She watched as it danced from petal to petal but stopped herself. *Stay on mission. Sabotage the Sublander.*

Forget everything else except getting your life back. There was nothing she could do about prophecies anyway. She and she alone held her future in her hands.

Everyone cheered when her father finished speaking. She scanned the crowd and found her little sister in a bright yellow dress. Lily waved a House Stromm banner and grinned from ear to ear. Avalynn smiled and waved back. She would protect Lily from danger or harm, even from their father. No matter what.

In her peripheral vision, an axe caught her attention, followed by a tuft of red hair. Wide-eyed, Kragar grinned and mouthed the word, "Sublander," and then ran his finger across his throat.

Okay... Message received. She moved to the starting point behind the large crate of Shadowblood foxes. Would they run in a pack? Toward the forest? She adjusted the bow and quiver strapped to her back. Or would the foxes splinter and spread in all directions? For that matter, how would she and the other hunters head out for the hunt? In a single line? Or in groups? As far as she knew, she still had an alliance with the other highborns. But her fake alliance with Mateo concerned her.

Something about his more than usual chilly demeanor screamed something was off, missing, awry, gone bad. She wasn't sure why he had changed, but she needed to fix that. Her experience with Mateo thus far indicated that a direct approach worked best.

She stepped next to Mateo. Heart thrumming, she glanced at him, and he met her stare. He wore his dark hair in his usual fashion, two strands braided in the front while the rest flowed down his back. With the stitched lip and the bandage near his eye, he still made her weak in the knees.

"You still with me?" She wore her hair in a long tight braid, and tucked a strand behind her ear.

He swallowed hard and then parted his perfect lips. "Yes, my princess."

Did he mean it? Something about the way he used the word 'princess' told her he might not. She would find out soon enough.

The hunters took their places behind a line of purple ribbon. Mateo to her right and Finnian to her left. She leaned into a running stance. The weight of the weapons on her back felt like a thousand anvils. She prayed to the Sun, Moon, and Stars to bless her effort as she blew out a shaky breath. She could do this. She *had* to do this. Her life's preparation for this moment was not lost on Avalynn.

The palace animal keeper positioned himself at the crate's latched opening. Fingers at the ready. The royal trumpeter took his place beside the hunters. He raised the horn to his mouth and stood perfectly still for the longest seconds. His cheeks filled with air and then, *Blaaare!*

The foxes bolted. The crowd roared. Avalynn took flight in a tight pack with the other hunters. Arms pumping, she kept her eye on the shiny black coats as they bounded across the open meadow through lush grass and scattered wildflowers.

The foxes quickly synchronized in a rhythmic pace as they veered toward the edge of the meadow. In a blink, they disappeared into the Summit Range trees. Catching up to the lethal skulk would challenge the best hunters, but not her. She knew this terrain like the back of her hand. And, she knew the secrets Kragar shared with her and her alone before the hunt.

Grunting and hollering made her look left. Mateo and Eiric were running side by side, jabbing each other with their elbows. They stopped as they locked arms, pushing and pulling like rival stags during mating season.

"Mateo, stop!" She needed him with her. That fool Eiric would only mess up everything. "Let him go."

Mateo threw her a look, lips pursed and nostrils flared. He shoved Eiric away.

"Lowborn scum!" Eiric hollered. Selene joined him, and they took off, their legs in harmonious stride.

Avalynn shook her head and sneered. Eiric and Selene, what a perfect couple. She should have known they'd stick together. To her surprise, Finnian stayed with her and Mateo, and together the trio dashed after Eiric and Selene into the forest's towering embrace.

The transition from open daylight to the dapple-shaded trees added an extra layer of challenge. But she had anticipated that and slowed down, waving for Mateo and Finnian to do the same. "We must be careful." She pulled her bow from her back and kept it in her hand. "There are dangers in this forest." Charging forward like hot-headed Eiric and reckless Selene would only lead them into greater peril.

"You are right." Mateo drew his dagger. "Foxes are crafty and deadly, the Shadowblood probably more so. Not to mention the other creatures lurking here."

Finnian tapped his spear into the ground and glanced about. "What's the plan?"

His question landed like an Enbarr's hoof and reminded her of what she had to do. "Well, we hunt." And she would distract Mateo from capturing or killing a Shadowblood.

"And I shall win," Mateo declared.

"Or I will," Finnian asserted.

She was unsure how to make Mateo last place while she came in first but held on to the idea that she would figure it out along the way. "You both can save yourselves the time and trouble. The first-place prize belongs to me."

Mateo seethed. "You highborns already have the prize." His voice rose. "You have everything. What more could you want?"

His words shook her awake, although she did not sleep. *Already had the prize?* She tightened her grip on her bow. He was right. The royals *did* have everything. What did his people have? Nothing... She must stop thinking about that. It did not matter. And it never would.

Snap! She drew an arrow and swung her bow. A flash of fur zipped by, and she unleashed. *Yip!* She gulped and stared at the others. Had she done it? Had she struck a Shadowblood?

"No way," Finnian uttered.

She shrugged. "Let's go see."

They raced in the direction of her aim and found the lifeless animal. A regular fox with red fur took its last breath.

With his boot, Finnian nudged the dead fox. "Great aim, wrong beast."

"This time," she said. She retrieved her arrow and readjusted her quiver. "We also didn't see the magic in the air. Remember?"

Mateo scanned the area. "Speaking of magic, where's the boundary?" He walked around and squinted as he studied the trees. Everyone did the same.

"Is it visible with the naked eye?" Finnian asked.

Before anyone could answer, Mateo called from a cluster of trees. "Over here. I think I see it."

She and Finnian followed Mateo to the spot. A glint waned in the air, almost like a beam of light struggling to break through the clouds. She pointed. "There. I saw a spark."

Mateo moved closer. "It won't hurt us, right?" His brows gathered and bunched. "I don't trust that red-headed axe wielder of yours."

"Trust and deception are different matters." Avalynn folded her arms. "Master Kragar would never say something untrue."

Stepping forward, Finnian stretched out his arm. "Only one way to find out."

"I would not do that," Avalynn cautioned with her hand on her hip.

The thick fae touched the barrier anyway. *Zap!* He stumbled backward but stayed upright. He examined his buzzed hand. "It definitely hurt, but not too bad." He rubbed his fingers. "Like dipping your hand in a bucket of bees."

Even though it wouldn't kill them, she'd rather avoid

being zapped. She held her bow, tip out. "We should hold out our weapons while we walk."

"Not a bad idea," Finnian agreed, holding out his spear. Mateo found a long sturdy-looking stick and held it out too but kept his dagger closer.

Avalynn walked with caution, searching for signs of prey. She found two sets of boot prints instead. "We are headed in the same direction as Eiric and Selene. Through the trees and to the Grand Valley."

Mateo frowned as he bent down. "Those are sprinting footprints. They're close together, and the pattern is linear." His gaze darted about, and he pointed. "Those are the Shadowblood tracks." And he took flight.

"Thunderation!" Avalynn charged after him. Was he going to win after all? Would she be the big loser? She kept him in view, not letting him get too far ahead. She dodged chunks of rocks and jumped over fallen branches. After running a good distance, the trees thinned, and she burst into a small clearing.

Blurs of black fur streaked around in a chaotic circle. Yips and barks filled the air. In the middle of the circle stood Selene and Eiric. Selene's eyes were wider than a canyon while Eiric jabbed his spear at the nearing foxes. They would be overrun soon.

Avalynn gulped. The Shadowbloods were deadly and smart. But were they smart enough to join forces for an attack? Did her father or Master Kragar or both know they would go after the hunters like this?

Mateo eased toward the frenzy and picked up Selene's thrown spear that had obviously missed its target. He started backtracking toward Avalynn and

Finnian, looking as if he wanted nothing to do with the deadly ambush.

But this was not what she had signed up for. She bit her lip. Eiric and Selene would probably not come to her aid in the same situation. But if she could help it, they would not suffer death by mauling.

She reached for an arrow, but Finnian yanked her arm down. "They will swarm us."

"But they will die out there."

"Or we will." Finnian shook his head as if she endangered them more. "We can't take that risk."

He was right. She lowered her hand. Hit or miss, those foxes might come after them if they were alerted.

Mateo backed up until he joined them. Spear readied, he focused his attention on the foxes. "What kind of devious prey did that lunatic Kragar pick for us to hunt?"

She sifted through what she knew of the Shadowbloods—solitary, intelligent, and hunted varmints like mice, rats, and rabbits. Then she sorted the stuff she knew, but the others did not. Bloodsuckers. They disappeared into the shadows, and their claws sometimes passed on a deadly toxin. But Kragar never said anything about behaving as a pack or hunting fae.

"I do not know." She hated the weakness of those four words.

Mateo balanced his newly acquired spear in his hands. He studied the pack of foxes. "I'm going in." He glared at Avalynn. "This is my shot, and I'm taking it."

Of course he would say that. "Fine. I am too." She drew her arrow and matched his vim and vigor. She could do anything he could do...better.

Finnian brandished his spear. "Me first." He ran toward Selene and Eiric.

Avalynn and Mateo locked eyes and then ran after him toward the melee. Neither Finnian nor Mateo were making the first kill. No. Way. That honor belonged to her. Forget the directive by her father. With the attacking prey, all bets were off. Her father would have to understand.

Avalynn darted toward the middle of the clearing. She carried her bow in one hand and an arrow in the other. The Shadowblood foxes had not noticed them emerging from the tree line, but they would soon.

Mateo raced upon the prey like a charging Enbarr. He quickly passed Finnian and hurled his spear. It soared on target for a Shadowblood, but the wily beast darted sideways at the moment of truth. The sharp silver tip grazed the fox's hind flank. The beast yelped and fixed on Mateo. Raising its head, the fox let loose an ear-piercing wail.

Avalynn stopped and mumbled, "What in thundera-tion?" The foxes circling Eiric and Selene began darting every which way, yipping and barking in a frenzy.

"Stop them!" Mateo hollered.

"Stop them? From what?" Avalynn quickly studied the scene and realized they were assembling like warriors for a battle. She nocked an arrow and aimed her bow, but foxes came from everywhere. *Impossible!* It was not only the Shadowbloods. She gulped and lowered her bow. Other foxes, some red and others dark, joined from the forest's edge. They were *helping* the prey. The hunters had become the hunted.

Mateo's back pressed against hers. "I am going to kill that Master of Arms of yours."

"Not if I manage it first." She saw a clear shot, aimed, and let fly. *Zip*. The arrow lodged straight through the skull of a regular red fox. That was a kill. She nocked the next arrow when a Shadowblood leaped toward her, growling, claws out, and baring sharp teeth. Its eyes blinked from beady black to bright red.

Mateo clutched her waist, spun her, and slammed his fist under the beast's mouth. With that uppercut, the Shadowblood buckled and then dropped with a thud. It sprang back to its feet, snorted, and snarled like it wanted more.

"Why are they working together?" More scurried at them, and Mateo kicked them away. "How is that even possible?"

"Magic!" Finnian moved closer, swinging his spear back and forth. "Must be magic!"

Selene and Eiric rushed in. Selene kicked at anything and everything that neared her boots. She grunted and hollered with each strike. Her wild red hair flew in every direction with each movement. "This hunt is a huge load of dung!"

"We cannot keep this up!" Eiric shouted as the foxes attacked, over and over with relentless abandon.

Avalynn reached for an arrow. *Zip*. It hit the hind of a Shadowblood, which howled and then raced off. No smoke in the air. That's an injury, not a kill, and not a winner.

Mateo brandished his dagger, slicing at anything that came close. Off lopped a bushy tail with a *thwack*.

Avalynn flicked another arrow when a scream made her freeze.

"No!" A Shadowblood raced up Eiric's leg, past his stomach, and latched on to his neck. He hollered like it was his last. "Get it off me!"

Mateo whipped around, gripped the beast's tail, and jerked it from Eiric's skin. He spun in two circles, gaining momentum, and flung the creature into the trees.

Blood jetted from Eiric's neck. He slammed his hand over the wound and then slumped to the ground.

"Eiric!" Selene planted herself in front of him. "Protect him!"

Avalynn fired her last arrow, taking out another regular fox. She choked up on her bow and started whacking. She flashed Mateo an unsure glance. Were they goners? No winner. No loser. Only five dead hunters. They would all tie for last. What a joke.

A snarl echoed, and a large black wolf burst onto the scene. Sharp teeth bared and claws unsheathed, it leaped on an unsuspecting fox. The wolf chomped and severed the fox's head with a mighty crunch. Growling and ferocious, it went after another and tore it to shreds. With furious frenzy, it clawed away at two more.

The advancing foxes yipped and scattered in all directions, retreating into the trees. But now they had a wolf to battle. She raised her bow. Her body trembled. Could they destroy a wolf that strong and that big? It was huge. She assumed a fighting stance, ready for whatever came next.

Mateo dropped his dagger. He fell to his knees. The

black wolf with a white streak down its back jumped him and then...licked his face?

"Stormy, girl!" He hugged her as she rested her big paws on his shoulders.

Avalynn lowered her bow. "You know this wolf?" Stormy tilted her head, sniffed, and then bounded from Mateo to Avalynn. It circled her legs, jumping and twirling. "Uh...what is it doing?"

Stormy raised up on her hind haunches and pounced on Avalynn, who fell back. The friendly wolf towered over her and licked her face. "My Stars." She moved her head to the side and held up her hands. "Does she greet everyone like this?"

"Stormy, off!" Mateo pulled the wolf away. His brows inched closer together. He squinted as if he didn't understand what his beast was doing.

"Eiric is bleeding!" Selene shouted. "Help him!"

Avalynn scrambled to her feet and joined Selene. Eiric's face had gone white as snow. His eyes were fixed and almost fully rolled back in his head. She touched his wrist. The thump of his pulse remained, but faint. "We need to move him somewhere safe." She scanned the forest. "And quick." But were the foxes waiting? Thank goodness for Mateo's wolf.

"I saw a cave close by." Selene pointed to the other side of the clearing. "Over there."

Mateo took charge. "Let's move."

Avalynn gathered her arrows while Mateo and Finnian lifted Eiric. They trudged into the woods, following Selene. Stormy stayed by Avalynn's side, as if assigned to her protection. She reached down and rubbed the wolf's head. "Thank you for saving us, Stormy." She could get used to this big, loveable beast.

Mateo's wolf moved closer, as if understanding her. Avalynn wanted to know more about the wolf and more about Mateo. His family, his home, where the wolf came from. She shook her head, snapping to her senses. Why? It would only make things harder when she did what she had to do. She had been ordered to sabatoge him and that directive still lingered.

He was a lowborn. Plain and simple. And that would never change. She was a highborn bound for the throne. And that would never change either.

CHAPTER FIFTEEN

Celyse left Faevenly for a life with Julio, and their love blossomed into a daughter—me, Gabriela... I am your mother.

Mateo shifted his grip on Eiric's legs while Finnian held his limp upper body. Selene led the way through the forest. She weaved her way through the overgrown brush, heading back the way they had come. So far, they avoided the magic boundary and another run-in with the foxes. Perhaps those deadly creatures needed a reprieve too.

Mateo never thought he'd be working with highborns, much less save one as detestable as Eiric Lind. But now, all hunters had a common enemy. What did that mean for the hunt? And for him winning? In order to capture one of the deadly foxes, he needed to survive. The only way to survive? Use the highborns to his advantage. Once he made his kill, they were on their own to figure out last place, death, and banishment of their people.

Even Avalynn.

He glanced over his shoulder at Stormshroud. Usually next to him, she was now trotting along with the princess. What a betrayal, but he could not entirely blame Stormy. If Mateo and Avalynn were not competitors, he would want to be with her too.

"Over here." Selene veered off to an area thick with vegetation, and the cave's mouth came into view.

Mateo had scoured plenty of caves with Stormshroud. They would check it before the others went in. "Stormy, go look." He whistled, and she bounded with a leap and then disappeared inside.

Avalynn approached. "She came all this way to be with you?"

He knew Stromshroud had come for him, but she seemed to stay for Avalynn. "Or you. I can't tell for sure." His wolf had been so eager to join him when he left the Sublands. But now, it was as if Stormy had laid eyes on a beautiful maiden and abandoned all senses.

A smile crept across Avalynn's face. She winked at Mateo. "Your wolf has good taste."

Stormy trotted out of the cave. Selene pointed at the cave's mouth and a dirt floor with plenty of fluffy leaves. "Lay him here." Selene slipped off her satchel and set it under Eiric's head. She looked up at Avalynn with pleading eyes. "What do we do?"

"Um...well..."

Did the highborns know nothing? They were too busy being pampered by maidservants and healers. He took off his satchel and found fruit, flat bread squares, water, and a small rag. It was a start. He took the water and the rag and approached Eiric.

Selene blocked his path. "How do I know you will not hurt him?"

"He is already hurt." Mateo shook his head. He approached with a rag, not a dagger.

"Come on, Selene." Gently, Avalynn pulled her back. "Let him help."

He knelt beside Eiric and pulled the blood-stained collar down. Coagulated blood caked around the bite. A clean water rinse provided a better view. The sharp, precise punctures dotted the skin in a curved line. Fresh blood began seeping from the wound. "He needs stitching. If the wounds are not closed, he will bleed out."

Eiric's eyes opened. "What is happening?" He looked around as if in a daze. "Where am I?"

Selene fell to her knees and wiped his brow. "One of those horrid foxes bit your neck. But you are going to be fine now." She glanced at Mateo. "Right?"

He shrugged, not knowing if the Shadowblood's bite was deadly. They'd know soon enough. "He should survive." He scooted back, then rose to his feet. "But I need something to close up the wound."

Vines, ferns, and moss-covered rock covered the cave's entrance. He walked the perimeter of the cave, searching for spider webs but found none. He'd have to go back into the trees.

Avalynn approached with Stormy, her new best friend, trotting at her side. "What are you looking for?"

"Webbing. For the cut." He shot Stormy a glare and then went outside the cave. He didn't have to walk far to see thin, silky threads stretched between two limbs of a giant oak. He grabbed a handful.

"How do you know about that?" Avalynn followed and observed.

"Because, princess, I am a Sublander and a lowborn. We are survivors. We don't have servants kissing our bruises and mending our wounds."

She grabbed his arm. "Will you stop, please? We are trying to survive this cursed hunt and must work together." She paused as if carefully crafting her next words. "Or we will *all* end up dead."

There it was. She needed him again. He stepped closer. Her sweet scent of roses and jasmine drifted around him, tempting him like sirens on a dangerous sea, her melodic call drawing him into uncharted depths and possible death. "No matter what we do, princess, one of us will surely end up in the Passing Place. And it won't be me." It *couldn't* be him. Too many people counted on him.

He went back to Eiric, who was sitting up and leaning against the cave wall. "This webbing will help seal your wound and prevent infection."

With Selene by his side, Eiric nodded. "Thank you." He gulped. "Mateo."

He smirked. Now that a lowborn Sublander could help, he had a name. It figured. He applied the spider threads and pressed them into the wound. When everything looked the way he wanted and the blood stopped spilling out of the bite, he went to the edge of the cave's mouth and inspected the trees. From the length of the shadows filtering through, the sun had passed over. If the Shadowbloods were like regular foxes, they had found a den to hunker down for the remainder of the day. They would come out at night. The cave offered some protection, but not enough.

Avalynn came up next to him, rock in hand. "We need to talk about what happened." She tossed the rock from one hand to the other. "And our next move. I say 'our' because it's us against those foxes."

"How did they know to work together?" Finnian approached with his satchel. He took out a piece of fruit. "Like they were part of one larger pack."

Eiric added through labored breaths, "I have neither seen nor heard of anything like it."

"I want to get out of here." Selene opened her satchel. "I never wanted to be in this wretched hunt anyway."

She did not even want to be here? Back home in the Sublands, his people were dying for a chance at the hunt. Mateo studied her foolish, whiny face. "You are the worst of the worst."

Selene recoiled and huffed. "No one cares what you think, lowborn."

"Stop." Avalynn glared at Selene. "Right now, we are not lowborns or highborns." Her voice rose. "We are not even hunters."

Mateo folded his arms. He hated to admit it, but the princess had a point. "You are right. We are now the hunted."

The silence returned like a shadow, dark and menacing. Tired of silence and tired of talking, Mateo wanted action. "We need to get back to being hunters." He drew his dagger. "We need more weapons." If they acted like prey, they would continue being that.

"Spears," Avalynn said. "You can make spears with your dagger."

"You could probably make some with the tip of your

arrow too." He pointed to her quiver. "How many do you have?"

"Only three." She kept one, handed one to Finnian, and the other she held out in front of Selene and Eiric. "Who wants to make spears?"

Selene took the arrow. "I will."

"I can fashion a defensive perimeter using whatever you all make," said Eiric.

Now they were getting somewhere. Mateo explained how the branches should be sturdy, straight, and at least eight feet long. Growing up in the Sublands certainly showed its advantages in this moment. And the highborns were actually listening. Survival mode at its finest.

Everyone took to the trees and started breaking branches. When they had about two dozen, they cleared the side branches and began whittling the ends to points. They handed their finished product to Eiric, who placed them around the cave's mouth.

When their hands ached and the sunlight had all but disappeared, they retreated back to the cave. "Now what?" Selene paced, her eyes darting as she scanned the surroundings.

"Now we build a fire, gather logs for seating, and take turns sleeping." He avoided Stormshroud, who stayed close to Avalynn still. "I will take the first watch." He would use the time to think about his next moves.

"I will join you," Avalynn offered right away.

Night fell quickly. Darkness engulfed the cave except for the crackling fire. Eiric and Selene lay close together in one corner. Finnian slept opposite them.

Assuming watch duty, Mateo sat close to the fire. He

kept his gaze on the flames, ignoring Avalynn by his side. There was nothing for them to talk about anyway. Despite the fire, the chill air clung to his skin, creating a layer of dampness. It even coated each breath he took. He missed the dry red rocks back home. And he especially missed his family. He patted the cross in his pocket. *Please, let them be okay.*

Stormshroud moved closer. She nudged her head under his hand. "Now you want to be best friends again," he whispered. He brought her close and stroked her thick fur. No hunter would be alive without Stormy. Her excellence brought back all the times they spent together on Spirit Butte. And thoughts of Spirit Butte pulled his mission to the forefront of his mind as the dancing flames filled his vision. "Everything is on fire," he whispered to himself. His overwhelming need to win and save his father and sister and everyone in the Sublands pulsed within him. "And so am I."

CHAPTER SIXTEEN

Your grandparents took me to Faevenly often. But when my life was threatened, we stopped going, and unease began spreading amongst the provinces.

valynn did not want to disturb Mateo, but at the same time she longed to know what he saw in the crackling fire. The red rocks from his Sublands home seemed the obvious choice. Death from another fox attack made the list. His wolf favoring and coming to her over him seemed most likely.

He patted his pocket, something she had seen him do at least a dozen times. Her mind toyed with what he carried inside that pocket. A coin? A trinket? Maybe a gem? Still, the news that Mateo might be a savior with powers weighed on her mind the most.

The wind whistled through breaches in the cave's bumpy stone walls. The smell of dewy earth hung thick. She had nudged Stormshroud and directed the wolf to join him. Now they were side by side, Stormy's head tucked under Mateo's hand. Avalynn's heart felt heavy, knowing Mateo's wolf responded to her like it did. Perhaps she was drawn to the floral rose and jasmine scents that trailed Avalynn. While they were dancing, Mateo responded to that same scent.

The pull between them that night was unmistakable. Still, she had no idea if he felt it now. Withdrawn, his words and actions were as complicated as the cave—a labyrinth leading her down a dark, winding, and secret path. She wanted and needed to know the *real* Mateo, but did he even know himself? Only time would answer that question. Though it seemed they were running out of that.

Leaves rustled from tall trees swaying outside the cave's mouth. Frogs called from somewhere out there. She cleared her throat and softened her tone. "I would like to know more about the Sublands, if you would so kindly indulge me."

"You? Princess of House Stromm?" His voice echoed in the dark cave. He fixed his eyes from the fire to her. "You want to know about the Sublands?" He lifted his chin. "It is the dreaded home of us lowborns—the ones not worthy of breathing the same air as the Stromms."

Her back stiffened. She and the royals deserved that response. But she didn't back down. "Why not tell me?" She moved closer. "You are the one who said we share this land, remember?" She would have shared anything with Mateo.

He threw a stick into the fire. "Our night with the Enbarr." The flames jumped with a crackle and a pop. His eyes followed the dancing sparks, and then his gaze landed on her. "I remember every word I say to you." He stared deep into her mighty soul. "And every word you say to me."

Heat flushed her face. It came not from the burning wood but from the waves of intensity from Mateo. His body angled closer to hers. A gust of wind whipped by, and pebbles crumbled from the cave's mouth. Their knees touched. Such a simple thing while sitting on a log sent a flutter within her. Should she stay or should she go —the eternal question. Her heart pulled in one direction and her duty in another.

"What do you want to know about the Sublands?" Mateo's relaxed face spoke volumes. The butterflies in her stomach lost their wings. He had dropped his defenses. This was her opportunity.

She wanted to know more about his family. Knowing them would help her understand him. "How about starting with your family? Your mother and father."

Brows pinched, he shifted away and returned his stare to the fire's flames. She had struck a troubled nerve. Her instinct said to retreat, but her heart said to stay. "We do not have to talk about them."

"No. They are important to me." With clasped hands, he swallowed and sighed. "I am here because of them."

She put her hand on his knee. His soft, aching tone. The way he leaned forward and clasped his hands together. Something awful must have happened to them. "You can tell me."

He bowed his head. "Eight years ago..." He drew in a deep breath. "A mysterious ailment came to the Sublands —Dragon's Bellow. Our healers knew no treatment, let alone a cure. Without enough healing seeds, our village suffered." His chin quivered. Two teardrops rolled down his cheeks, and he wiped them away with the back of his hand. "It took my mother."

Seeds. Mateo said the highborns already had all the rewards they needed. He meant those healing seeds. He competed for those. A sickness whirlpooled in her gut, followed by the deepest sadness that soured her insides.

"Her cough grew worse until *that* morning. She could barely breathe." He wiped his tear-streaked face. "My father sent me to the healer for whatever seeds she had." His jawline tightened. He clutched his knees. "I ran so fast."

Avalynn dreaded how the story ended. Terrified for what was next. She could see a desperate race that was lost.

"I took the healer's small stash, hurried home, burst through the door, but..." He squeezed his eyes shut and shook his head. "I was too late. She was gone."

He had lost his mother and blamed himself. Her heart broke. She had never beheld a sadder sight or heard a more sorrowful story. "It's not your fault." A pang of sorrow gripped her. No wonder he hated the highborns. She now saw the hunt in a different light. She competed for the Stromm name and for acceptance as the future queen. She hunted for duty and glory. Mateo competed for the prize of providing life-saving seeds. He hunted for life itself.

"Since *that* day, a fire has burned inside me and I have been running." He made a fist and pounded his leg. "Running so that I would be faster than any other hunter." He double-tapped over his heart. "I hunt for the sake of my mother's memory. I hunt for my father, sister, and other Sublanders who are sick." He looked up at the sky. "Winning means everything."

She swallowed the lump of heartache in her throat. Mateo loved his family so completely he risked death for them. And she was responsible for making sure he died. For what? Her father's approval? A mother who never spoke to her? A crown that would one day be hers *if* it pleased her father? A dark cloud covered her soul as tears streamed from her eyes. She was no better than her father.

"Hey. Wait." He wiped those tears with a gentle touch. "Why are you crying?"

She stared at her boots, shaking her head. Her tears fell for their twisted fates, which could not be unraveled without utter destruction. She cried for the person she was and for all the things she must do at her father's command. "I am sorry about your mother, your father, and your sister. I am sorry for all of it." She would never forgive herself.

His finger trailed down the side of her face. He lifted her chin. Their eyes locked. His energy spread through her like wildfire. "It's not your fault. Do not cry for me or my people."

She wiped her face, feeling worse than before. "I am not normally this emotional, but..."

"But what?" He searched her eyes.

She trembled as her heart skipped a beat. "You have an effect on me."

"What kind of effect?" He scooted closer and licked his luscious lips.

"You know the kind," she breathed.

"I do." He placed his fingertips on her throat, then trailed his hand around to the back of her neck. His lips parted, and she closed her eyes. His musky scent sent her skyward, but he suddenly stopped. He pulled back with widened eyes, then grabbed a spear.

Dead leaves crackled near her feet. She lunged for her bow and snatched an arrow. "What is it?" Paws shuffled over the cave's floor. A flock of birds flew away outside. A yip sounded. Followed by another. Thunderation. The foxes. They were back.

Mateo's nostrils flared. He choked up on the wood, looking deadly and beautiful with his long dark hair gleaming in the firelight. "Wake the others," he urged Avalynn.

Stormshroud faced the cave opening with a growl while Avalynn sprinted toward the cave's back. "Up! Now!" She nudged the hunters with her bow's tip. "Foxes are here!"

Finnian shot up, grabbed his spear, and then darted to the mouth of the cave. Selene and Eiric followed him. The yips grew louder. Mateo and Finnian added handfuls and then armfuls of brush to the fire. The flames nearly engulfed the entire opening. With their weapons out, everyone stepped back. The yips were silenced.

"Are they gone?" Selene drew closer to Eiric. Her eyes darted about the cave in a zigzag pattern.

"I think so," Mateo replied. But then there was another yip, this time from behind them.

Avalynn's heart raced as she spun. Had a Shadowblood vanished into the shadows and slipped past when she and Mateo sat together? She needed to warn the others. They would hate her, but they needed to know. "You all should know the Shadowbloods are invisible in the shadows."

Mateo leveled her with a death glare. "You knew this all along and did not tell us?"

He didn't take the news as well as she'd hoped. "Let's move past that."

He squinted and seethed. "The worst of the highborns."

Selene smirked like a child. "She is a Stromm. What did you expect?"

"Stop this," yelled Finnian. "Everybody back-to-back. Stay sharp, or we are all dead."

They formed a tight circle. Stormshroud growled, fangs out, body lowered, fur bristled along her back. Standing beside Avalynn, Mateo shot her a side-eye. "Are they totally invisible?"

Her mind zipped back to her session with Kragar. When he threw the blanket over the cage, the Shadowblood had disappeared. But was any part of it visible? Had she paid well enough attention? "I'm not sure." She should have asked Master Kragar that question.

Another yip, followed by two more. Stormshroud's growl grew louder, her wolf body ready to spring.

"Those devious creatures play with us," whispered Eiric. "Stay sharp."

The yips continued. Right. Left. Closer and closer. Their circle tightened as Avalynn's muscles tensed. How many foxes were in the cave? Were the regular foxes here too? Maybe in the way back? Adrenaline rushed through her veins. Her senses beamed on high alert. She poked her foot around, searching for furry animals. Where were the damned foxes?

Illuminated by the flames, a ball of black fur shot from the darkness. Mateo lunged and speared it through. The beast yelped and jetted out of the cave. Stormshroud pounced after it.

A regular fox came at them. Selene swung, but missed it by a hair. Eiric followed with a thrust to the head. *Shunk!* Got it.

Howling yips shrieked as two more foxes charged. One made a beeline for Eiric. The other zeroed in on Avalynn. She nocked an arrow and let fly. The arrow pierced the fox's eye, but the creature continued rushing her. Mateo pulled Avalynn behind him. He slammed his spear against the creature. It dropped, howled, and then sprang back to its feet. Flying high, it soared over Mateo. The beast's claws scraped through Avalynn's hair as she ducked. Mateo grabbed it by the tail and hurled it into the fire. A piercing squeal filled the night air. Engulfed in flames, the beast cooked with a pop and a sizzle.

Bent over, hands on her knees, Avalynn labored for air. "Is that it? We got them?"

"The regular fox that went after me escaped," Eiric said between panting bursts. "The Shadowblood did not even *try* attacking."

"Devious and intelligent." Mateo kept a firm grasp on his weapon. "The other foxes are doing their dirty work."

"Maybe this was only a warning," Finnian suggested in a low voice, as if the creatures, wherever they were, would hear him and get ideas.

"A what?" Selene recoiled, her shoulders pulling up to her ears. "Please, no."

Spears out, Mateo, Finnian, and Eiric walked the cave's perimeter. Stormshroud bounded back in time to join them.

Avalynn and Selene stayed by the fire and tossed more branches in. The fox inside flamed. The stench from burnt fur turned her queasy stomach. She covered her mouth and nose and faced away from the flames.

Everyone gathered around. "The cave is clear," announced Finnian.

Mateo tacked on, "For now."

Was it really? She prayed to the Sun, Moon, and Stars the foxes stayed clear until the sun rose. So far, they had been fortunate, even lucky. Yet Avalynn feared their fortune and luck ran on short supply.

CHAPTER SEVENTEEN

*Draven's evil returned to Faerenly,
and your grandparents went missing.*

Mateo's eyes remained fixed past the fire and on the cave's mouth. Without blinking, he gripped his spear. Those damned foxes were never getting past him again. He should have never let himself get drawn into Avalynn like that. He'd said too much—exposed himself like never before. And never would again. Especially not with her. A highborn. A Stromm. She withheld vital information about the Shadowblood. She could have gotten them all killed.

What else was she hiding?

His grip tightened around the spear's rough wood. *Do not let her get in the way.* Who cared if Stormshroud had a thing for her? Or that she smelled *so* good? Or that she was stunning?

Finnian sat next to him on one side. Avalynn sat on the other side. In front of them, the fire burned but not like before. Eiric and Selene tended it the best they could with the brush and branches they had gathered earlier. Yet their supply dwindled.

The fire's flames peaked low. The ember's orange glow faded. Mateo prayed to the Sun, Moon, and Stars they had enough kindling to make it to sunrise. He placed his hand on his pocket, on the cross nestled there, and prayed to his father's God too.

Selene tossed a handful of leaves onto the smoldering fire and scrunched her face. "I am so tired of this hunt business." Her complaining had started hours earlier. At first, Eiric appeased her. Now, even he ignored her. She had proven herself unworthy as a hunter and a fae. She should have never been included.

Mateo kept his stare fixed on the darkness beyond the cave's mouth. He shifted his weight, then noticed a silvery haze. Faint at first, it grew bigger and brighter. A bird chirped, followed by another. A rabbit scampered nearby. Finally, daylight had arrived.

Avalynn exhaled as if relieved. "Thank the Stars, we made it."

"The Stars?" *Pfft*. They did nothing. "We fought to make it through the night." Mateo knew the foxes were still out there, planning another attack. He rose, his legs tingling and stiff. "Now we need to make it through today." That could be the challenge of a lifetime. Selene was worthless, Eiric was injured, and Avalynn had her own designs. Maybe Finnian had some worth.

With a grunt, Finnian got up and stretched his legs. "So...we resume the hunt as normal, then?"

In a flash, Eiric and Selene darted from the cave's

mouth. Avalynn tumbled to the ground from a push. "Hey!"

Mateo helped her up. What fools. "Forget them. They will not last an hour out there." He dusted her off. "Let them go, they will—"

"Ahhhh!" A holler echoed from the trees.

Avalynn shot Mateo a wide-eyed look. "Selene."

They raced from the cave's mouth with weapons out. A few paces into the trees, they found Eiric, face down and lifeless, one of the spears through his neck. Selene hovered over him. Her hands shook, and tears streamed down her face. "This hunt is cursed!"

Avalynn moved closer to Selene and rested her hand on her shoulder. "This was an accident. Nothing more."

Studying the scene, Mateo could tell 'the accident' was more foolishness than curse. In a mad rush to get ahead of him and the others, Eiric tripped and impaled himself on his own defense barrier. His blundering deprived him of an honorable death. He got what he deserved.

"Do not just stand there!" Selene pleaded. "Do something!"

With Finnian's help, Mateo flipped over Eirics's body. His crooked mouth hung open, and he looked pained. His fixed eyes appeared hollow, like an empty nest. Blood drained from his neck wound down his tunic. He was gone. No one spoke for a few long seconds.

"We need to prepare him for the Passing Place," Selene said between tears.

Prepare him? With the foxes afoot, Mateo saw the danger. "No. There's no time and it's too risky." Eiric did nothing to deserve either a preparation or a ceremony. "Let him be taken the way he is."

Selene's voice hardened. "You say that because you are a lowborn with human blood." She spat toward Mateo. "You have no respect for our customs."

"*Our* customs?" Mateo's blood boiled. "Like I am not one of you!" He was sick of Selene. "I know the customs, and I care for them." He stabbed his finger toward Eiric's body. "But someone like him..." He stepped closer to Selene. "And someone like you, for that matter, commands no respect."

"Stop. Both of you." Avalynn sidled between them. "We will do it fast, and then we'll figure out our next move."

"We? Do you have a maidservant in your pocket?" Mateo crossed his arms. He didn't care one way or the other that Eiric died or what happened to his body. "I want no part of Eiric Lind of Cuesta and his end-of-life send-off."

"Why you—" Selene muttered with pursed lips.

Avalynn raised her hand toward Selene but kept her softened blue eyes on Mateo. "Will you at least keep watch then?" Her brows lifted, and Stormshroud's followed. "While we prepare our fallen hunter?"

Really? His wolf supported the effort? "Fine. But hurry. Foxes do hunt us, remember?"

Spear in hand, Mateo walked the perimeter. He kept one eye on the tree line and the other on Avalynn. Stormshroud joined him and matched his stride. He glared at the wolf and muttered under his breath, "Now you want to be with me?" Stormshroud's ears lay flat, and her head lowered. "You *should* feel bad. I am the one who saved you as a pup, not her." She sat back on her haunches. *Great.* Now he was the one feeling bad. He sighed. "Come on, girl."

With Stormy back in her regular position at his heels, they kept watch while Avalynn, Selene, and Finnian prepared Eiric for his afterlife journey.

Finnian removed the spear from his neck with slow, easy tugs. He wiped the blood off on the grass and set the long stick next to Eiric's body. Then he scooped up a pinch of dirt and packed it into the circular wound. Another scoop of soil and the opening was sealed.

Avalynn worked on his clothing. She started with his tunic. She smoothed out the fabric and fixed his sleeves, whisking away any wrinkles with her hands. The blood would have to stay, though. Next, she moved to his pant legs, straightening them and then dusting them off.

The last part came from Selene. She closed Eiric's eyelids, one at a time. With a gentle-looking touch, she closed his mouth, then fidgeted with his lips until they looked the way she wanted. Next, she took the cloth from her bag and wiped the blood from his neck, taking care not to disturb the packed dirt in the wound. She then cleaned his chin, cheeks, nose, and forehead. When she'd cleaned as much as she could, she threaded her finger through his long silver hair, making sure each strand was in place.

When Eiric appeared as if he were merely sleeping, the three went to a nearby Mountain Laurel shrub. They picked white clusters of flowers from the broad green leaves. The clusters smelled of sweet honey, and they came back and placed the blooms around his body.

Mateo eyed the mountain paths. The Enbarr transported the dead to the Passing Place for a new life. Would his and Avalynn's Enbarr come and take Eiric? Or maybe a different one would do the job? Of course, he preferred any Enbarr other than theirs.

When the last flower was placed, Selene kissed Eiric's lips, rose, and then wiped the tears from her cheeks. Avalynn and Finnian moved behind her. This was it. Selene would deliver the last words. It would be difficult for her to invent an honorable or good death for Eiric. What would she say?

Mateo moved closer and clasped his hands behind his back. The Enbarrs and the Passing Place commanded his respect. Nothing more.

Instead of facing the fallen Eiric to deliver her farewell, Selene turned and faced them. She pushed her long flaming red hair out of her face and held her head high. "I am leaving this forsaken hunt."

What? Stunned silence filled the air. She was abandoning the hunt? "Has this ever happened before? Is it allowed?" He couldn't believe it. He looked to Avalynn for answers. Her frozen features told him this was new to her too.

"But Selene." Avalynn stepped toward her. "You cannot. My father, he will…"

Selene threw her head back and laughed. "He will do nothing to me or my house. He needs us to do his bidding and his dirty work." She squinted, and her brow furrowed. "And we are very good at it. But the bargain I struck with him is now void. So, my work here is done."

Mateo approached Avalynn, his mind racing in a million different directions. Her furrowed brow told him hers was doing the same.

Avalynn finally spoke. "What bargain? With whom?"

Selene smirked, "Finally asking the right questions." Her hands on her hips, Selene laid bare the undercurrent that caused a riptide. "You were promised to Eiric in a deal struck with the Linds years ago." She stared into the distance. "But Eiric and I had our own plans. So, my father asked your father for reconsideration. He said he would agree if I accepted a bargain."

Avalynn shook her head. "Oh no, Selene. You bargained with my father?"

"I did. In exchange for an arrangement with Eiric, I agreed to enter this hunt, not to win, but to ensure the lowborn came in last."

Avalynn sucked in a quick breath of air. "What?"

Mateo's head spun. Time slowed down. He closed his eyes. Of course, the High King put Selene in the hunt to sabotage him. No highborn could beat him fair and square. The High King knew that and resorted to maneuvering. Underhanded. Lowdown and dirty—the Stromm way.

Selene secured her satchel and scoffed. "With Eiric gone, the bargain is null and void." She picked up two spears. "And now I am leaving this chuffing hunt and taking my chances that the foxes will keep their attention on you all while I escape this horrid forest. I'd wish you all luck, but I don't really care."

After one last mournful look at Eiric, she took off into the woods.

Mateo turned away from Eiric's body. The highborns played games and targeted him, not the foxes or each other. He slammed his spear across his knee and cracked it in half. His arms shook like a reed in a fast current. What else were the highborns keeping from him? Likely enough to cause his decimation.

With the jagged edges of his spear ready, he spun and faced Finnian and Avalynn. "Who else is working against me?"

Stormshroud growled. She planted herself between him and Avalynn and bared her fangs. The sight of his wolf turning on him sent a boulder through his chest and crushed his soul.

Avalynn's palms shot up. "Stop. Please, Mateo. There are only three of us left. We need to work together to make it out of here alive."

He slammed one half of the spear into the ground. "You think me a fool? You two will sabotage me. I will come in last, and then my life will be wasted." He dipped his chin and spoke directly to Avalynn. "You know my people need me to win. And you know why."

Finnian inched closer. "I assure you that I am not here to sabotage you." He held out his spear. "I provide my weapon to you to prove it."

Whatever. Finnian's offer meant nothing to Mateo. It changed nothing. *Yip*. His head swung in the sound's direction. He snatched Finnian's spear. If they were against him, then he needed to distance himself from them and get his prey. "The hunt is on, and I am winning."

CHAPTER EIGHTEEN

Every last Strong descendant, as well as the future of the Sublands, was at risk upon Draven's return.

Avalynn grabbed her gear and ran out after Mateo who'd quickly disappeared into the trees. Finnian kept pace along with Stormshroud. "Really, wolf?" About to shoo her away, she stopped. Mateo's wolf could come in handy. The beast wiped the floor with regular foxes.

They ran and jumped over roots and branches as she reflected on her arranged betrothal to Eiric. Sickened, her mind swirled with questions. How could her mother and father keep that from her? Why would they? And what else did they keep hidden? She side-eyed Finnian. Did he make a deal with her father, too?

She slowed and closed the gap between them. "Did you bargain to sabotage the lowborn like Selene?" Of the highborn fae from the other provinces, she always thought him the most honorable. She hoped her assessment was on the mark because right about now she needed someone to trust.

He pumped his arms, his face red and sweaty. Kragar

had said Finnian was as slow as a turtle. Now she believed him. He barely kept up with her. "No, did you?"

She did not count on the question being lobbed back at her. A half-truth would suffice. "I am here to win." She owed him nothing at this point.

"Guess that makes three of us."

They skidded to a halt at a fork in the path. Unsure of which direction Mateo had gone, she tested her theory with Stormshroud. "Find Mateo!"

To the left and up the mountain, the wolf bounded, graceful and elegant.

"Good girl." Avalynn and Finnian followed. She spotted the shimmery boundary to her right. Beyond that trickled a stream feeding into the Summit Crest River. They were near the Great Valley with its open meadow, no trees and nowhere to hide. Mateo had no experience with this land or its terrain. The foxes could have lured him into a trap.

Stormshroud skidded to a halt. She spun in a mad circle, belted out an ear-piercing howl, and then bolted like a streak of lightning. Avalynn's heart skipped a beat. Mateo was in danger. She left Finnian in her wake and raced until she broke into a clearing.

The sight stunned her.

Mateo battled in the middle of the field. His spear out and spinning in a graceful yet deadly dance, he smacked and hacked at a swarm of attacking foxes. Stormshroud pounced from the rear, clawing and biting anything with fur.

Bow out and arrow nocked, Avalynn charged. *Zip.* One of the foxes fell. *Zip. Zip.* Two more.

Hollering a battle cry, Finnian sprang into action from behind her. He barreled forward, whacking at the foxes.

She lined up another shot when a fox jumped on her back. It ripped off her satchel and quiver and dug its claws into her skin, raking them down her spine. "Ahh!" She reached with an arrow and jabbed at the vicious creature. "Off!" Another fox latched onto her thigh. Things were going from bad to worse. She swung her leg and stomped her feet but could not free herself of the deadly foxes.

Mateo's whistle pierced the tense air. "Stormshroud! Avalynn!"

The wolf charged and pounced. She flung the fox from Avalynn's leg with a chomp. Swooping in with a yell, Mateo wrestled the other fox off her back with his bare hands. He snatched the arrow from her grasp, stabbed the fox through the skull, and flung it aside.

But there was no magic. The kills were regular foxes.

Whirr! A gust of wind whipped through the valley. Avalynn's long braided hair had unraveled from its binding and wrapped around her face. The foxes froze and poked their tiny muzzles into the air.

"Great." She held her bow and gasped as her ears rang. "Now what?" The mark on her back was warm and wet and starting to itch.

"I have no idea." Mateo scanned the valley. "But it can't be good."

Finnian joined them, panting. His face had been clawed from his brow to his chin. "You are right. It can't be good."

The wind shifted directions, and a storm's rumble resonated through the valley. Avalynn looked to the skies. Puffy white clouds dotted the bright expanse. The sky was bright blue. Failing to detect any foul weather, she exchanged worried glances with Mateo and Finnian as the three packed together.

A deafening roar ripped through the valley and vibrated deep inside Avalynn. It sent shockwaves of shivers through her. A flock of squawking birds sang death hymns from the treetops, fluttering away in a frenzied exodus. The foxes crisscrossed in a mad dash, sprinting out of the valley. Stormshroud whined and crouched down. The air stilled like right before a tornado.

Like a beacon illuminated, Avalynn remembered Engrendorn and the North. Fear pricked her body. "Dragon!"

From the mountain range, a massive beast rose into the sky. Iridescent scales glinted against the sunlight. It whooshed its massive wings downward, then upward again, creating tendrils of chaos through the clouds.

Avalynn grabbed Mateo and Finnian. "Run!" This was a battle they would never win.

They raced for the tree line as the dragon glided down into the valley. It opened its mouth and sprayed a torrent of flames at the running foxes. Fire doused the ground, swallowing the devious foxes in a river of red and orange. Thick, acrid smoke and the pungent scent of scorched fur filled the air.

Stormshroud leaped into the tree line in a streak of

black and white. Mateo pushed Avalynn forward. "Go, go, go!"

Another dragon's roar—so close this time her body shook and her teeth chattered. Faster, she pumped her arms and prayed to the Sun, Moon, and Stars with each stride. With wings outstretched, the dragon soared over the tall trees. It cast an ominous shadow while following them.

Avalynn sensed safety in one place and one place only. "The cave! Get to the cave!"

Turning at the fork in the path, she spotted the protective chamber. "Hurry!" With Stormshroud ahead and Mateo at her side, they dove through the cave's mouth. Her face hit the dirt with a smack. Spitting dust, she rolled over. She took stock of her companions. Mateo. Stormshroud. Finnian? "Where is Finnian?"

Mateo swallowed and said through ragged breaths, "Behind me."

She clambered to her feet and saw Finnian's muscular frame pounding their way. "Come on, Finnian!"

The dragon descended. Its long claws reached down and snatched Finnian, lifting him like a helpless puppet.

She dashed out of the cave. "Finnian!"

Mateo raced toward her. "Nooo!"

But it was too late. The dragon jetted upward, kicked its wings back, and then dive-bombed, mouth open, red fire bubbling in its throat. She and Mateo grabbed each other and fell to the ground.

She slammed her eyes shut. Mateo—the Only One— they needed his power. She clutched him and squeezed.

Now. Now. Now. An image of blue light flooded her mind. A swathe of protection, a peaceful yet powerful sensation. Her body warmed, and her insides tingled. A pleasing glow swirled in her stomach like a summer sun.

He was doing it!

She cracked open an eye. Blue, all around like an electric sky, and beyond the haze roared an inferno. She looked toward Mateo, but his gaze fixed on her.

His mouth hung open. "It's you."

"Me?" She looked down at her hands. Electric blue swirled from her palms and spread around her and Mateo. *She* was doing this? She was *really* releasing the light?

The dragon screeched and then soared out of sight. The blue power around them dissolved. Avalynn struggled for air. Her head spun like an ancient windmill. A cold rush flowed from her head to her toes.

Mateo held her. "How did you do that?"

"I, uh..." Weakness sapped her words. The searing pain at her back registered. The fox had jumped her and raked its nails down her back. Her adrenaline from the dragon attack must have numbed her injuries. With the threat gone, the pain plowed deeper.

Stormshroud whimpered and circled Avalynn. Mateo brought her in close. "Are you okay?"

She studied his long dark hair, steely gray eyes, and perfectly chiseled face. Beautiful. Irritating. "Do I look okay?" She slumped onto his chest.

He wrapped his arms around her. "Thunderation. You are bleeding...but yes. You look like a thousand sunrises all at once."

She smiled, then struggled to form words. She had powers and deflected the dragon's blast. But she could not heal her possibly fatal wounds. "The fox... its claws..." Without the proper attention, she would soon see the Enbarr and never again lay eyes on breathtaking Mateo.

Gently, he laid her on the ground, cradling her head with a soft touch. "What do I do?"

She swallowed as her vision dimmed and her eyes closed. "You win. If it had to be anybody else, I'm glad it's you."

CHAPTER NINETEEN

Leaf, Faevenly's fiercest warrior, was sent to the human realm to protect me... He is your father.

Mateo panicked. Avalynn had powers. She saved them from the dragon. Now she was dying from a claw wound? Master Kragar had mentioned the Shadowblood's claws could contain poisonous toxins. Perhaps she got injected by one of those deadly claws.

He touched the side of her neck. Her heartbeat thumped ever so softly, but still steady. Avalynn was beautiful both inside and out. He responded to her in a way he had never known. But she was a Stromm. A highborn. An enemy. He needed to win the hunt. Saving her could ruin that. But he didn't care. His mother was gone. His father and Floriana struggled. His heart said enough death.

Avalynn must live.

Stormshroud whimpered. She sniffed Avalynn's face and then dragged her smooth, wet tongue across her cheek. She nudged Mateo and pawed him, digging her thick nails into his arm as if pleading for him to do something. He patted her head. "I know, girl."

"Who's calling me girl?"

Mateo warmed at the sight of Avalynn's eyes opening. "You're okay."

She shook her head and winced. "I need help."

"What can I do?" He could carry her out of the hunt. Or even run back for a healer. But those options would leave him vulnerable and maybe even cause her wicked High King father to blame him for her state. He would surely end him on the spot. Yet still, he was pulled to help her.

"My satchel." She closed her eyes and pointed into the distance. "In the meadow. I have a vial of healing water from the Green Falls."

He raised his brows. He didn't think the hunters could bring anything outside of what they were provided. Yet Avalynn had a vial of saving water. Typical. She'd also withheld the Shadowblood's disappearing qualities. Besides magical powers, what other advantage did she have?

"Stormshroud will get it." He slipped off his, showed Stormy, and then pointed to the meadow. "Get Avalynn's satchel."

The wolf raced off in a flash while Mateo stayed with Avalynn. Eyes closed, her chest moved slowly up and then slowly down, as if she neared the endless sleep. He held her hand and traced her palm. Should he keep her awake? Or let her rest?

Leaves rustled, and Stormshroud bounded back with Avalynn's scorched bag dangling from her jaws. He took it and shoved his hand inside. Empty. He flipped it and shook. Nothing. The contents must have spilled out and burned.

"Not my lucky day?" Her head barely lifted.

He wiped the sweat beads from his forehead. "No."

"Great." She fanned her fingers. "Help me sit up."

He clasped her hand and helped her with a gentle pull. "What are you doing?"

She took a labored breath. Her trembling finger pointed toward the spot where they had left Eiric's body. "See if Eiric is still there."

He hurried over and found the body gone. He came back in a dash. "He's vanished."

"That's good." Her muscles relaxed. "Either my Enbarr or another knows this spot." She winced with each word. "I will call and see if it will come back and take me to the Green Falls."

"You know how to make that call?" He moved closer so she could lean on him.

She groaned. "Not exactly. But I must try."

Stormshroud let out a short howl and spun in place. Mateo scanned the tree line. As if on cue, the majestic Enbarr strode through the tree trunks. Avalynn had not even tried to summon it, yet here it was with its gleaming white and silver coat and fluttering long lashes.

Avalynn smiled. "My beautiful friend. How did you know?" It stopped beside her and brayed. "I am injured and must go to the Green Falls. Will you take me?"

The magical beast whinnied, then lowered its front legs so she could climb on.

Mateo helped Avalynn stand. But as soon as he let go,

her legs buckled. He swooped her up in his arms. "Let me know if I'm hurting you."

She spoke in a weak tone. "I am mostly numb."

"I can work with that." With extreme care, he lifted her and sat her on the horse. He stepped back. The Enbarr swung its head. It nipped at Mateo's tunic and pulled him close. "I am not going. Only Avalynn." The Enbarr ignored his command and kept snorting and nipping.

"Get on," Avalynn said in a strained voice. "You know how she is."

Oh, he knew. The Enbarr was stubborn and seemed to have strong feelings about them. So, he climbed onto the beast and snuggled in front of Avalynn. She wrapped her arms around his waist and leaned her head against his back.

She whispered, "Thank you, Mateo."

He stroked her hands so gently, the overwhelming need to protect her flooding through him like an irresistible tide and pulling him into a sea of unspoken devotion. This time, he did not fight it. This time, he wanted her to know. "I would do anything for you."

A soft laugh came out of her. "Now you tell me."

Stormy barked. He glanced her way with a nod. "Stay here, girl. We'll be back soon."

With a whinny, the Enbarr took slow and steady steps through the trees, each movement faster than the one before until it sped over the terrain with the grace of a summer breeze.

Avalynn tightened her squeeze around Mateo's waist while he gripped the Enbarr's mane, eyes shut, head down. Avalynn's perfect curves pressed against him, sending a pleasing warmth throughout his body. There were those lightning bugs again, swirling in his stomach. But he could not let them stay. He would help with her wounds, but then they would return to the hunt where he must take first, get those healing seeds, and then go home to the Sublands. He had to believe her High King father would spare her from the last place death penalty. She was his daughter after all. He touched the cross in his pocket. *Please, let him spare her.* It wasn't too much to ask.

The Enbarr's speed slowed, and Mateo's cramped hands released its thick mane. He stretched and popped his stiff and sore fingers. He had no idea how far they had traveled, but it seemed far enough for them to be on the other side of Faevenly.

With a shake of its head and a satisfying snort, the Enbarr came to rest. Mateo slid off and then helped Avalynn down. "Can you walk?"

"I think so."

He slowly released her, but her legs had no strength. He scooped her up and held her close, then quickly caught his bearings. He heard water trickle and scanned the lush green grass and tall majestic trees for the waterfall. He detected aromas of moisture, soil, and water logged wood from upwind. His chin swung in the direction of the source. "Up there."

Cradling her in his arms, he swiftly made his way over branches and roots. A few paces more and they came upon an open area with a looming magnificent cliff. The smallest trail of liquid dripped down the rocks and barely splashed into a small green-hued pond with water lilies floating on the surface.

"So," Mateo said, "the Green Falls are indeed dying. I have heard the rumors."

Avalynn teared up at the sight. "I had no idea it was so bad. Nia said it once roared like mighty thunder."

They walked along a muddy bank strewn with dandelions, bluebells, and clover blooms. Leaves and waterlogged sticks floated along the pond's lip. Minnows and tadpoles swam in the shallows. Algae fuzzed on the nearby rocks. He walked into the water then stopped.

"Shall I set you down here?" he asked.

"Please." He eased her to her feet, but kept his arm around her waist. "Nia said submerging in the water works best. I need help removing my tunic. I can do the rest."

The lightning bugs returned to his belly tenfold. "Of course." He hid a swallow. He had never undressed a maiden, let alone beheld the undergarments of a princess. Unsure of himself, he flashed her a frozen smile, but neither of them moved a muscle or spoke. She must have thought him an immature sprite.

"Help me tug it over my head," she said.

He faced her, untucked her tunic, and lifted it with care over her head. Her long dark hair spilled over her shoulders and rested on the delicate lacework covering her bosom. He averted his eyes and spotted a purple splotch on her wrist. Perhaps the poison? But then he saw the bruises that trailed up her arms and made a perfect hand pattern. His gaze locked on hers. He could not unsee that damage to Avalynn.

She curled her arms to her chest. "It is nothing."

His blood boiled inside his fearless and intrepid veins. Someone would pay for hurting her. "Who did this to you? Was it Eiric?" He was dead, but Mateo would travel to the Passing Place to batter his body.

"It is none of your business."

"I beg to differ, princess." He turned her arm, exposing the bruising. "*This* right here...is *always* my business." He might have needed to win the hunt, but he could not and would not ignore that someone had hurt this princess. She irritated him to no end. Still, all he wanted to do was hold her close, kiss her lips, and tell her that nobody would ever hurt her again.

With downcast eyes she whispered, "I do not need or want your worry."

He lowered her arm gently. "I do not understand you. Or myself when I am with you."

Her head shook. "There is nothing to understand." She huffed, and her arms clasped close to her chest, hiding her bruises again. "They came from an accident. Now please, turn around while I remove the remainder of my clothing and enter the water."

He did not believe her for one second. *Accident?* He had seen the hand marks but did as she asked and turned around. He focused on a nearby boulder. Eiric the abuser luckily died, or Mateo would've choked the life from him. How dare anybody abuse Avalynn, ever.

Her boots thudded on the ground. A soft rumple of clothing hit the dirt. As she stepped into the pond, the water rippled and wings flapped from noisy water birds taking flight. He rubbed the back of his neck. The pond water splashed. His insides burned from something deeper now—desire.

He wanted to look. He needed to see. His eyes felt magnetized, and he fought that natural pull to—wait. She was injured. Wrong thing, wrong time. He needed to move away. "I will wait at that boulder ahead."

"Thank you. I will come to you when I am finished."

He trudged to and then climbed the massive rock. Eyes forward, his back remained to the pond. The sunbaked rock warmed his backside while the cool wind against his face lowered his internal temperature. He must stop thinking about her and turned his focus to the terrain.

Scanning the horizon, he saw their silver Enbarr grazing nearby. It swished its long tail while birds flitted from branch to branch. His gaze drifted to the clear skies. The dragon... where had it come from?

But the question that repeated the loudest in his head... Avalynn's blue light that came out of her... How did she do that?

With a gust of wind, the note slipped under his door sprang to mind. *Protect Princess Avalynn.*

Panicking, he swung his head on a swivel. Avalynn floated in the pond. Dragonflies skated on the surface next to her figure. Her long hair spread on the water like a silken veil. His breathing steadied. He wanted to talk to her. He needed answers for himself. The time for secrets between them had passed. They were beyond that now.

The pond's cool water slipped over Avalynn's skin, caressing her like smooth silk. Its purity eased the pain in her back, diminishing it to a dull ache. The pond's muddy bottom squished between her toes. She closed her eyes and soaked herself in the gentle waves. If she were home in her bath, she would have opened her eyes and seen the blurred Stromm crest on her ceiling. Perhaps that image was more than an optical illusion.

Maybe her home was not what she thought it was. Her father left bruises on her. And those Shadowbloods... Surely, her father knew that the hunt could end her life. Perhaps that was his plan all along—kill every single hunter. That would have ensured her father could always claim the Sublander came in last, no matter what. Gullible Lily would then be next in line for the throne. He could manipulate her with ease. Would he hurt her? She trembled at the sinister thoughts that shook her to the core.

She rose from the water and examined her palms. How did that blue energy power come out of her? If the power lived within her, maybe she was the Only One, not Mateo. But how? And wouldn't she have known? The notes that came under the door into her bedchamber must have meant something.

Trust your instincts, not your past.

Be brave, for a new path is on the horizon.

Instincts. Path. What did it mean? Maybe Mateo had ideas. Maybe he channeled his power through her. She stretched her legs and arms underwater. She twisted her torso from side to side. Feeling as good as new, she made her way to the pond's edge and walked out.

Water dripped from her naked form, the sun warming her like a wood stove. She slipped on her lower lacework and then her upper lacework. But her blood-stained, filthy tunic and dirty pants lay crumpled on the spongy grass. Scooping them up, she returned to the water. After a quick scrub, she laid the clothing out on a flat stone. Time to talk to Mateo.

Grasshoppers jumped as she picked her way through the wildflower-filled grass. Mateo turned and dusted off his pants when she approached. Standing tall on the rock with the sun shining down on him, he looked like a radiant god—a vision of perfection. He smiled and crouched down, stretching his arm out toward her. "Please, let me help you."

She took his hand. Tingles raced all over her body at his touch. His strong gaze roamed her face and then darted to her lacy chest covering and exposed middle. She welcomed his glance and hoped he would never stop. Standing before him on the rock, she wasn't sure what would happen next because suddenly her mind drifted to their dance. The closeness of their bodies. Their almost kiss.

But Mateo had other things on his mind. "Are you better?" He motioned toward her back.

"A little achy, but that is all. The water did its job." She sat, and he joined her.

His forehead furrowed. "A lot has happened, and we have much to discuss."

"I was thinking the same thing." Pushing aside her desires, she tucked wet strands of hair behind her pointed ears. Everything she wanted to talk about cluttered her mind, with one thing overriding all the others. She held her palms up. "How did I do that?"

"I don't know." He hovered his hands over hers for a few seconds. "From the moment I stepped into the carriage to come here, I have been told that I am this so-called Only One. The witch from my village even claimed I had Strong blood in my veins. But they must have meant you. They must have meant Stromm."

"Strong blood? As in Strong Haven?" That did not make sense. Her closest and most trusted confidant, Nia, told her Mateo was the Only One. "I, too, have been told that about you. But I never heard anything about the Strongs. That bloodline is extinct."

Mateo sat back. Intensity darkened his gaze. His jaw tightened. "No one decides my fate. Not a prophecy and not a witch." His piercing stare returned to her. "All we have is the here and now. The hunt. We must go back." His voice lowered. "One of us must win, one must lose."

He was right. A sick feeling churned inside her gut. Powers aside, they needed to finish what they started. And they were the last two. She found a stick and started tracing the surface of the boulder. She repeated his words in a whisper, "One of us must win, one must lose."

He let out a sigh. "That is right."

A trio of wood sprites swooped downward toward the pond. They flitted with high-pitched laughter, skirting the top of the water before soaring away. Watching the tiny creatures, she longed to go back to her life before the hunt. Back to a time where her life wasn't at risk and her crown wasn't in jeopardy.

She pulled her legs to her chest and wrapped her

arms around her knees. There had to be a way for both of them to get what they wanted—the seeds for Mateo and the victory for her. The command to ensure Mateo's last place finish be damned. They needed a plan, a solution.

Her thoughts returned to the hunt's qualifier. She and Engrendorn were neck and neck the entire event until she got distracted at the last minute by a butterfly. He swooped in and dashed across the finish line first. But what if they had crossed the finish line at the same time? What would have happened?

Hope sprang inside her. She grabbed Mateo's arms. "I know what to do."

"What?"

"We each capture our prey and finish the hunt together."

He paused and furrowed his brows. "A draw? So, we both get the rewards *and* avoid the death penalty?" He cupped and stroked his chin. "Has something like that ever happened?"

"I do not believe so. But as the Stromm princess and daughter of the High King, I will get you however many seeds you need, regardless of whether there is an issue with the reward. For your family and for all of the Sublands. We just need to cross the finish line together."

His mouth parted, and he sat back, looking almost dazed. "You would do that for a lowborn half-fae from the Sublands?"

"I would do that for you." She placed her warm hand on his awaiting knee.

He scooted away and rose to his feet. He faced the falls. A soft breeze whisked between them. The water trickled. Had she upset him with her suggestion? Said the wrong thing? She hoped not. She joined him at the boulder's edge but stayed silent, waiting for him to speak.

He sighed and stared into the distance. "All my life, I have carried a hatred for you Stromms." His words came out like a whispered confession. "And now here I stand with one who is willing to help me and my people." He faced her, his intense gaze igniting a flurry of desire within her. "I stand with the one who makes my insides flutter like fireflies." He wrung his hands. "She makes me forget who I am. I am wholly unworthy of her."

His vulnerability tugged at her like a fierce current, pulling her into the depths of his truth and the profound abyss of his being. Echoes of pain emanated from Mateo, like a haunting and rhythmic melody. That pain, combined with reservoirs of immense strength, meant he had weathered countless storms and would weather countless more. Through all his complex ways, she felt as if she was seeing him—the *real* Mateo, for the first time. But seeing him was not enough. She needed to feel him.

Her pulse quickened. Should she open her heart to him? Tell him how he burned a fire inside her? How she would toss her duty and her station in life for him? But what would happen to her then? Her solution was simple for the hunt. But this force that united them was like their dance, intricate and unpredictable, where every step held the weight of the unknown. A war raged inside of her—what she should do versus what her heart wanted. Duty or love.

The walls he had lowered were slowly rebuilding.

His face hardening. He stepped away. "I have said too much."

She should've let him walk away. She should've never crossed that boundary to the point of no return. But she locked her hand inside his arm. "You make me forget who I am too." Her words came out fast and unbridled. "And you do more to me than merely take my breath away."

His eyes took on a smoldering look. Her body trembled in reply. He wrapped his arms around her waist and tugged her closer. "What do I do to you, princess?"

She could not describe in words the passion bubbling inside of her. She could not tell him the things she longed for him to do with and to her. No words could have expressed the way he moved her. She would show him. They might never have this moment again.

"You do *this* to me." She took his hand and placed it on her cheek. She closed her eyes. Her hand guided his across her mouth and then down her neck. With quick, shallow breaths, her chest heaved as the fire for him burned so deep within her she thought it might consume her. With his hand hovering over her laces, she opened her eyes. "I am yours, Mateo."

"Are you sure?" He searched her eyes with tenderness.

She pressed his hand against her thumping heart. "Yes, I am sure."

His lips met hers, softly at first, then harder and filled with passion. And she wanted all of it—taste, scent, sight of the one who had worked his way into her heart. His hands explored her body, and hers did the same. They had been stripped to nothing but two simple souls brought together against all odds. Nothing else existed, not a hunt, or a dragon, or a prophecy...not even time.

On that boulder, with the sun basking down on them, the water birds trilling, and the waterfall splashing, she drowned herself completely in Mateo. And they shared it all.

CHAPTER TWENTY

Wielding my power, and with the help of a witch named Lady Sonia, I faced Draven and restored peace. This same power lives in you.

Their passion-fueled day stretched into the night, a symphony of shared desires and whispered promises. And when they had no more to give, they drifted into a peaceful slumber beneath the stars. But as the first rays of dawn pierced the forest canopy, their harsh reality set in.

The hunt awaited them.

"I don't want this to end," Avalynn moaned into his neck.

"I don't either," he said, tracing her silky-smooth skin as she snuggled closer.

His fingertips moved from her neck, down her back, and up again in a circular pattern. Being with her was everything, but at the same time it was terrifying. She was a Stromm. A highborn. He was a lowborn from the Sublands. What would become of them after this? He had no idea. But he was sure of one thing. Nothing would ever be the same again, but they would always have the Green Falls.

They must re-enter the hunt. They would each capture a Shadowblood without being killed. There was also the dragon to worry about. Not to mention Avalynn's villainous High King father. What would he or his witch do when they crossed that finish line together? His stomach twisted into knots. He had no way of knowing how any of it would unfold.

He stopped his tracing motion. Avalynn glanced up at him. "What is it?"

His hand caressed her jawline. So beautiful. So brave. So strong. He could do anything with her by his side. "We must finish this thing."

She leaned in and kissed his lips. "Let's do it."

They dressed in a hurry, climbed down their boulder, and joined the Enbarr. Once again on the magical beast, they snuggled in for the journey back to the hunt. They raced with the wind, the fresh air enveloping them as they dashed toward the cave. Her arms were wrapped around his waist. The pair of them melded and rode the regal horse as one. Her touch had new meaning. They spoke no words. Everything had been said on that boulder.

Mateo's memory turned to Rhyka in the carriage ride to Stromm Palace. She warned him that she had foreseen that he and the hunter from House Stromm would be linked in the hunt. She had threaded her fingers and folded them into a joined fist and spoke the prophetic words, *"Two destinies tied, making one future."* Now he knew what she meant. Her premonition had come true. His future would always be tied to Avalynn Stromm. The Green Falls ensured that. Now all they needed to do was survive the hunt, and step over that finish line together.

In what seemed like no time, they arrived back at the cave. Stormshroud circled them, jumping and wagging her tail. Avalynn slipped off the horse, knelt, and rubbed Stormy behind the ears. The wolf replied with a thick lick across her face that nearly toppled her. "I missed you too, girl."

Mateo crossed his arms. "What about me?" Stormshroud lifted herself up on her hind legs and placed her paws on his shoulders. "So, you do remember me." All was not lost with his trusty wolf.

Leaving them, Avalynn approached the Enbarr. She rested her head against its front flank and stroked its gleaming white and silver mane. "Thank you for helping me."

The majestic beast snorted and sauntered into the trees with a flick of its long tail.

Time to focus. Mateo turned his attention to the new mission. With the sun already dipping, the bright blue expanse morphed into muted purples. He did not mean to leave the Green Falls so late, and now they were running low on daylight. But there was still plenty of time to prepare if they hurried.

"We need weapons." He spotted the makeshift spears they had whittled earlier. He kept one and gave Avalynn two.

She tightened her hands around the wood. "I have an idea." Her gaze remained distant.

"What is it" Anything she offered would have been welcomed.

She circled the cave's mouth. "Master Kragar prepared me for the prey beforehand, as you know." She flashed him an apologetic look. "He showed me how the Shadowbloods disappear. I had never seen such a thing and wondered how such a creature could be hunted." She stopped circling and faced him. "He claimed he had told me the answer already, but I never figured it out."

"A clue..." Mateo raised his eyebrows. He nodded, and his voice grew louder. "The madman gave you a clue."

"He must have." She scrunched her face and scratched her head. "Though at the time, I could not decipher it in his words."

"What exactly did he say to you?" Two minds focused on the same purpose were always better than one. "Leave nothing out."

Avalynn paced with her finger on her lip. "They're from the far north. They're cunning and devious. They disappear in the shadows. They can inject a deadly toxin with their claws." She paused, closed her eyes, and then exhaled. "They're vampiric, feed on small animals, and their favorite meal is rabbit."

"Their favorite?" The answer came to Mateo in a flash of inspired genius. "That dwarf Kragar *did* give you the answer." It was obvious to any experienced hunter.

"He did?" Her head tilted sideways, and she squinted. "Perhaps I'm not seeing what you do."

Mateo knew exactly what Kragar meant with that sly piece of information—Rabbit could be bait. "If they love rabbits, we can use their cravings against them. Instead of tracking the Shadowblood, we will *summon* the creatures. All we need is a rabbit or two."

Her brows furrowed. "What do you mean by summon?"

He, Lirien, and Gareth had used still hunting before. Messy yet effective, it worked well against intelligent prey. "We smear rabbit blood on our bodies. If we wear the pelts, the Shadowbloods will think we are rabbits and come close, and then we will attack them."

She closed her eyes and swallowed. "That's what I thought you meant."

He glanced at the darkening sky, then set his spear on the ground. "Stormshroud will hunt for rabbits. We will stay here." He lowered himself in front of Stormy. He held his hands to his head with the backs of his hands facing out. Then he raised his middle and index fingers and twitched like rabbit ears. "Rabbits. Fetch."

His wolf knew this routine well and excelled at the task. She barked and then darted from the cave's mouth.

"How do you know how to communicate with your hands like that?"

"My friend back home, Gareth, is mute and speaks with his hands. Over the years, I have learned and taught Stormshroud. It is most effective in hunting when silence is needed."

"That is actually quite amazing. I hope to meet this Gareth one day."

He wanted to believe she would have that chance. "I hope so too." Again, he glanced at the sky. "We should spread out sticks and leaves so we can hear the foxes approaching."

"Good idea."

They gathered armfuls of kindling and spread their haul over the cave's floor like a rug. He glanced at the remnants of the fire they had burned with the other hunters. Eiric and Finnian were dead, and Selene had most likely joined them. He and Avalynn could suffer the same fate. His empty stomach grumbled as he suspected they would. His gloomy thoughts remained hidden from view. As a lowborn Sublander, life had trained him to hope for the best yet expect the worst. The Summit Range Hunt would be no different.

Avalynn leaned into him. Her floral scent delivered him from his morbid thoughts. "What is in your pocket? You keep touching it."

His hand clutched his outer pocket, holding the cross within. How long had he been doing that? He loosened his grip, slipped his fingers inside, and removed his wooden cross. He placed it on his palm.

"It's a cross. My father made it for me when I was a child." He dismissed all notions of anyone else being his father. He belonged to Manny and Faeryn. Their beliefs belonged to him, too. "It is a symbol of my father's human religion."

"May I hold it?" Avalynn held out her hand.

He passed it to her. "Of course."

She brought it closer and studied it, rubbing her thumb and forefinger over the smooth surface. "Such a simple thing. Does it hold any power?"

"No. It is only a shape, but wielded by a believer, it

symbolizes the greatest power of all." His father explained his religion once a week for all the years of his young life. When Mateo grew to the age where he would account for his own actions, his father's teachings ceased.

At this moment, here with Avalynn in the cave, he regretted not learning more from his father. Yet he remembered every lesson. "The cross represents the sacrifice of a savior from the human realm. One with great power. This symbol is a sign of hope and love."

"Really?" Her eyes widened as she turned the wood over in her hand. "A savior with power?" She handed the cross back. "Do you touch it hoping it will provide you that power?"

"I touch it for hope." Everything about his life as a lowborn and his place in the hunt had him feeling powerless. But he kept his fears hidden and slipped the cross back where it belonged.

"Do we need hope?"

"We all need hope. It inspires courage. My father says faith is a warrior." Without being killed, they needed to capture two Shadowbloods and cross the finish line together. Hope was important, especially now. "Hope ignites resilience and influences destinies. In times of total darkness, hope is that small sliver of light visible only when you look hard enough."

"Faith is a warrior." Her lips curled with a smile. "You *are* a savior like that. You bring hope."

He chuckled. "No, I am most definitely not." Mateo had too many villainous tendencies to earn a title like savior. He kissed her lips. "But thank you for thinking so."

"Well then, you are a messenger of hope."

His stomach whined like a trapped wolf. Sharp hunger pangs coursed through him. He placed his hand over his grumbling midsection. "I think the only messenger here is my empty stomach."

Avalynn's belly joined in on the chorus. "Mine feels the same way."

With Stormy hunting, they had some time to search for berries. They would need the energy. He ventured out of the cave's mouth, scanning the thick and thorny brush. "There are berries out here. I know it. But where?"

She pointed to the west and the setting sun. "I saw some mystic moonberries over there. Not too far at all."

Spears in hand, Mateo followed Avalynn into the oak groves. Fifty paces in, they came across a cluster of bushes filled with sweet white berries. They each grabbed a handful and wasted no time eating them.

"*So* good." Mateo couldn't remember the last time he'd had a mystic moonberry. It tasted better than the food he'd sustained himself on in the Sublands.

Juice squirted from the ripe berry. Syrup dribbled down Avalynn's chin. "So excellent." She wiped her berry-stained lips. "But let's not overdo it. We don't want to go from empty to achy."

"Good point." Mateo wiped his hands on his pants. "We need to return for Stormshroud anyway."

They were heading back when Mateo detected a rumble underfoot. He stopped and pulled Avalynn closer. "Do you feel that?"

"I do." Her brows pinched. She squinted and inspected the trees. "Please, not the dragon."

The rumble grew louder. The force of it vibrated through Mateo's legs. Soft at first, it grew in intensity. Panic seized him. *Stampede!*

He grabbed Avalynn, shoved her back against the nearest oak, and shielded her body with his. A frenzied herd of elk streamed past. The ground shook with the drumbeat of a thousand pounding hooves. Avalynn buried her face in the crook of his neck and held on for dear life.

A cacophony of bugling, barking, and whistling mixed with thunderous stomping and branches cracking filled the air. Pushing closer and holding her tighter, his body shook and his teeth chattered. But then Mateo heard something else. A roar. He peered up through the criss-crossing branches and spotted the dragon's broad, soaring wings. The elk... they were stampeding away from the fire-breathing foe. Avalynn looked up, following his line of sight. Her eyes widened. She spotted it too.

The dragon dove. It swooped down into an open space and snagged a galloping steed with a roar. Avalynn clapped her hands around her ears as the sound battered them. When the roar tempered, a gust of fire sprayed down, trailing the herd. The frightened and furious stampede charged even faster.

Mateo peered over Avalynn's shoulder just in time to spot a speeding elk galloping their way. Heart pounding, he spun Avalynn away from the tree. With the antlers lowered, the mountainous creature barreled into the tree at full speed. *Thwack!* The oak's strong trunk shattered. The dragon's head swiveled toward them.

"Run!" Avalynn hollered.

They jetted into the herd, darting between the crazed elk in search of the cave's safety. They skirted thudding hooves and edged out swinging antlers. Breaking free of the drove, they zigzagged through the trees and dove through the cave's mouth as flames shot across like a fire shield.

Laying on the warm dirt floor, Mateo gasped for air. He squeezed Avalynn's hand. They stayed like that until the melee was over and the danger had passed. "That was close."

Panting, she squeezed back. "Beyond close." She sat up and pulled twigs and leaves from her long hair. "But we are still here. So that hope you spoke of is still with us."

Avalynn had a point, and he took their survival as a good sign. The Passing Place would have to wait another day. Yet the challenge of capturing the Shadowbloods still remained. They needed to nab their prey and be done with it before anything else happened.

CHAPTER TWENTY-ONE

Raw and unlimited, your power will always come forth in your times of need.

Stormshroud trotted toward them with her tail swishing. Two dead rabbits dangled from her drooling jaws. Steam rose from her muzzle as she nudged Mateo. "Hey, Stormy. You missed the elks and the dragon." She tilted her head. "Never mind," he said with a pat to her head.

Mateo and Avalynn scrambled to their feet, dusting each other off. While the rabbits' blood dripped to the ground, Mateo studied the sky's deepening darkness. "We need to hurry."

The full moon had begun its slow rise. The temperature had dropped. Time to turn the tides and get their prey before any other creature discovered their cave.

He tugged the kill from Stormshroud's loosened jaws and looked at Avalynn in the cave's half-light. "You may want to turn away."

She moved closer to Stormshroud and faced the trees. "Go ahead."

With his boot heel lodged against the rabbit's neck, he jerked and ripped the head from its body. He repeated the exercise with the other one. "Okay, you can come over now."

With the carcasses, he covered her tunic and pants with warm blood. For the finishing touch, he smeared it across her face. He repeated the process on himself. When there was no blood left, he draped one carcass around Avalynn's neck and the other around his own. They were ready for a still hunt of the Shadowblood foxes.

"Now what?" she asked.

"Now we wait."

Stormshroud stayed in the woods while they positioned themselves in the dark around the unlit fire pit. In hushed silence, they sat on the logs with their spears resting on their laps. Side by side, they faced the cave's mouth, which showed a moonlit panorama of the tree line. They stayed still, hands wrapped together, and waited. Seconds turned to minutes. Minutes turned to hours. Mateo knew the stillness represented the calm before the storm.

An owl hooted in the distance. Maybe the Shadowbloods were too smart for a still hunt. A flock of nocturnal nightweavers flew through parting clouds. Perhaps the Shadowbloods had all been wiped out during the dragon melee. A breeze whisked around them. The vinegary stink of rabbit decay kicked in the air. The pungent stench turned Mateo's stomach. He side-eyed Avalynn. Her nose wrinkled, and her lips pursed shut. At the end of all this, after they crossed the finish line together, could he somehow keep her by his side? He pushed those ideas aside. They needed to survive first.

Crunch. At the sound, Mateo's eyes shot to the cave's mouth. It came from where they had scattered leaves and twigs. *Crunch. Crunch. Snap.* His hands tightened around his stick spear. He heard them, but he couldn't see them. *Snap. Snap.*

That's right. Come on. Come get your snack, you devils.

The still hunt had begun.

A large ball of wire-like fur leaped out of nowhere onto Mateo's chest. His spear wrenched from his hands and rolled to the ground. He flew to his feet and clutched at the beast. But the more he pulled, the deeper the beast's claws sunk into his skin. He gathered all his strength and might for one last yank. Writhing in pain, he jerked the beast loose by ripping it away. Tiny bits of bloody flesh flickered in the cave's glow as he flung it from his body. He patted his chest. Flesh wound. He would survive.

His eyes scanned the melee for Avalynn. Her weapon whooshed. She yelled and grunted, but he couldn't help her yet. He whistled and shouted, "Stormshroud!"

With a swipe of her claw and a crunch at the neck, the wolf finished off one of the creatures then bounded toward Avalynn with a ferocious growl.

Another Shadowblood attached itself to his thigh. With a left hook and a straight right, he slammed his fists against the beast's wicked jaws. It shrieked, released its hold, and dropped to the ground with a loud thud. Mateo raised his boot, but the creature scurried off, circled, and then latched back on to his arm. "You want more? You get more." He tried to do it the humane way. But this beast demanded a dramatic end... So he got it.

Mateo grabbed the beast by the jawline. Staring into its dark beady eyes, he spun toward the cave's wall and smashed it against the solid rock. The beast whimpered, but Mateo slammed it again and again. With a murmur, its eyes fixed, and the Shadowblood beast went limp.

He breathed a sigh of relief and tossed it aside. As it touched down, a burst of blinding white light erupted from underneath its rigid flesh. The light danced in a dazzling and twirling display all around the cave's walls. Then, like a shooting star, it shot out of the cave's mouth, leaving a luminous trail. It raced upward over the trees and into the night sky. He felt a part of him rising with that star. He was the light—the shooting star.

He destroyed a Shadowblood, the hunt's prey. He had done it. First place and all the pride and satisfaction that came along with it. A life of hopes, dreams, wishes and hard work came together in that one glorious moment. He had bested all the highborns, all the naysayers, all the nonbelievers...

"Hey! A little help here!" Avalynn stood on the log, waving her spears toward two advancing Shadowbloods. Nearby, Stormshroud wrestled two regular foxes.

Mateo scooped up his spear. He got a running start, leaped with all his might to his highest point, and then descended with his weapon into the back of an advancing Shadowblood. It howled, yipped, then wobbled out of the cave.

He spun around to assist Avalynn, but she rolled away the final beast with a kick. She balanced the spear in her hand, then hurled it. The wood spear carved a hole through the Shadowblood's skull. It teetered and fell on its side with a whump. The same white light exploded from the downed beast. It whirled throughout the cave in a glorious streak, and then shot into the dark night and up over the trees.

Silence filled the cave as Stormshroud joined them. Gulping for air, the trio waited and anticipated the next attack, which never came.

"My Stars," she whispered. Soft whimpering came from her as he held her tight. The emotion of the hunt finally spilling out. "We did it."

He squeezed and pulled her closer. The weight he'd been carrying since he arrived at Stromm Palace slowly dissolved. "We did."

CHAPTER TWENTY-TWO

There are still those who seek to disturb the balance in Faevenly, and thus a lasting prophecy was born. Your prophecy.

A valynn held Mateo tight. She didn't care about the rabbits' blood, guts, or stink. All she cared about was being close to him and holding on and not letting go. The hunt was over. They killed their prey. All that remained was carrying their prizes to the finish line. She dreaded the thought of it.

Everything would change from that moment.

Mateo would get the healing seeds he needed and return to his life in the Sublands. She would resume her position as Princess of House Stromm, heir to the throne of Faevenly. It felt as if duty bound shackles around her heart, and she shuddered at the weight and significance of her pending return to the palace. Her father and mother surely would not approve of any ties with or to a lowborn Sublander. They wouldn't understand what she had come to know about him. She also knew they would never listen to her enlightened views on the Sublands.

He cocked his head sideways. "What is it?"

She mustered a small smile. "I am relieved, that is all." Beyond the cave's mouth, daylight sliced through the night and unraveled the inky darkness. It painted the forest with a hazy gray sheen. She ached from the night's stress and physicality. But mostly, she ached at the thought of never seeing Mateo's face again. Never touching him. Never kissing him. "I am exhausted as well."

"I am tired too." He hoisted the Shadowblood carcasses on two spears. He handed one to Avalynn and kept the other. "Let's get out of here and claim our prizes."

She rested the wood on her shoulder. It was time to face the inevitable—her father and the other royal families. With Eiric and Finnian gone, there would surely be a formal inquiry. She would find out soon enough if Selene had made it back safely or met her end in the forest.

"Yes, we have no choice. We must go." Life and duty awaited. She could love and live with Mateo in the Green Falls forever.

Mateo led the way out of the cave. The sky brightened to a soft blue as the sun kept rising.

She peered into the early morning sky. "I wonder where that dragon hides?"

"No idea. But if we stay in the trees, we will be fine. Do you think your father knew about it?"

"It is a possibility." She had learned the ways her father undermined and manipulated her. He'd arranged a secret marriage to Eiric and bargained with Selene. "But maybe more like a probability." The hunt had only heightened her mistrust of her father, the High King of Faevenly.

With each step through the forest, something odd and strangely sad happened between her and Mateo. A tragic distancing like a widening abyss between their souls. Like the echo of a fading melody. She sensed the silent erasure of their cherished moments together. They spoke little, walked feet apart, and their strides fell out of sync. Perhaps it was over before it began.

It was just as well.

Stormshroud recognized the inscrutable shift too. She sauntered closer to Mateo, then closer to Avalynn, as if having a hard time choosing between the two. Did Mateo feel it? The slow breaking of their connection, and her heart? If his silence was any indicator, then she had to believe he did.

The tall and clustered trees grew further apart. The dirt and leaves underfoot became grass and flowers. The sweet smell of hyacinth and daffodils tickled her nose. A kaleidoscope of butterflies flitted across her path. She wondered where they went and foolishly imagined scooping Mateo's hand and chasing after them. What would it be like to run away with him?

She would never know.

They broke from the forest and faced the flat meadow that led to the palace gardens. They faced the hunt's finish line—back to where they started. The brilliant sun rays overhead offered a bright homecoming, while inside of her darkness loomed.

Her father would not approve when she and Mateo

presented their kills together. If he threatened her after she danced with Mateo at the ball and left bruises on her body, what would he do when they crossed the finish line at the same time? He would escalate the harm for sure. She would be lucky to live out her life in the dungeons while Lily took her place atop the throne. More likely, she would be disqualified for violating the High King's orders, rules, and edicts. She would be drawn and quartered like the other enemies of the Stromm crown. Maybe even banished.

Raelor the witch would react even worse. At her father's command, he could compel Mateo again, drag him across the meadow with his magic. Her father might even declare him the last place finisher and end him on the spot, along with her.

This would not end well for her or Mateo.

Mateo stopped walking. He faced Avalynn. "My world is no longer on fire. You should know that the Green Falls meant *everything* to me."

She nodded. "Me too... Everything." That's why she would never forgive herself if she did not try to save them both.

Closing the distance to the palace grounds, the massive structure with ivory and gold turrets and spires came into view. It sparkled like a precious stone, glinting under the sun and casting a radiant hue over the horizon.

Royal fanfare drifted toward them on the wind. Trumpets blared, and people cheered. The crowd gathered in front of the dais. With banners flapping, they formed a long walkway that stopped in front of her High

King father and High Queen mother. Lily stood beside them, dressed in purple. Avalynn was not yet close enough to see their expressions, but she could well imagine her father's and mother's angry glares. She could see Lily's snicker at seeing her big sister with Mateo.

Avalynn's heart raced.

As they neared the first batch of revelers, the cheering tapered. Banners lowered. Quiet gasps and noisy whispers found her ears. The word *lowborn* spread like a nasty contagion and quickly rose to a din. The atmosphere morphed from celebratory to turbulent.

Heat flushed her cheeks. She needed to remember that she was Princess Avalynn Stromm of the highest house. Highborn. She was next in line to the throne. Straightening her shoulders, she lifted her chin and focused on the dais. Her hair in disarray, her clothing bloodied with rabbit guts, she walked as if she wore her finest threads. A regal dress of silver and gold, a crown perched on her head. She was royalty and would act every bit the part.

Close enough now, her father zoomed into perfect focus. His face filled with the fury of fifty Shadowbloods. His eyes blazed with dangerous intensity. That look sent shivers down her pond-healed spine. Every line across his rippled forehead screamed savagery. She had been right. His furrowed brow meant only one thing. He would not tolerate her defiance. The air crackled with his rage. With a twisted and evil smile, he patted Lily's head.

Lily... Her father threatened her little sister now. But she could not veer from her chosen path. She controlled the outcome. As queen, she would do things differently. Until then, she would use her considerable influence to justify doing the right thing.

She remembered when Kragar asked about her weaknesses while reviewing the hunters during training. She told herself she possessed none and placated him with the easy answer. "My weakness is confidence." But she had been wrong and knew the correct answer today, right now. Her decisions would always favor honor over self preservation. She could not forsake her duties in favor of her heart—doomed to a life of an unloved slave to her crown.

She slowed her pace. The purple finish-line ribbon crossed the pathway. It flittered and furled in a crosswind. Her mind shut off. She set love aside. Duty kicked in. She swiped her leg across Mateo's ankles, shoved him to the ground, and then darted through the ribbon.

The crowd erupted with excited cheers and even wilder laughter. She turned and saw Mateo on his knees, eyes wide and mouth open. At her betrayal, his face hardened. He locked eyes with her. "Avalynn!"

His cry cut deep into her soul as Stormshroud howled and darted between her and Mateo. Like the Enbarr on that first night, Stormy tried to bridge the gap between them. But that was impossible now. It was over. She had chosen. To protect Lily, and hopefully Mateo, she had to preserve herself first.

"I am sorry," she whispered as her vision blurred with tears and Stormy howled. If she kept her position, she could work on her father. Maybe with her intervention, she could convince him to spare the Sublands and provide them with much-needed healing seeds. She needed to survive her father to make that happen. She was no good to Mateo, Lily, or the Sublands if she was in a dungeon or dead. But alive and as a winner of the hunt with much power, she could affect a different outcome. If Mateo had won, the same could not be said about his ability to save her, Lily, or the Sublands. She hadn't seen it until now.

Brandishing his axe, Master Kragar rushed to Avalynn's side. He waved his cold weapon toward Mateo. "Take him to the dungeon! And his wolf too!"

A troop of guards sprang into action.

Mateo jumped to his feet. He jabbed his spear toward the guards. "Stormy, go!" He hollered. The wolf bolted through the guards' grasp while Mateo collapsed under the entire troop's weight.

Avalynn blinked her tears away. Her heart shattered into a million tiny pieces. She turned away, unable to watch. She had fallen madly in love with Mateo and, for the first time, shared herself in the most intimate way. And now she'd betrayed him to save herself. What a wicked choice.

Kragar slammed his hand against her healed back. She thought of the waters of Green Falls as Kragar scooted her forward. "Present your prize, my princess." He winked. "First place finisher."

She had witnessed the formal presentation of the prize dozens of times. She had dreamed of this moment— herself in the winner's circle. Now that it was here, her gut twisted so hard she thought she might retch. Who had she become? Peering at her father's smug face, the answer was easy. She was her father's daughter, bruises and all. She disgusted herself and wished she'd never won.

She ripped the Shadowblood Fox from the spear's tip. She balanced it in her hands. She approached the dais. She bowed and extended her kill. "It is my great honor to present to the High King and High Queen the first place kill for this year's Summit Range Hunt."

The crowd exploded with hooting and hollering. A wicked grin spread across her father's face. Her mother offered the slightest of nods. Lily jumped up and down with a grin so wide Avalynn thought she might rip her little lips.

Behind her father loomed Raelor. His diamond eyes were sparkling with menace. A hunt attendant dashed forward with a silver tray. He took the Shadowblood, placed it on top, and stepped back.

Her father rose and raised his hand. The crowd quieted. His voice boomed. "The High Queen and I accept the prize as offered by Princess Avalynn Stromm of Summit Range. She is recognized as the first-place finisher." He turned to the left. "We also accept the forfeit of Selene Baffin of Sand Bluff. *Without* penalty." He turned to the right. "We honor the bravery *and* sacrifice of Eiric Lind of Cuesta and Finnian Baffin of High Meadow."

A series of trumpet blasts and the cheering cranked back up. She searched the crowd for Selene but didn't see her. Not that it mattered.

Her father raised both hands. As the crowd quieted again, he shot Avalynn an ominous glare. His lips curled at the edges. "The High Queen and I declare the Sublander as the last place finisher. Execution of their hunter in three days and banishment of the province in thirty days hence. As it is declared, so let it be done."

THE
IMPACT

CHAPTER TWENTY-THREE

In the twilight of transformation, there will arise like a mighty storm, one born of the union between realms. With a sword of blue in hand and the heart of a champion, this Only One will restore peace to Faevenly and forever unite the bloodlines.

A forgotten flame ignited inside of Mateo. Once again, everything was on fire. Guards pinned him to the grass while he flailed, writhed, and kicked. A guard's boot smashed into his back, another pressed his cheek into the sod while two more subdued his wrists. But at least Stormshroud had darted off and gotten away.

Thunderous crowd cheers rang out. With his face half planted, he watched from the corner of his eye as Avalynn presented her kill to her father. Although somewhat muffled, he heard the High King's edict for his execution and the decree of his province's banishment.

Time slowed down. His fate had been decided. Avalynn had deceived him.

He flushed away the memories of the Green Falls. He should have known better than to trust her—vile and wicked highborn—just like every last one of them.

A thick black boot along with a thick axe slammed into the dirt beside his face. Master Kragar, the Mad

Dwarf. "Lowborns never win," he sneered and waved his hand. "Take him away."

Arms yanked Mateo to his feet. He needed the counsel of his travel companions. "Lady Verona and Rhyka! I demand to see them!"

An angry mob gathered around him. The guards pushed him forward into the fray. Gobs of spit pelted his cheek. A petite hand reached through the rabid mass. Maid Nia's face popped into view. "I will tell your companions," she said hastily, trotting beside him as the guards pulled him toward the palace. "I will tell them right away."

Nia provided him with a sliver of hope. "Thank you."

Perhaps Lady Verona or Rhyka could reverse his fate. He knew no others at Stromm Palace other than Avalynn, the betrayer. As if she would or could help him. She had chosen. So much for protecting Princess Avalynn. What a joke.

Guards yanked and dragged Mateo through the gardens, past the main palace, toward a tall, skinny tower. They shoved him through a thick wooden door and forced him down a torch-lit corridor that smelled of sweat and urine. At the end of the hallway awaited a room with bars, a bucket, and a cot. The guards crammed him into the cell. *Clink.* The prison door closed with a final insult. "Lowborn scum."

Breathless, Mateo froze, yet a tidal wave rushed throughout him. His hands shook. His heart screamed. *Bonk.* He banged his head against the cool metal bars. He trusted Avalynn, and she betrayed him. *Bonk.* She manipulated him and seduced him. *Bonk.* She spewed enough lies to make him do exactly what she wanted—a Stromm, through and through. *Bonk. Bonk.* Blood dripped down his face. He would be executed and his people banished from the Sublands...all because of her. *Bonk.* Maybe his father, Floriana, and Poppy had died already. Did it even matter now? He killed the first Shadowblood and ended up with last place. His quest was doomed from the beginning. He was defeated before the hunt began. The High King always got what he wanted in the end.

Backing away from the bars, he slumped onto the wooden cot. He leaned over with his elbows on his legs and his hands clasped tight in front of him. A solitary tear joined the blood streaming down his face. One tear led to another, then another. He had disappointed his people, and it sickened him. His only saving grace was that they wouldn't know how he had trusted and was then betrayed by a highborn, a Stromm princess.

From down the corridor came a tinkering echo, followed by stomping boots. A trio of guards escorted Lady Verona and Rhyka toward his cell. "Only a few minutes." The guard backed away but stayed in view.

His hope brightened. They wouldn't have come without information or a plan. He clenched the cold bars and whispered while pressing his face close. "You have to get me out of here." Surely there was something one or the other of them could do. They were his only chance.

Lady Verona pulled a linen square from her pocket and passed it to him without meeting his eyes. "There is nothing we can do. We are to be escorted from the palace grounds and sent home immediately after we leave you here, with orders to prepare the Sublands for an exodus."

His hand hovered in midair. He was stunned but not entirely surprised. What did he expect? He took the linen square and gave into his plight. "I understand." He wiped the square across his bloody face.

Rhyka spoke in a hushed tone. "There is still something that *you* can do." Her crooked finger poked through the bars. "Summon your power."

Still with that? He shook his head. This witch's earlier claims were nothing more than mere guesses. "You were right about the powers, but you were wrong about the person."

Rhyka leaned in and dipped her chin. "What do you mean?"

"My betrayer, Princess Avalynn, has the power you speak of. The blue light came from her when a dragon attacked us in the forest." She'd probably only saved him so she could betray him and hand him over as the last place finisher. Keep your enemies close, and then even closer.

Lady Verona turned to Rhyka. "A dragon? From the North? They're back?"

Rhyka's sparkling eyes blinked. "I have heard but did not know the veracity of the rumor. I will look into it." She brought her attention back to Mateo. "But what about these powers? Are you sure of what you saw?"

Verona added, "Yes, the powers. Tell us."

"Perhaps he saw an illusion," Rhyka said to Verona. "Maybe his power channeled through her."

"Enough!" He tossed the bloodied square. "It does

not matter! If you can't help me, then I am done for in three days' time. Your words, your prophecies, your madness... They are all for naught!" He steadied his breathing. He slowed his thundering heart. He wanted them to leave him be. They could not help and were of no use to him any longer. He needed to be alone now.

"Of course," Verona said.

"Please. My final wish and command is that you see after my family, especially my father, Manny, and my little sister, Floriana. They are not well." Another tear spilled. With a quick swipe, he wiped it away. "Tell them I am sorry and that I love them."

Lady Verona's chin quivered as she stepped back. "Whatever we can do, we will. You have my word on that as a Sublander."

Whatever she *can* do? She had no power. She could *do* nothing but talk. The carriage ride back to the Sublands would take three days. They would arrive on the day of his death. There would be no celebration in the Sublands, no parade greeting the carriage, no *pan de volvo* from big sister Camilla, and no *piñata* or painted flowers from little Floriana.

Lady Verona and Rhyka would deliver another cautionary tale to the people of the Sublanders. The tale had been told so many times it'd be another version of the same warning—never trust a highborn, especially if they happened to be a Stromm.

He didn't want to sound ungrateful to Lady Verona. His father would not approve. "Thank you for your help. I couldn't have gotten this far without you."

As they walked away, he dropped back down onto his

cot and took the cross out of his pocket. His grip dug the cross into his skin. He placed his shaky hand on his forehead, then on his chest, and moved it from shoulder to shoulder like his father taught him. If there was any time to call on the earthly God, this was it.

"If you're up there, if you can hear me, please send help. I really need it right now."

CHAPTER TWENTY-FOUR

There is great power in you, my love. Now the time has come for you to claim your destiny. Know that your father and I will always be with you. You will never be alone.

Avalynn took slow and steady steps away from the merry music and the bustling celebration. She left the garden far behind. Her muted mind found solace in the echoing silence. Nothing could dim that numbing ache in her soul. Or mend the scattered shards of her heart. Mateo was his name. Mateo Vela. He would be executed. It was her fault. She had no choice but to protect herself...and Lily.

"Avalynn! Avalynn!" Lily skipped toward her. Her little sister beamed with that familiar smile, bowed, and then curtsied. "My big sister did it!"

She forced a smile. The innocent child had no idea what Avalynn had *really* done. And she never would. "That I did. But now I must bathe and rest." And cry a thousand tears.

Lily's twinkle dulled. Her innocent face seemed to harden. "The way you betrayed the lovely lowborn, that was special."

A dagger sunk deep inside Avalynn's heart—not special, not by a long shot. Lily's age meant she did not understand what she was saying. Or did she? That notion frightened her to her core. "It was not special, little princess. It was wretched. But it was necessary for many reasons."

Lily twirled, as if not even hearing her. "Very special!" Then she held her nose. She waved her dainty hand in front of her face. "You need a bath. You smell like a troll!" She backed away with a giggle. "Come find me when you smell like a garden. I want to hear more about how you tricked the lowborn."

Avalynn watched as Lily swayed her dress and skipped back to the celebration's revelry. Her little sister could not know her words as she had not one care or concern in the world. Avalynn would never be carefree like that again. And she didn't want to be.

She would never forgive herself for Mateo.

She sighed, and a flood of tears welled in her eyes. Her throat clogged, and she mumbled, "Do not lose it. Not here." She picked up her pace toward the palace when she heard a whimper. She stopped dead in her tracks. She heard it again.

Her attention zipped to the far end of the palace. In the shadowy area lined with trees, she saw movement. She narrowed her gaze. A muzzle and then a thick paw. "Stormshroud?" She glanced about. Reassured she was alone, she hurried over to the wolf, who waited at a cluster of tall bushes. "Stormy, it's you!"

The wolf's eyes darted about as she backed further and further into the bushes.

"It's me, girl. It's Avalynn."

From behind her, a hand slammed across Avalynn's mouth. A cloth wad went between her teeth. A hood whooshed over her head, plunging her into darkness. A scream lodged in her throat. The taste of bitter herbs flooded her mouth. A sharp chill coursed throughout her body. Toxin. Someone poisoned her. They were taking her, and Stormy did nothing.

Her abductor swept her off her feet. He cradled her and spoke in a pressing tone. "You will be okay, Princess."

Her head buzzed as her energy drained. She knew that voice. But for the life of her, she could not place it. "Who are you?" Her slurred words sounded unlike her. She was fading...

Her abductor's tone softened. "You are safe, Princess. Sleep now."

Sleep? She didn't want to sleep. She wanted to fight her abductor. Yet, her mind and body disagreed. Her breathing slowed. Her muscles relaxed. No matter how hard she fought closing her eyes, she dropped into a dark slumber.

Tickling her cheek like a butterfly's kiss, a tiny ray of sunshine warmed Avalynn's face. But she wanted more sleep. Her mind and body were *that* tired. She flipped on her side and pulled the silk sheets over her face. Her questioning hand lingered on the fabric. Stiff and scratchy did not equal silk. Someone was having a bit of fun at her expense while she slept. Everyone in the palace knew her sheets were made of silk only.

A flood of events exploded in her mind—the hunt, Mateo, the finish line, the poison in her mouth.

Her eyes snapped open. She sat up. She lay on a simple, narrow bed in the corner of a small room with thick, beige stone walls. This place was no palace. Surely, she was still dreaming. Sunlight shone through a narrow window. The smells of soil, pine, and burning wood drifted about. Awake, she had no clue where she had ended up. Yet, she sensed peace, calm, and cleanliness. She touched her smooth and washed face. Her hands and arms showed that someone had scrubbed away the hunt's grime.

A soft rap sounded on the door. She had been taken. She looked for a weapon but found none. She grabbed the small pillow, held it up, and jumped into a fighting stance. As if the soft square could do anything. "Uh, you can come in, but I must warn you that I have a weapon."

The door swung open. Stormshroud darted in and tackled her with a wet kiss to her face. Behind Stormy came Maid Nia. "Nia!" She hugged her so tight it squeezed a grunt out of the petite maidservant.

Nia squeezed back with a laugh. "My lady, it is so wonderful to see you awake."

Awake...the horrors of the hunt and what she had done to Mateo flooded her mind and her heart. She could not avoid her painful acts or the reality of Lily admiring Mateo's destruction at the hands of her devious big sister. It all fell on her like a crushing weight.

This time, she didn't stop the tears. They flowed like

a rapid and relentless river as she explained to Nia. "Mateo..." Her shoulders shook. "I stepped across first." Her words were clogged. "He will die." She cried harder, her words registering like a skipped stone on a calm pond. "Because...of...*me*."

"There, there. My princess, it will be okay." Nia patted Avalynn's back.

Nia's calm soothed her, but it triggered her as well. How would anything be okay again? Where were they anyway? Avalynn stepped back and wiped her face with the sleeves of a plain brown tunic. She didn't recognize it. "Where am I?"

"In the Sublands—at Mateo's home. This place belongs to his father, Manny Vela."

"What?" Had a trickle of wind passed through the bedchamber, she would have fallen over. "Where?"

"There is much for me to tell you." Nia handed her a small brown box. "But it is best if you go through this first."

Avalynn blinked as she studied the intricate wooden box. Carved with leaves around the borders, it boasted a swirly and fancy 'S' etched in the middle. She wrapped her hands around it. "What is this?"

"You will see." Nia left the room and closed the door behind her.

Avalynn lowered herself onto the bed's edge. Stormshroud circled the room and then plopped on the floor. Her paws landed on Avalynn's bare toes.

She ran her fingers over the smooth wood. She traced the raised letter and whispered to Stormy, "Should we be scared?" Surely the elaborate 'S' stood for Stromm. A gift perhaps? She trusted Nia completely. Still, the box made her uneasy. As if it contained dormant whispers of something ancient simply waiting to be awakened.

She drew in a deep breath, then blew it out nice and slow. She'd faced a dragon, a vicious swarm of Shadowbloods, and an elk stampede. She would face this wooden box.

She opened it. Inside she found a platinum necklace with a cross pendant like the one Mateo carried. She palmed it and removed the parchment underneath—a note addressed to *My Love.*

When you read this, know that your father and I love you more than life itself. I pray you accept this with peace and understanding in your heart. To appreciate your birthright, it's important to start at the beginning. Before you were conceived.

At one time, there existed harmony between the fae realm and the human realm, with access to both realms made possible through shimmery portals. Over time, humans sought to conquer the fae, which culminated in the Great Shimmer War. But humans were no match for the fae.

The Great Shimmer War ended swiftly, and humans were branded as enemies. The Strongs, the ruling house of Faevenly, used a glamour to erase the war from human memory. They then stored every portal on Torch Lake and forbade their use henceforth.

Over time, there came to be twin princesses in the Strong family—ambitious Princess Malena and curious

Princess Celyse... Celyse is your grandmother. Princess Celyse found a shimmer portal and peeked at the human realm, where she met Julio Avila... He is your grandfather.

When the courting season approached, Celyse hid her portal and ignored Julio, choosing duty over heart. Celyse later learned of a threat to humans involving the shimmers. Using her own, she crossed into the human realm, seeking Julio's help in unraveling the mystery.

Celyse, Julio, and Julio's best friend, Manny Vela, discovered one of the royal families was manipulating the shimmers in a way that would harm humans forever. Celyse, Julio, and Manny, along with allies from the Sublands, stood against this family and their evil witch, Draven. After many lives were lost, the Sublanders were victorious, and peace returned to Faevenly. The Sublands' victory hinged on Julio's blue energy power and his innate human witch abilities.

Celyse left Faevenly for a life with Julio, and their love blossomed into a daughter—me, Gabriela... I am your mother.

Your grandparents took me to Faevenly often. But when my life was threatened, we stopped going, and unease began spreading amongst the provinces. Draven's evil returned to Faevenly, and your grandparents went missing. Every last Strong descendant, as well as the future of the Sublands, was at risk upon Draven's return.

Leaf, Faevenly's fiercest warrior, was sent to the human realm to protect me... He is your father.

Wielding my power, and with the help of a witch named Lady Sonia, I faced Draven and restored peace.

This same power lives in you. Raw and unlimited, your power will always come forth in your times of need.

There are still those who seek to disturb the balance in Faevenly, and thus a lasting prophecy was born. Your prophecy.

In the twilight of transformation, there will arise like a mighty storm, one born of the union between realms. With a sword of blue in hand and the heart of a champion, this Only One will restore peace to Faevenly and forever unite the bloodlines.

There is great power in you, my love. Now the time has come for you to claim your destiny. Know that your father and I will always be with you. You will never be alone.

Avalynn's hands shook like a feather in a windstorm. She dropped the cross and the note. Her gut clenched tight. She was not the person in this writing. She snatched the parchment from the floor and reread it. No way. This message was not meant for her. She bolted to her feet and jerked open the door.

Maid Nia came right away with raised brows. "Did you read the note?"

"Yes. This is not for me." Avalynn slammed it back into the box. She carefully placed the cross on top and handed it back. "I am a *Stromm*—S-T-R-O-M-M—not a *Strong*. There's been a mistake."

"There is no mistake." Nia patted Avalynn's arm.

"You are a Strong from Strong Haven." She set the box on the bed. "Every single word in that note is true."

Heat rose in her cheeks. This was absurd. She might despise her parents, but she knew her identity, and no maidservant could tell her otherwise. "How would you know?"

"Because, I am Lady Sonia."

CHAPTER TWENTY-FIVE

Everything slowed—Avalynn's heart, her breathing, even time itself. It was as if the Sun, Moon, and Stars had pressed pause on the realm and her life. "No, no, no," she muttered. "I know who you are."

She studied Maid Nia's features—silver hair, heart-shaped face, petite frame... Everything remained the same. "You are my maidservant and friend and have been for years." She shook her head as if clearing the mental haze caused by the note. "And I am Avalynn Stromm of Summit Range."

"Indeed. I am your friend, and that will never change." Nia stepped to the middle of the small room. "Allow me, and I will show you who I *really* am. And then perhaps we can discuss who you *really* are."

Show her? She backed away from Nia. Her body trembled. Her mind reeling. Show her what?

Stormshroud stuck to Avalynn's leg like a protective blanket as Nia closed her eyes. Her ivory skin sparkled with a soft glow. Her features blurred and then rippled like a pool of shimmering water. Her long silver hair flowed further down her back and then darkened until a jet-black sheen took hold. Her petite frame stretched, becoming longer, her features elegant and enchanting. The wave of magic pulsed so strong it sent a warm tingle across Avalynn's scalp, down her neck, and then to her ears. When Nia's shifting and blurring stopped, a completely different person remained in the room. Statuesque and beautiful, she wore a long blue dress with a black cape.

Avalynn's mouth dropped. "This is..." Her words stuck in her throat like a knotted ball of yarn. "The real Nia?" She had just witnessed a glamour lowering. A sight few had witnessed, and only powerful fae and strong witches could do it.

"I am Lady Sonia, eternal friend to your mother and father, and your mother's mother and father. This is my true form. My glamour was connected to the one I placed on you." She motioned to a small mirror on the wall. "If you look, you will see a change in your hair and ears."

Her fingers felt her ears. Usually sharply pointed, they rounded to her touch. Human ears. Lowborn. Sun, Moon, and Stars, what had happened to her? Backing up, she slammed her back into the wall. She was becoming someone and something else. "I-I-I'm no longer...myself?"

A gentle shake of the head and Nia, or Lady Sonia, said, "You are finally your true self on the outside. Who you are in the inside remains the same." She motioned to Avalynn's head. "Your mother had white streaks in her hair. You have a similar streak."

Avalynn lifted a thick strand of her long hair. White nestled within the brown, the dark midnight gone. She turned and faced the mirror. The white swathe started at the roots and flowed to the tips.

"You look like Princess Gabriela, your mother. Yet your tall physique is that of your father, Leaf of the Sublands. Your mother was quite petite."

Reaching behind her as if she had lost her sight, Avalynn found the bed's edge and lowered herself inch by inch. A hurricane wind of confusion swirled in her mind. "My mother was petite. A royal. A princess from House Strong." She wanted to touch her ears again yet kept her hands on her lap. "My father was a Sublander. An outcast and a lowborn, like Mateo." She lifted her gaze back to Lady Sonia. "How?"

"How did you come to be raised as a Stromm? And Mateo, a true Stromm, came to be raised as a Vela?"

"Mateo is a true Stromm?" Why hadn't she thought of that? He resembled a full-blooded fae through and through, and even acted like one. She'd figured whatever fae blood he had in him dominated his human ancestry. "He is a highborn with no human blood?"

"That is correct." She nodded. "He is a pure blood. When you are ready, I will show you how it happened."

She rubbed her sweaty palms on the skirt of her crude brown dress. Stormshroud pawed at her foot, as if signaling all would be well. But would it? Even if it frightened her, she wanted and needed the truth. She steadied her shaking hands. "I am ready. I must know."

Lady Sonia took a small wooden stool from the corner of the room. She sat in front of Avalynn and rubbed her hands together. "I will use my magic to take you to the time and place of your birth and the switch." She reached out. "I will do so by touching your forehead." The witch's graceful fingers grew closer. "I will be with you in the vision, and we will be able to speak to each other. Understand?"

Avalynn nodded. "Understand."

The witch placed her cool fingertips on Avalynn's forehead. Silence descended as weightlessness swept her off her feet and her vision tunneled to black. Her heart catapulted against her chest for a few long seconds until she met solid ground.

"You may open your eyes," Lady Sonia said from within her head. "I am right here with you."

One at a time, Avalynn cracked open her eyelids. She saw a thick wall of gray mist. "What is this?"

"Magic," Lady Sonia said. "It will clear."

A small bedchamber came into view. It looked like the one she was in now—thick, beige stone walls and a narrow window. A lady lay motionless on a bed, eyes closed. White-streaked brown hair clung to her face. Avalynn's soul sank at the sight of blood-stained sheets between the lady's legs.

A dwarf dressed in all-white moved from side to side, shushing a swaddled baby. A small maidservant huddled nearby. They assisted the lady.

Avalynn touched her own hair, which matched that of the motionless lady. "My mother?"

"Yes. That is your mother, Princess Gabriela." Lady Sonia pointed at the dwarf. "That is a trusted friend and maidservant, Maid Gidna. The infant in her arms is you."

With a gentle hand, she covered her gaping mouth. Her mother died giving her life. The sight crushed her. "Wh-wh-what happened to her?" she stuttered.

"We suspect the Kanes spelled her or somehow slipped her a poison. Their mission was always to end the Strong bloodline."

"And my father? What happened to him?"

"Soulbound to your mother. When she breathed her last breath, so did he. Leaf's Enbarr, Silverhoof, led us to him."

"Silverhoof?" She snapped her eyes toward Lady Sonia. The Enbarr, the one in the forest. The one that separated her and Mateo, then later carried them to the Green Falls. It belonged to her father?

Lady Sonia nodded. "Silverhoof is the Enbarr you have been seeing. She has been watching over you."

Tears welled in her eyes, blurring her vision. This whole time her father, her real father, had been helping her. Her hands moved to her arms, to the skin where the man she thought was her father had bruised her. Her fake father. The man who threatened and hurt her. She was sure Leaf would have never done that. A flow of tears escaped her eyes for never having known him and her mother.

Inside the vision, movement from the doorway drew her attention. Lady Sonia from the past dashed into the room.

"She is gone, she is gone," the maidservant Lady Gidna cried.

Lady Sonia wrapped her arms around the maidservant. She held her and the baby close for a few long seconds. She pulled back and placed her hand on the maidservant's shoulder. "But the child. The child is not gone. We must activate our plan."

"Yes. Let us do that before we are too late." The dwarf maid kissed the infant's tiny head. "Please, protect her."

Avalynn tore her gaze away from the scene and looked at the Lady Sonia standing beside her. "You all knew this might happen and had a plan?"

"We did." Lady Sonia paused as if waiting for a reaction. But Avalynn gave none. "We had been keeping watch on the lady of House Stromm. She was with child, and I had foreseen that hers would not be born alive. So, we planned to hide you in plain sight as their offspring. You would be safe there. I had already established myself as Maid Nia in Stromm Palace so that we could facilitate the switch."

"But..." Avalynn's mind scrambled at the unfolding events. "How did Mateo come to be in the Sublands if he was not born alive?"

"Keep watching. You will see."

Lady Sonia of the past reached into her cape's pocket. She pulled out a shimmery glow. Placing her fingertips on the edges, she stretched it out until it took on the shape of a doorway.

Avalynn gaped in wild wonder—the shimmery portal she had read about in the note. She had heard of them but had never seen one. According to the history tellings, they were all destroyed. From where she stood, she could make out the Chrysalis Chamber of Stromm Palace, where newborns were taken for cleaning. Lady Sonia secured the baby in her arms, kissed Gidna's cheek, and then stepped through the portal.

Avalynn held her breath. The switch. With her gaze fixed on the opened portal, she watched Lady Sonia and herself as an infant disappear from view. Biting down on her lip, she clasped her hands tightly in front of her. This had already happened, but Avalynn felt perched on the edge of a knife anyway.

A few seconds later, Lady Sonia appeared in her Maid Nia form with a swaddled infant in her arms. She passed the bundle to Maid Gidna through the shimmery haze, then shot back through the opening. She closed the portal with a swipe of her arm.

Avalynn's heart raced. She stepped closer to the maidservant holding the infant. Mateo. She bit her lip and waited for a sign of life. Nothing. And then, a cry from the swaddling. Maid Gidna turned to the maiden in the corner. "The babe lives!" The pair scurried out of the room.

With the room emptied, Avalynn scanned the surroundings. Her attention landed on a tall, dark wooden chest with intricate flower and leaf carvings. The wooden box with the same 'S' sat on top. Next to it rested the platinum chain and cross.

"Have you seen enough?" Lady Sonia wrenched her hands. "I am not able to hold the vision much longer."

Avalynn studied the room and took one last mental picture. "I have."

Lady Sonia waved her arm, and the scene dissolved. The two were back in the room. Lady Sonia on the stool, and Avalynn on the bed.

"Are you all right?" Lady Sonia lowered her hand from Avalynn's forehead. She rose and stepped back, giving her space.

All right? How does one even answer that question after witnessing such a life altering moment? She picked up the box, the same one from the vision. She draped the necklace with her *real* mother's cross over her hand. Deceived and hidden for all these years as a princess of House Stromm, she was actually the daughter of Gabriela of House Strong and Leaf of the Sublands. Like she had thought of Mateo, she was a Sublander, a lowborn. Hated by many.

But she was unsure where the Only One fit in. She faced Lady Sonia. "Who foretold the prophecy? And what does it mean?"

"It came to Princess Gabriela in a dream, from your grandmother, Princess Celyse. For your safety, we have kept it hidden and were mostly successful until whisperings of the Only One began circulating."

A knock sounded on the door. It jarred Avalynn from the conversation.

"I want to see her, Sonia." It was a man's voice.

"You will, Manny. Give us a little more time here."

Avalynn touched Sonia on the shoulder. "Mateo's father?" She could not face him after what she had done to his son. She hoped to never face the man Mateo loved so much.

"Yes, Manny Vela. He is Mateo's father by choice. He raised Mateo with all the love of a real father. His friendship for your grandfather knew no bounds. He practically raised your mother as well. He has been a faithful servant of the Strong family for a century's mid-moon."

Mateo's face at the finish line sprang to her mind. It took three days by carriage from Summit Range to the Sublands, and Mateo had three days until he was executed. Did that mean he was... Avalynn gulped, and a burning pain pierced her heart. "I must know what became of Mateo."

"He is safe for now." Lady Sonia's eyes softened. "Pending a formal inquiry regarding the hunt's events and your disappearance, his execution has been stayed."

She breathed a sigh of relief. Mateo was still alive. But for how long? His execution had still been ordered and would still happen. And it was her fault. But then another dawning recognition hit her...Mateo was home. He was a Stromm. A member of the family he despised. And no one knew.

With a reach and a pull on the sleeve, Avalynn asked. "Does this family know the truth that I have just now learned?"

"They do, but only because I told them when you arrived. It was done this way for your protection and Mateo's, and at Gabriela's insistence."

Manny knocked again, but this time harder. "I need answers. Now."

Avalynn clutched the cross. Would it give her protection like it did Mateo? Mateo adored and cherished these people, this family. She was certain they felt the same way about him, even if he was sired by highborns. How could they not? He was born and raised here. She slipped the cross necklace on.

Lady Sonia eyed the precious heirloom with a smile, then placed her hand on Avalynn's shoulder. "There is still much for us to discuss. But we must include Manny and the family. Are you ready?"

Was she ready? She gulped. Her nerves were a chaotic whirlwind. She would never be ready but needed to face the man they called Manny. "I will need this man of loyalty to my mother and father and grand sires. Most of all, I need the man who raised Mateo Vela."

If she was the Only One, then her lowborn story had just begun in the Sublands. And she needed Manny.

CHAPTER TWENTY-SIX

Could he be executed already? The dim dungeon wrapped him like a fog, the blood and guts from the rabbit stuck to him like a second skin, and the bucket of his excrement in the corner steamed with stink. Being put out of his misery would be better than this. A scrap of bread here, a drop of water there... His final moments could not come fast enough.

He stopped caring about Avalynn's betrayal two days ago. His shock and anguish transformed until it evolved into a resilient shield that guarded the remnants of his heart. She was nothing more than a phantom now, lost in the shadow of his memories. A rotten piece of fruit left to wither on the vine of his past. A Stromm. He never wanted to see her again, though he was sure she'd be at his execution. Front row for his death by beheading. He would not give her the satisfaction of knowing how deeply she cut him. He would not glance her way. Or maybe he would... Maybe he would level her with a stare until the bitter end. He shook his head. As if she would even care.

With his hands clasped in front of him, his family and friends sprang to mind. He hoped they were okay and that the news of his fate hadn't troubled them too much. They all knew the risk of the hunt. But still...

A clunking sound pulled him to his feet, followed by pounding boots. It was day three. Time to put an end to all things. A trio of guards opened his cage. Two pointed their spears at him; the other held out a stack of clothes. Simple brown garments.

"Your High King and Queen would like me to change my clothing for my big send-off? I am not opposed to it, of course." He stepped out of his cell. "Perhaps I could have a final meal as well? I'm not sure how these things are carried out since this is all new to me, but a spread would be nice."

"Silence," the tallest one warned.

With the spears pressed to his back, he made his way down the corridor. Outside, the bright sun blinded him, the warmth welcome against his cold and grimy skin. They walked down a crushed granite path that hugged the outer gardens and winded to a small brick building Mateo hadn't noticed before. "Will I be changing here? Or do you have something else planned for me, like some sort of pre-execution torture?"

The guards nudged him inside, and he found himself in a small bathhouse. Tan brick lined the walls, and white marble covered the floor. In the middle sat a large tub filled with steamy hot water. Mateo's shoulders dropped as a sigh escaped his lips. "Please tell me that is for me."

The guard set the clean clothes on a stool. "It is."

He didn't care why he was getting a bath or who stayed to watch. He was already stripping down and climbing in. With a soft groan, he submerged himself in the water and stayed there as long as he could hold his breath. His hands moved across his chest over the raised and bumpy cuts and scrapes inflicted by the Shadow-blood Fox. Their scuffle in the cave seemed so long ago, that time with Avalynn like a dream. Though now more like a nightmare.

Mateo broke the ripples with an exhale and took the cloth draped over the edge of the tub. He began scrubbing, and the towel sudsed with notes of lavender and sage. He undid his braids and ran his fingers through his dark strands. The crystal-clear water soon turned murky as the dark and chunky remains of the hunt floated atop. He thought of that foul creature Eiric and how Selene, Avalynn, and Finnian did their best to clean him before his departure. He was grateful to have the same opportunity.

A spear knocked on the edge of the tub. "Out."

With a final rinse, Mateo got out, dried himself, and put on clean clothes. He snatched his cross from the pocket of his dirty pants and placed it in his clean one. Feeling almost like himself, he followed the guards out of the bathhouse. Instead of heading to the back of the garden, where he'd thought his execution would take place, the guards prodded him to the palace.

"Why are we going to the palace?" He eyed the guards. "A final meal? Perhaps some meat and fresh bread?"

They kept their silence as they entered the rear door and escorted Mateo to the receiving room. The thick, heavy doors were closed, and outside waited Master Kragar. Mateo nearly tripped over his feet at the sight of the mad dwarf. *What did he want?*

His scowl dug deep into his face, his red hair greased down and woven into several small braids. He waved his axe in Mateo's face. "You listen up, lowborn. You have been summoned to a meeting of the Royal Council to answer questions about what happened to the missing hunters. You will be truthful or—"

"—I will be executed? Oops, too late."

Kragar's blade came within a hair's breadth of his nose. "You will be truthful, or you will be tortured slowly for over an eon until all of your blood is emptied drop by drop. You understand?"

Mateo flared his nostrils, feigning indifference while his gut clenched. "Whatever you say, Master Dwarf."

What was going on? An air of panic and desperation laced the dwarf's voice. Dark circles had formed under his eyes. He hadn't slept. Something must have happened, no doubt a result of Selene's early departure from the hunt. Would her actions favor him in some way? Could he be that lucky? He pushed that idea aside. Lowborns didn't have luck, especially those that finished last.

Kragar swung open the heavy door. The High King and High Queen sat in their day thrones in the front of the room. The view took him back to the presentation of the hunters on his arrival, when he strode past everyone, knocked Avalynn with his shoulder, and entered the room first. He almost chuckled at their reversal of roles. Had his little act inspired her? He would never know. Even if he wanted to ask, she was not there. Maybe she was counting her silver and gold, ordering people around like Lirien said when he and his friends were on Spirit Butte. He was going to miss them and that place.

A row of seats with lesser royals in formal attire was lined before the king and queen. To the side was a lone servant's chair of simple wood. Kragar nudged Mateo in its direction, and he sat. A stretch of silence filled the room as all eyes bore into him. What were they waiting for?

The dreaded witch Raelor rose from his seat behind the High King. He flicked his long dark robe behind him and moved in front of Mateo. His long white hair hung loose. He wore his usual all black, matching the molten-colored staff in his hand.

Mateo raised his brow and narrowed his stare. He was already dead, so he didn't hold back. "What does the royal henchman want?" He spat on the gold-flecked marble. "Another plaything to occupy your time? Are your rats boring you?"

A growl escaped the witch's thin lips.

"Oh!" Mateo quickly added. "I know! You are the master servant of the palace. I would enjoy a glass of wine and a plate of cheese, please."

Raelor's diamond eyes darkened like an endless void. He raised his crooked fingers.

"Stop!" commanded the High Queen, shutting him down. She sat tall on her sparkling wood throne, dressed in all green and wearing a simple crown of silver and crystal. Her dark hair draped over her ivory shoulders. All eyes shot her way. Even the King's. "Ask your questions, Raelor."

Mateo thought the High King had all the power. But maybe it was the High Queen. Not that it mattered.

The witch took a few steps, repositioning himself. "Mateo Vela of the Sublands. You have been brought here to answer questions about the Summit Range Hunt and the disappearance of Princess Avalynn."

His nerves shot on edge as his head spun. *Disappearance?* A shiver ran down his spine, causing a slight tremor in his hands. "What do you mean, is she missing?"

Ignoring Mateo, Raelor tapped his staff against the marble floor and began asking a series of questions about the hunt and Avalynn, Eiric, Selene, and Finnian. Were any of them in an alliance with Avalynn? Did any of them speak privately with her? Was she ever alone? How did Eiric meet his end? How did Finnian, and what did Selene say when she left the group?

There were also questions about the regular foxes, the Shadowbloods, the dragons, the elk, and even Stormshroud. The witch went on and on as the day turned to night. Some of his questions were repeated, others asked in different ways. But one thing remained constant, the truth of Mateo's answers. Missing or not, he owed Avalynn the betrayer nothing. He didn't hold anything back and answered each question as best as he could. Until...

"Did any of the hunters engage in romantic activities?"

He drew in his chin. Why ask that? Did they somehow know about him and Avalynn and their time at the Green Falls? Could Raelor read minds? He shut off his, just in case. *The hunt... Focus on that. Answer in the vaguest way possible.* "I did not pay them any heed as I was trying to win and not get killed."

"Did Princess Avalynn ever indicate having any romantic attraction to any of the hunters?"

Were they on to them? Did they know what they had done on that boulder? He raged inside. What he and Avalynn did was none of their business. "She was hard to read."

"Hard to read? So she never spoke about romantic interludes?"

"She hated me, and I hated her." It was true in the beginning, and true now.

"Does that mean she never spoke about romantic interludes?"

He fumed. "She is missing, and you want to know if she was having sex?"

"Sex, sexual relations, romantic interludes, romantic interactions. Call it what you will. Did any of your fellow hunters have any of those interactions with the princess?"

He jumped to his feet. "We were trying to survive your vicious and rigged hunt!"

Kragar slammed his hand on Mateo's shoulder and forced him to sit. "Down with you!"

Mateo heaved, ready to charge the crazed dwarf.

Desperate to slam his fist against his pudgy face when a guard from behind held his arms behind his back.

"Did you have any of those interactions with the princess?"

Mateo's heartbeat quickened. So far he had avoided mention of her wounds, her blue light, the Enbarr and the Green Falls and how they had shared each other. That part of the hunt was theirs and theirs alone. It did not belong to anyone else. His brow raised sharply while he tapped his right foot, ready to explode out of the chair, even if it meant the witch would end him on the spot.

The High Queen quickly rose to her feet. She waved her arm. "Everyone out!"

As if on cue, the High King joined her. "Now!"

Kragar swung his axe in the air. "Move it, move it!" He jabbed it at Mateo. "Except you. You stay put."

He gulped. What now? The royals practically knocked each other over as they shuffled out of the room. Only the King, Queen, Raelor, and Kragar remained.

Raelor tilted his head at the queen. "My Queen, are you not pleased with the inquiry?"

She dismissed him with a flick of her fingers. She left her throne and moved toward Mateo. Her steps were slow, graceful, and deadly. Her gaze scanned him from head to toe as if she had never really looked at him before. She shooed the guard from behind Mateo away.

He swallowed but refused to bow down or look away. He met her steely gaze. "Did you only now realize that I am in the room?"

With her glare on Mateo, she uttered, "The lift of the brow, the tapping of the foot." She turned and addressed the King and Raelor. "The dark hair, the gray eyes. Even the physique."

The King sidled forward. He studied Mateo as if picking him apart. "It is not possible."

"Is it not?" The High Queen faced Raelor. "Possible? You yourself said she never really quite fit."

Mateo's thoughts collided like a storm, a mental scramble to process what they were saying. *She Avalynn? Fit what?* "What are you all talking about?"

The witch took slow steps around Mateo but ignored his question. "I can test it if you would like, my Queen," Raelor said.

"I would like."

Was the witch about to spell him? And why were they staring at him like that? His leg bounced. If he got up, could he dart out of the room before being caught?

Kragar slammed his thick hands on Mateo's shoulders and squeezed. "Oh no, you don't."

Raelor grabbed Mateo's arm, pushed up his sleeve, and raked his long nail across his skin. "Hey!" A line of blood thickened. "What is this?" Mateo tried to squirm out of Kragar's grasp as the blood oozed down his arm. "Why did you do that?"

The witch took the queen's arm and did the same. With a swipe of his finger, he scooped a dollop of her blood and placed it on his tongue, then did the same with Mateo's blood.

Mateo shivered as pinpricks raced down his spine. He had heard of the ancient procedure for testing lineage, but why were they doing it to him and the High Queen?

Raelor's eyes widened as he swirled the blood in his mouth and then swallowed. He blinked. He studied Mateo before turning to face the High King and High Queen. He tipped his head. "High King and High Queen, this"—he indicated Mateo with a deep bow—"is your son."

CHAPTER TWENTY-SEVEN

Mateo's mind swirled like a cyclone. Lady Verona and Rhyka had worked tirelessly to try and convince him he was of Strong blood. He had not believed them, not for a second. But this... this was proven. Raelor's test showed *Stromm* blood ran through his veins, and blood never lied. But it was more than that. Staring at the King and Queen, he saw the similarities pointed out by the Queen. He felt them too. All of his villainous thoughts finally making sense.

Time stood still. Raelor's claim repeated in his mind. *This is your son.*

His hands shook. This truth resonated within him like a long-forgotten tune, a favorite scent, or a cherished heirloom. It fit, even though he hated it.

Mateo rose to his feet, and Kragar's axe lifted. Mateo simply shot him a palm. "Down, Dwarf."

"Step aside, Master Kragar," ordered the High Queen while waving the stocky dwarf away. "The fae standing before you is no mere Sublander. He is the Prince of Stromm Palace."

Kragar's bushy red eyebrows raised. "But my Queen—"

"Step aside."

Kragar rested his axe on his shoulder with a huff but stayed close.

Mateo studied the High Queen. Their similarities zoomed into focus. Her features were highlighted as if a muted beam like a spotlight flicked on above her. Dark hair, ivory skin, graceful features, and steely gray eyes. Was this his mother? Which of his tendencies came from her?

He backed away and eyed the High King. Was this his father? What part of him did he share?

The Stromms hated lowborns. They hated the Sublands. They kept people like him down. Despite his blood, he was raised a Sublander. "No." He cast away Raelor's blood truth like rotten kill. He forced himself to push the King and Queen from his mind and focused on Faeryn and Manny. *They* were his mother and father.

Manny's dark skin, small frame, brown eyes... Mateo did not resemble him. But that did not matter. He'd always been told he favored Faeryn. What did she look like? He searched his memory for her, but her image was lost. It had drifted away. She had gone to the Passing Place so long ago he could not even conjure up her face anymore. His gut sank. How long had he not been able to see her?

"You know the truth." The High Queen's tone softened. "I can see it in your eyes, my beautiful son."

Mateo shook his head and looked away, not wanting to see himself in her eyes. Yet he could not help himself. "Suppose I dared to believe such a wicked tale, I must understand how." He made eye contact and pleaded with his mother. "How did you let this happen to me?"

Raelor moved about the room, circling Mateo from a wide berth as if studying a new species. "Powerful magic is the only explanation. Someone with extraordinary gifts wanted you in the Sublands and Avalynn here." The witch cupped his pointed chin. "A Sublander, I presume, since that is your origin. It would explain who abducted Avalynn and where she has been taken. It would shed light on much about her, as well."

They suspected she had been taken to the Sublands —his home, where the red rocks, desert landscape, and Spirit Butte belonged to him. The highborns struck a nerve in Mateo. "Explain yourself. What would being from the Sublands say about her?"

"Her softness," the witch clarified. "Her hesitancy with hard choices—"

The High King interrupted with a sneer. "Her weakness. Always with her head in the clouds following butterflies. She was never a Stromm. But you..." His eyes widened and lit up. "When you brushed aside all the hunters in the receiving room, stepped forward, and declared yourself as the impending winner—those were Stromm moves. I knew you were special."

"Never mind all that." The High Queen moved closer. She placed her long, elegant hands on Mateo's shoulders. The blood from her arm had dried up already. Only a remnant of red remained. "You must be exhausted and famished. You have been through so much, my son."

She called for a maidservant. "Take the prince to his bedchamber. Provide him a proper bath. Prepare his royal threads. Feed him a feast until he can no longer swallow." From his shoulders, her hands hugged his neck. She pulled closer and whispered into his ear, "We will talk more later. You are home, my prince."

The King slapped Mateo's back. "Tomorrow, we shall celebrate the homecoming of the Son of Summit Range!"

A voice inside Mateo's head said to leave, flee the palace, demand a horse, and race to the Sublands. The blood test was wrong. Still, another voice sang in soprano, "*Stay!*" The blood test was right.

Split between the Sublands and Stromm Palace, he felt an overriding desire to experience highborn life, if only for a day or two. There was also that deep rumble in his stomach from three days in the dungeon that needed addressing. Staying and indulging the High Queen certainly would not hurt his situation. Besides, the High Queen did not seem the highborn he had always thought of her. Maybe she was not so bad after all. "If I stay, it will be for a short while only."

"As you wish." The queen nodded with a smile.

As he wished? Interesting. If he truly belonged to them as the Prince of House Stromm, then he had the power to help his Sublands family. He straightened his shoulders and lifted his chin. "As the Prince of House Stromm, I demand a wagon of healing seeds and nutritious food be sent to the Sublands under the care of Lady Verona. This is to be done with all due haste.

Today." He had no idea if that would work but prayed it would.

"I will see to it." Again, the High Queen nodded with a smile.

He blinked so fast his vision blurred. Was it that easy? Making good on his request, the High Queen ordered Master Kragar to bring in her personal servant, someone named Marina. Tall and thick with a bumpy face, the hulking servant resembled a small troll. The queen issued orders for the things Mateo requested while he merely approved each one.

With no further orders, Mateo followed another maidservant, Penny, upstairs. She reminded him of Maid Nia, but smaller. She wore a white dress. Flowers adorned her short-clipped brown hair. Hands clasped in front of her slender waist, she strolled to the second floor and spoke in a tiny voice, "This floor is where the royal guests stay. It has a sitting room, a library, and a study. It is open to you should you wish to explore it."

When they reached the third floor, she paused at the landing. "To my left is the private chamber of the High King and High Queen. They have their own sitting room and study."

She beckoned him to follow her down the corridor to the right. "This side of the floor has the royal family's bedchambers. For their offspring and family visitors." She passed a closed door. "This is the bedchamber for Princess Ava—" She stopped and pressed her fingers over her lips. She lowered her head. "My deepest apologies. She is not...that is, not..."

"It's okay, Penny." They were already scrubbing

Princess Avalynn, now merely Avalynn, from the palace. He had plenty to say but kept it to himself. He would not burden Penny, who picked up where she left off and continued walking.

Stopping at the next door, she bowed her head. "This is your bedchamber, my prince. Everything you need is inside." She motioned ahead. "Down the corridor, you will find a stairwell that leads up to the fourth floor and the servants' quarters. Should you require my assistance, there is a bell beside your bed. Though we can sense when we are needed. We are here to serve you." A quick curtsy and she walked away.

Mateo stared at the fancy wood-carved door that led to his bedchamber. They had already prepared a place for him. With a long exhale, he wrapped his hand around the gold knob and entered the biggest bedchamber he had ever seen—it would have swallowed his entire Sublands home with room to spare.

Rich, burled chocolate-brown walnut wood lined the walls. Underfoot sparkled dark marble floors with thick gold flecks. A fireplace with two purple fabric chairs took up the space on the left. A fire flickered, casting a warm glow throughout.

In front of the fire's flames sat a sturdy marble table with a spread of meats, cheeses, fruit, and a clear goblet filled with red wine. He made a beeline for the table and shoved the feast into his hungry mouth. He'd never been so starved.

After he had his fill of food and finished with the wine, he explored the rest of the bedchamber. As he strolled through the magnificent room, his new reality hammered at him like a tidal wave. What was he doing here? He thought of Avalynn—they were switched at birth. Someone powerful had exchanged their fates, but who and why? He needed to return home, and to her, but paused his thoughts.

Their positions did not change the fact that she was still his betrayer. The greatest deceiver. She wanted him dead and did not bat an eye at his downfall.

A soft knock at the door and he turned to see the High Queen. She no longer wore her ceremonial garb and crown. Instead, she opted for a simple royal green dress. If he didn't know any better, he would think her a regular lady and not a high queen. Still, he did know better.

She carried a stack of clothes and shoes. "May I enter?"

"Of course." He glanced down at his bare feet. His mucked boots were left at the bathhouse. He didn't need them for his execution...but now he was a prince.

She lifted the clothes as if presenting an offering. "Some things have been laid out for you in the washroom, but I thought I would bring more."

He faced her somewhat clumsily, without knowing the proper greeting. "Thank you. After I wash and change, I would like immediate transport to my home in the Sublands." He leaned in closer and whispered, "I do not belong here."

She set the stack of clothes on a cabinet near the door and made her way to the fire. She sat, then motioned for Mateo to join her. She folded her hands on her lap as he settled into his seat. "The revelation of your identity must be difficult. It is for all of us. Especially me, your mother. After all these years, to think that someone so cruelly ripped you away from me and kept you hidden." A lone tear trickled down her cheek. "It is unthinkable."

He swallowed the lump in his throat. He had not thought of that yet. He'd never considered the severity of the pain inflicted on her—a mother's child taken and replaced. And for what? He still did not understand. He cleared his throat. "Why would the Sublands want to switch a lowborn with a highborn?"

The fire crackled. His birth mother shifted in her seat. "An ancient question—why do the Sublanders do what they do?" She sighed, a heavy sound. "We have tried for so long to help that province. But they refuse our aid. They hold fast to the long-forgotten prophecy of an Only One—a uniter of the bloodlines who will supposedly bring peace to all of Faevenly."

Mateo thought of Avalynn and how she repelled the dragon with those powerful blue lights and saved them from fate's certain destruction like Finnian and the elk steed. Did that make her the Only One? He still did not understand it all. But he knew disclosing that information would put her at further risk. He wasn't ready for that... just yet. So he kept his silence.

Her brows pinched together. "The poor Sublanders don't understand that peace exists in Faevenly already. Their denial of the Stromms only harms themselves and the entire realm."

"Denial?" He did not know what she meant. Surely, the Sublanders were blameless. *Right?*

"We offered them a seat on the Royal Court years

ago. The lowborn that calls herself Lady Verona informed us that the Sublands refused. That is why the province struggles. That is why they are lacking. It is their own doing."

Pinpricks raced up and down his spine. Goose bumps lined his skin. The Sublands had been offered a seat? "Why refuse a seat? That makes no sense."

"I agree with you. It was senseless then and remains senseless now. Your father and I have grappled with that question too. All we can do is accept their independence and leave them be."

Heat flushed his face. "Leave them be?" His voice rose. "You tried to manipulate the competition to assure my last place finish and my execution and the Sublands' banishment! How is that leaving anything be?"

She shook her head. "Your father... He means well, but he is impulsive and does not always think things through or implement the best strategies. Our inner council decided that, since the Sublanders could not co-exist with us and the rest of the realm, then it was best for them to leave. They refused, and your father took matters into his own hands."

Mateo had stepped into an alternate reality where everything he knew was turned on its head. And yet, everything the queen said made perfect sense. The Sublands could not complain that they lacked a seat at the table when it had been offered and refused. Such damning information should have been made public throughout the Sublands. It should not have been a secret. No doubt the political maneuvering of Lady Verona and Rhyka.

With regret in her eyes, she patted his hand. "We never meant to hurt the Sublanders. You must believe me, my son."

Believe her? Although he wished not to trust a word, her explanation contained logic. Besides, if she really meant the Sublanders harm, she would not have approved and ordered the delivery of the much-needed seeds and food per his instructions. That kindness alone proved her good faith to him.

"I have taken up too much of your time." Her tender voice soothed his aching spirit. "I will let you return to your rest. But, my son, will you please stay? If only for a little while?" She reached out and touched the slice on his arm that Raelor had made. It had stopped bleeding, like hers. "Perhaps your presence here can bring about a new understanding with the Sublanders. Isn't that what you want?"

He placed his hand on top of hers. What would it hurt to stay and understand this royal life? He could even do what Lady Verona and Rhyka could not— really and truly help the Sublands. "Yes, I will stay for a little while."

When she left the room, he turned back toward the fire. He found his life inside the flames again. "Everything is on fire." Yet this time, his world burned without him knowing who he was or what to believe.

CHAPTER TWENTY-EIGHT

Avalynn opened the door to a frail child with long dark hair, big brown eyes, and tan skin. Behind the little girl stood the man they called Manny. He was of small stature and had the same dark features, but he was stooped over and holding a cane. Long gray hair hung past his shoulders. He leveled Avalynn with a narrowed glare that quickly softened. His eyes welled with tears. He pressed his closed hand to his mouth. "*Dios mío*. You look just like her—my Gabriela."

Lady Sonia gripped his shoulder and made the introductions. "Manny, this is Avalynn, Gabriela and Leaf's child. Avalynn, this is Manny Vela. He raised Mateo." Lady Sonia rubbed the little girl's head. "And this is Floriana, Manny's child from his union with a fae named Faeyra who is no longer alive."

Deep dark circles lined the skin under their eyes. They were bone thin. Their hair was brittle and breaking. A tear spilled down Avalynn's cheek. She wiped it away, nodded, and then swallowed. "Hello." Mateo had said they were ill with Dragon's Bellow. It showed, and she saw why Mateo had risked his life. And now, because of her, there were no healing seeds. "It is nice to meet you all. Mateo told me all about you." She wiped away another tear. "I am very sorry about your illness."

Manny motioned to Lady Sonia. "We are okay. When Sonia brought you here, she had healing seeds with her. You needn't worry yourself with us."

"As Nia, I did not know Dragon's Bellow was ravaging the Sublands until Mateo arrived," Lady Sonia explained. "The Stromms keep news of the Sublands province hidden from the rest of the realm."

"The Stromms," Manny hissed. "They have my boy. *Mi hijo.*"

"I want my brother back," cried little Floriana.

So, Avalynn was right. They still regarded Mateo as theirs. It was the definition of true love.

"We'll get him back, *mija.*" Manny stroked Floriana's brown hair. "Don't you worry." He held her closer, then brought his gaze back to Avalynn. His bottom lip trembled. "Can she do what Gabriela and Julio could do?"

"She can," Lady Sonia answered.

Avalynn cleared her throat. "Do you mean the blue light?"

"Yes," Manny whispered. "The fae called your mother and grandfather human witches. But really, it's only your aura. The light is all around you, all the time. Like an invisible cloud that can be used as a weapon or a shield. The gift to manipulate it is passed down through your human side, and it seems you possess it too."

"You can also see spirits," Lady Sonia added.

She was descended from human witches and had powers this whole time and didn't know? And she could see spirit forms? Her gaze drifted to Sonia. "The blue power came out of me. But I cannot see spirits." She grappled with these abilities. "That part is not true."

"The drink I gave you every morning suppressed your human witch abilities. And then, in your time of danger in the hunt, and having not had the potion, it came out. You should be able to see spirits too. You probably already have, yet did not know."

Avalynn glanced around as if in a daze. "I need to sit down."

Lady Sonia wrapped her arm around Avalynn's waist, like in the past when the maid recognized her sadness or conflict. Or, as in this case, confusion. "Let us go to the sitting room, and we can discuss everything."

With Stormshroud at her heels, Avalynn followed Lady Sonia down the short corridor to a small and cozy sitting room with thick beige walls. Blue and purple woven rugs covered the rocky floors. Stacks of books were piled in the corners. A fire burned in the fireplace, and lit oil lamps hung from the walls.

Back at the place where she was raised, everything sparkled with gold and marble and polished wood. Nothing could be touched that servants didn't follow up with a cleaning cloth. With all the fuss, the palace bore little resemblance to a space where a family lived. However, here, the atmosphere exuded warmth and comfort. She'd never felt more at peace or more at home.

Chairs and stools were arranged around a small

round table. Manny eased himself into a padded chair. Floriana sat on his lap. A slightly older maiden who resembled Manny and Floriana entered the room with a tray, the scents of lavender and lemon filling the room. She must be Mateo's older sister. Her tray contained small white cookies, wooden cups, and a wooden pitcher. She flared her nostrils at Avalynn. Her venom found no hiding place.

Lady Sonia made the formal introduction. "Avalynn, this is Camilla. She is the eldest sibling in the Vela family. Camilla, this is Avalynn."

Avalynn nodded despite the hate stares that came her way. She could not blame Camilla or any of them if they despised her. "Nice to meet you."

Camilla made no eye contact with Avalynn. She set the tray on the table with a clunk and took her place beside Manny and Floriana. "That is Mateo's wolf, not yours." She patted her leg. "Stormshroud, come."

The beast ignored her and moved closer to Avalynn. "Sorry about that." Avalynn nudged Stormshroud toward Camilla, but the wolf wouldn't budge. "She's been stuck to me like this ever since I met her."

"Because she is a wolfbeast," Lady Sonia explained. "They are bound to the Strongs. And Stormshroud just might be the last surviving one."

Avalynn pulled her chin in. The revelation made sense with all the times Stormshroud had favored her over Mateo. "Oh. I had no idea." She scratched Stormy behind the ears. "But it fits with what I have learned about this fine wolf. She saved mine and Mateo's life—"

With her arms crossed, Camilla cut in with a huff.

"Are we going to sit around and act as if she isn't the cause of our Mateo being thrown into a dungeon awaiting execution? We need to go get him!"

Avalynn froze. They despised her. She was foolish to think they wouldn't. They also didn't care that Mateo was a full Stromm. He was still their son and brother. The High King and Queen had never regarded her with such affection. Were they looking for her now? Doubtful. Were they glad she was gone? Probably.

"*Mija...*" Manny rubbed his forehead. "We promised Lady Sonia we would listen. This is Gabriela and Leaf's girl. She is one of us. Come on, now."

Avalynn could not feel any worse. She deserved Camilla's antagonism. Mateo's fate was on her. "I did not ask to be switched at birth. And I'm sorry about what I did to Mateo. But I had no choice. My life and that of my little sister were at risk."

Floriana perked up at the mention of a little sister. "You have a little sister like me?"

"Yes." Avalynn smiled. "Very much like you. Her name is Lily." She had to believe that Lily was okay and safe from the High King.

Manny hugged Floriana tight. "I cannot even imagine the position you were put in, Avalynn. My heart aches for you and what you endured with those Stromm monsters." He angled toward Lady Sonia. "But Camilla is right! We need to get my boy, Mateo. I will wait no longer!"

Everything she and Mateo had shared at the Green Falls replayed in her mind—the laughter, the tenderness, the intimacy. Fear for his safety and what he must be enduring in the dungeon stabbed at her heart like a razor-sharp knife. She needed to fix this situation. She would prove to this family what Mateo meant to her. "Yes, no more waiting. Let's go get him."

Scooting to the edge of his seat, Manny slammed his hands together. "Yes!"

Lady Sonia nodded. "That is the idea. But first, Avalynn needs to claim what is hers, as foretold by the prophecy." Sonia faced Avalynn and a hush fell on the room. Her voice lowered. "Left by your mother and grandfather, Julio, and held in the Passing Place, the last remaining piece of aquoise."

The words of the prophecy repeated in Avalynn's mind. "The sword of blue. So the blue is the aquoise? The power stone? I thought it didn't exist anymore."

"The last remaining piece was kept inside of Gabriela. She and her father put it there with their combined magic. My witch coven sisters and I removed it from her and infused it into the blade to protect her and to keep it safe. My sisters and I believe it will enhance your power."

"I see," Avalynn swallowed, not completely understanding it all but trusting Lady Sonia. "But what about the Passing Place? To go there, do I have to...die?"

"Works for me," Camilla muttered.

Manny shot his eldest a look that Camilla shrugged off before rattling off a phrase in a foreign and indecipherable tongue.

Manny must've caught Avalynn's confusion. "It's Spanish, my native language from the human realm. I'm

Hispanic, you are part Hispanic too, from your mother's side."

Her brain was cluttered with all the things about herself she didn't know. She felt lost. Drifting alone in an endless and unknown sea. "I have a lot to learn."

"Everything will make sense with time." Lady Sonia touched Avalynn's arm. "But for now, we need to focus on the mission. Retrieve the sword, then rescue Mateo. If you are ready, please follow me to the bedchamber."

No amount of preparation would have prepared her for any of this. It was as if someone had been writing a great tale and then suddenly ripped out the pages and started over halfway through. Was she prepared for those new pages?

She was about to find out.

CHAPTER TWENTY-NINE

Avalynn and Stormshroud followed Lady Sonia back to the room where she had awoken. She sat on the bed and folded then refolded her hands on her lap. Her gaze roamed the plain stone walls.

"Is this Mateo's room?" She knew the answer because she sensed him here. Notes of spicy vanilla mixed with sandalwood drifted amidst the earthy aroma, but she asked anyway.

"It is."

Mateo slept here, dreamed here. He hoped and prayed here. He probably also plotted and planned how he'd win the Summit Range Hunt here. Stormshroud's strong body pressing against her leg pulled her away from those thoughts and back to Lady Sonia. "So, how is this going to work?"

Retaking the stool, Lady Sonia explained. "It will work with your unique human witch powers combined with your fae strength. All you need to do is focus your energy, your blue light, on your parents, Gabriela and Leaf. You do not know them, but your heart and soul do."

"Um, what?" Avalynn shook her head. "I have no idea what that even means, let alone how to do it."

"Trust me, Avalynn. And trust yourself." Lady Sonia placed her hand on tops of hers. The gentle touch stilled her trembling. Was this part of Lady Sonia's magic? "Your gifts will never let you down."

"Okay." Avalynn blew out a breath. "I will try."

"Very well." Lady Sonia released her hands and sat back. "Close your eyes and repeat the names of your mother and father in your head. Gabriela and Leaf. Focus on feelings of family and love."

Family and love—concepts she didn't understand, but desperately longed for. She closed her eyes. *Gabriela and Leaf.* The ones who gave her life. They loved her so much and did everything to protect her. A tingle spread across the top of her head. *Gabriela and Leaf.* She had brown hair with a white streak like her mother and a tall and slender fae build like her father. The tingle coursed down her body in soft waves. *Gabriela and Leaf.* They were in the Passing Place, taken there by the Enbarr. Possibly her father's. Her name was Silverhoof and after all this time she had watched over her.

A swirl churned in her stomach. *Go there*, she commanded the mysterious sensation that tickled all over like sunshine. *Go to them.*

Weightlessness claimed her. Her body dropped, and her stomach tumbled. She soared through darkness until she crashed face-first on a soft surface. She opened her eyes. A lavender-filled meadow hazed over with soft sunlight spread out all around her. She spit out bits of grass and flowers as she propped herself up on her elbows.

Was this it? The Passing Place? She climbed to her feet and dusted herself off. A creaking sound met her ears. She turned to see an Enbarr pulling a wagon. Not her magical beast, but another. Inside lay two bodies dressed in all white. The horse's lavender eyes roamed to hers before shifting back to its path toward the bright horizon.

So, it was the Passing Place. She had made it. But where were her mother and father? She meandered about the meadow until she saw a hedge with tall trees beyond. Picking up the hem of her skirt, she crossed over the thick brush. There, under the canopy of an apple tree, sat a petite maiden with long white-streaked brown hair and a tall fae with long dark hair and piercing blue eyes. The same color as hers. Their attention snapped her way.

In a stunned wave, Avalynn raised her hand slowly. "Hello."

The maiden's hands clutched the fae's leg. "Sun, Moon, and Stars."

They rose to their feet, hand in hand, and approached her. The maiden smiled, and her eyes glistened like shaking stars. "*Mija*," she uttered. "It's you. My girl and my love." She touched Avalynn's face. Starting at her forehead, her fingertips moved down to her eyes, cheeks, and then her chin. "You are finally here."

"She looks like you," her father said, beaming with pride. "The hair and the features."

"But tall like you, my love," her mother added. Then she chuckled. "I always wanted to be tall."

A laugh came from Avalynn, and soon the three of them were hugging each other so tight Avalynn could hardly breathe. For the first time in her life, she sensed love, care, safety, and protection. It filled her heart and soul like an overflowing cup of blessings and happiness. She had her family. She didn't want to ever leave this circle and longed to stay with them forever in this place, but she had a mission. *Mateo.* Despite what she had done, he was to her what her father was to her mother. She would one day join her parents in the Passing Place to stay. But today was not that day. Until then, she must return and rescue the one who filled her heart.

It was Leaf, her real father, who pulled back first. His chiseled and handsome face took on a serious expression. "Are you alive?"

"I am. Lady Sonia helped me come here."

He glanced at Gabriela, her real mother, with concern before focusing on her again. "Then Faevenly needs you and your power."

Avalynn nodded. "It does." There was so much she wanted to say, but she had no idea how long she had. She needed to be quick. "The Stromms rule all of Faevenly, and they want to banish the Sublands forever."

Leaf and Gabriela glanced at each other. "The realm needs peace, once and for all," Leaf said.

"Is it even possible?" Avalynn asked. "After all this time of so much hatred and maneuvering and fighting, can it ever be?"

Her mother took her hand. "Your grandmother, Princess Celyse, says it is. We must take you to her."

Avalynn could not explain touch in this place, but it didn't matter. She was grateful for the connection. The three linked hands. They walked through the trees until they reached a babbling brook. They followed the stream until it opened into a crystal-clear lake. Purple reeds and wheat-styled long grasses swayed along the lake's edge. Along the still surface, geese and swans bathed and preened. Avalynn smelled wild mint and sweet clover.

"Wow," she breathed. "Faevenly is beautiful. But this, this is something else entirely."

"It is, my love." Her mother squeezed her hand. "But this is as far as your father and I can go. Your grandmother, Celyse, is in the water not much further ahead, at the shallow end. She will give you what you need and tell you what you need to know."

There was a tale there, how her grandmother ended up in the lake, but now was not the time for that.

Her mother and father wrapped her in their arms. They held her for something that seemed like an eternity, but was really only seconds. "You are so strong, my beautiful girl," her father said. "Do not forget that."

Gabriela stepped back. She kissed each cheek and then touched the cross around Avalynn's neck. "Faith is a warrior."

"It is," she whispered.

She left her parents and continued along the edge of the water. A soft breeze whisked about her, sifting through her long brown and white strands. She wasn't quite sure how the waters worked but thought she should take off her slippers. Kicking them aside, she edged her toes into the water, finding the lake to have the perfect cool temperature. She walked in until the water covered her ankles. A few more paces in, a glint and a gleam beneath the water's surface caught her eye. She edged closer. A beautiful woman under the glassy surface, with silver strands and a blue dress, came into view. She appeared ethereal and magical, and she held a sword in her hands.

Avalynn gasped. Of all the magical things she had seen, this outshone all the others. "Celyse. My grandmother."

The woman opened her green eyes and gazed at her with timeless affection. "I am her. Princess Celyse of House Strong. Betrothed to Julio Avila, a powerful witch from the human realm. Mother to Princess Gabriela. Grandmother to you, Princess Avalynn." She opened and closed her eyes. "I knew your name before it was ever spoken, and I have been waiting for this moment for the fortnight's eternity."

Avalynn neared, not knowing what to say or do. "I am so honored to meet you."

She smiled and tipped her head. With her brows slightly lifted, she said, "Beautiful Avalynn, Only One. It is you who will unite the human and fae bloodlines once and for all. As the last remaining heir of House Strong, and with your innate human witch abilities, you walk both realms. It is upon you to step into your destiny. You shall not turn away from this sacred duty."

She extended the sword. It broke through the water with a slice, sending droplets of water dripping from it like a cascade of a thousand diamonds. Blue etchings that lined the black onyx blade glinted under the bright sun. The hue snaked its way up into the guard and gathered at the blue-gemmed pommel.

Avalynn's hands shook, and she gaped. The power from the blade coursed through the air like a magical current, every hair on her body standing on edge. She reached out. She slipped her hand around the grip and held on as a blast of blue exploded around her, covering her sight like a charged fog.

With a gasp, she opened her eyes. Her body was back in Mateo's bedchamber, lying on the bed. Her hands gripped the sword's hilt that rested on her chest. She gulped and looked into Lady Sonia's anxious eyes. "I... did it."

Lady Sonia smiled back. "You did."

She and Lady Sonia returned to the room where Manny, Floriana, and Camilla were waiting. Their eyes widened when they saw the black and blue sword.

"The Only One," Floriana whispered.

The sword felt natural in Avalynn's hand, as if it had been with her, its true owner, her whole life. Her spirit and this sword said she was invincible. She moved it from one hand to the other. She would not turn from her duty. She would fulfill her destiny and unite the two realms.

The love of her life awaited death in a dungeon. She was the Only One and would not be stopped.

"Let's go get Mateo."

CHAPTER THIRTY

High Queen Lysandra Stromm closed Mateo's bedchamber door with a soft touch. With her chin held high and her shoulders pushed back, she clasped her hands together in front of her and made her way to the private library in her wing of the palace.

Her newfound son was eating out of the palm of her hand like a lost puppy. With wide eyes, he hung on to her every word, like a stray seeking comfort and security from its newfound owner. *Poor thing.* She could not imagine the atrocities of living he must have endured in the dreaded Sublands. To not have any luxuries or wealth at all. She shuddered. Why he would ever want to return to that way of existence was beyond her. She needed to make sure he had everything his heart desired for him to remain. As their only male heir, her bloodline and the future of House Stromm depended on it.

She swept into the library. Floor-to-ceiling rich wood

bookshelves filled with ancient texts, maps, and journals of Faevenly's stories and histories lined the four walls. A thick rug of red and gold with flowers and leaves covered the dark marble floors. The High King and Raelor the witch were waiting as instructed. They sat on the curved plush chairs in front of the crackling fire and rose to their feet when she entered.

"Sit," she commanded with a wave.

"Did all go well?" her High King mate Sylrick asked as he settled back into his seat. He had changed from his ceremonial threads into a simple silver tunic with black satin pants. One leg crossed over the other, his half empty goblet dangled from his thick fingers. "How does he seem?"

Raelor eased into his seat too, but kept his tongue and waited for her reply. Always plotting, that one. As long as it served her, she did not mind. Though he should have detected Avalynn's deception. And Maid Nia's too for that matter. Why must she do everything?

She went to the small table near the fireplace and poured herself a goblet full of red wine. "He is better than well." Her son craved his family like a desert wanderer desired an oasis. "It will not be hard at all to keep him here." She sipped the sweet liquid while facing Raelor. "Did you and Marina send the seeds and the food as I instructed?"

Raelor tipped his head. "We have." His grin grew and curled at the edges. "And I have arranged for their most unfortunate and untimely destruction along the way. With none the wiser." He closed his eyes and nodded.

"You can truthfully say that the High Queen made good on her promise to her son."

"Very good, Raelor." Finally, he'd done something right. She still could not believe Maid Nia had been aligned with the Sublanders and had gone undetected by the witch after all these years. Sometimes he was more trouble than he was worth.

The High King shifted in his seat. "What will we do about Avalynn? Now that we know she is a lowborn and possesses much information about our lives and palace business, something must be done about her."

"We have nothing to worry about," Lysandra sneered. The High King knew nothing about strategy. All he was good for was doling out intimidating glares and brutal handiwork. "The girl knows nothing. She always had her head in the clouds and paid little attention to the palace updates. Remember?"

"That is true," he agreed. "Worthless and unworthy."

She glanced at the fading cut on her arm. Her speedy fae healing had all but erased the mark. Yet rage simmered inside of her at the reminder of the abduction of her prince. Her offspring. How dare someone force her to endure a lowborn impostor in her palace for nineteen years. The audacity. "As for what we will do about her? Nothing. She will come to us. And then we will deal with her."

She had Mateo and would use his love for Avalynn to her advantage. The spark in his eye at the mention of her name was enough to make him weak and vulnerable. Like a foolish Sublander. She needed to bring out his

Stromm-ness. It was in there, they had seen many glimpses. It merely needed to be unburied.

"And the Sublanders? The ones who performed the dastardly deed of switching one of theirs for one of ours? We were robbed of our son!" The king leaned forward, eyebrows tightly furrowed. He hurled his goblet into the fire then balled his hands into fists. Between clenched teeth he seethed. "We must find those responsible. Someone must pay for this injustice."

"Oh, we will find them, and they will pay," the queen soothed. "Every last one. The entire Sublands province will pay. They will still be banished. The ones that survive the Dragon's Bellow, that is. The hunt may have ruined our plans, but we will find another way. The light will come to me." Like it always did.

"I have no doubt, my Queen," he agreed in a much calmer voice. With his brow smoothing, he crossed his arms. "No doubt at all."

Lowering his voice, Raelor scooted to the edge of his seat. His diamond eyes dimmed to a sinister glow. "And what of the prophecy of the Only One?" His voice lowered even further. "Do you think this person is Avalynn?"

She had no doubt the person existed, and she fully suspected it was Avalynn. Why else would she have been hidden within her palace walls? And then later abducted away? There was more to Avalynn than they knew.

The Queen took a long drink of her wine. "Do as I say, when I say, and then all will be well." She grew tired of their questions and failures of foresight. "Only One or not, House Stromm will remain on top."

. . .

Conclusion of Book One, A Storm Rises
Continue the Bloodlines Legacy with
A Shadow Falls

LETTER TO THE STRONG HEIR

My Love,

When you read this, know that your father and I love you more than life itself. I pray you accept this with peace and understanding in your heart. To appreciate your birthright, it's important to start at the beginning. Before you were conceived.

At one time, there existed harmony between the fae realm and the human realm, with access to both realms made possible through shimmery portals. Over time, humans sought to conquer the fae, which culminated in the Great Shimmer War. But humans were no match for the fae.

The Great Shimmer War ended swiftly, and humans were branded as enemies. The Strongs, the ruling house of Faevenly, used a glamour to erase the war from human memory. They then stored every portal on Torch Lake and forbade their use henceforth.

Over time, there came to be twin princesses in the Strong family—ambitious Princess Malena and curious Princess Celyse... Celyse is your grandmother. Princess Celyse found a shimmer portal and peeked at the human realm, where she met Julio Avila... He is your grandfather.

When the courting season approached, Celyse hid her portal and ignored Julio, choosing duty over heart. Celyse later learned of a threat to humans involving the shimmers. Using her own, she crossed into the human realm, seeking Julio's help in unraveling the mystery.

Celyse, Julio, and Julio's best friend, Manny Vela, discovered one of the royal families was manipulating the shimmers in a way that would harm humans forever. Celyse, Julio, and Manny, along with allies from the Sublands, stood against this family and their evil witch, Draven. After many lives were lost, the Sublanders were victorious, and peace returned to Faevenly. The Sublands' victory hinged on Julio's blue energy power and his innate human witch abilities.

Celyse left Faevenly for a life with Julio,

and their love blossomed into a daughter—me, Gabriela... I am your mother.

Your grandparents took me to Faevenly often. But when my life was threatened, we stopped going, and unease began spreading amongst the provinces. Draven's evil returned to Faevenly, and your grandparents went missing. Every last Strong descendant, as well as the future of the Sublands, was at risk upon Draven's return.

Leaf, Faevenly's fiercest warrior, was sent to the human realm to protect me... He is your father.

Wielding my power, and with the help of a witch named Lady Sonia, I faced Draven and restored peace. This same power lives in you. Raw and unlimited, your power will always come forth in your times of need.

There are still those who seek to disturb the balance in Faevenly, and thus a lasting prophecy was born. Your prophecy.

In the twilight of transformation, there will arise like a mighty storm, one born of the union between realms. With a sword of blue in hand and the heart of a champion, this Only One will restore peace to Faevenly and forever unite the bloodlines.

There is great power in you, my love. Now the time has come for you to claim your destiny. Know that your father and I will always be with you. You will never be alone.

ACKNOWLEDGMENTS

Wow, here it is, A Storm Rises! I have literally been talking about this story and these characters FOR YEARS. But then I got involved with writing in the Havenwood Falls world, then I wrote the four book in the Fae Bloodlines Series (which ended up being the perfect prequel series to A Storm Rises), and then I wrote a script for a TV pilot (which I'm still working on). And then and then and then... I just kept doing other things. Oh, and puppies! I've rescued a few. Lol

But finally, after all of that, this book is out in the wild. And I'm so very proud of it! I have a ton of people to thank for this one; but first and foremost I have to thank my son, Jake. Waaay back when, when I first started writing, I started a book called The Anarchist. It was a dystopian book with a main character named Peter, a best friend named Hammy, a love interest named Marie, and a foot race for a prize that included medicine. The timing wasn't right for that story, but the characters and their plight never left me, or Jake.

So, after Fae Bloodlines, I promised I would go back to Peter and reimagine his story. After a ton of brainstorming, A Storm Rises was born. But it took a lot of wonderful friends to get this story to the finish line. They're the wind beneath my wings!

To Garland Keith Grady. From law school friends to writing besties, I can't even begin to express how blessed

I am to have you in my corner! You sharpened my words like a master craftsmen, all while encouraging me and cheering me on with your colorful F-bombs and delightful Texas twang. You are like NO other! I am so lucky to have you as a writing partner.

To my incredible readers that I was able to include in this story early on for some valuable feedback–Jessica Ramirez and Ashley Nicole, thank you both for always supporting me!

To my incredible Rose Bud readers... Y'all mean SO MUCH TO ME! Some of y'all have been with me since the beginning, some are new, but it doesn't change the fact that we are familia. Brought together by stories and love for my books. I am forever grateful for each and everyone one of you!

It goes without saying that NONE of this would be possible without my faith, and without the unconditional support and love from my family and friends. You know who you are!

I could go on and on and on... but let me just say in final words to you, the person reading this acknowledgement all the way through... THANK YOU!

ALSO BY ROSE GARCIA

BLOODLINES LEGACY SERIES

A Storm Rises, book 1

A Shadow Falls, book 2

A Legacy Forged, book 3

FAE BLOODLINES SERIES

(Prequel Series to the Bloodlines Legacy Series)

Fae Away, book 1

Fae Fractured, book 2

Fae Hunted, book 3

Fae Rising, book 4

FINAL LIFE SERIES

(Prequel Series to the Fae Bloodlines Series)

Final Life, book 1

Final Stand, book 2

Final Death, book 3

First Life, book 4

For a full list of Rose's books and how they are connected, please visit

www.RoseGarciaBooks.com/garciaverse.

ABOUT THE AUTHOR

Rose Garcia is an award-winning USA Today bestselling author and screenwriter. She believes that no matter how dark the world may seem, there is always a sliver of light if you look hard enough. This theme permeates every aspect of her being and threads itself through the fabric of her stories.

A lawyer turned writer, Rose writes Young Adult and New Adult Fantasy with Hispanic characters, complicated romance, powerful families, and dynamic friendships. She is known for bringing richly diverse characters to life as she draws on her own cultural experiences.

Rose lives in Houston with her husband and overly needy fur babies. If she's not writing, she's either reading or watching a show. She might even be eating tacos because tacos are life!

For more on Rose, visit www.rosegarciabooks.com.

A final request: please review her books and spread

the word about her stories. She would be most appreciative!

Join Rose's Facebook Fan Group!
www.facebook.com/groups/TheRoseBudSociety

Subscribe to Rose's Newsletter!
www.rosegarciabooks.com/newsletter

- facebook.com/AuthorRoseGarcia
- instagram.com/rosegarciabooks
- tiktok.com/@rosegarciabooks
- bookbub.com/authors/rose-garcia